AF427461

COME *Back*

The Organization-Book Four

M.K. MANSON

One Night Publishing

COME BACK
Copyright 2026 M.K. Manson

The characters and events portrayed in this book are fictitious. Any similarity to real person, living or dead, or events is coincidental and not intended by the author.

No part of this book may be reproduced in any form or by any electronic or mechanical means. It may not be stored in a retrieval system, or transmitted in any form or by any means, electronic, mechanical, photocopying, recording, or otherwise, without express written permission by the author.

The use of any part of this book and its associated text, descriptions, artwork, maps, graphics, fonts, and metadata to train any form of artificial intelligence (AI) to generate text, images, and any digital output is expressly prohibited. All AI licensing rights are reserved by the author. This notice in no way limits the author's exclusive rights under copyright.

All rights reserved
ISBN: 979-8-999-3141-6-1
LCCN: 2025923510

Edited by: Editing4Indies
Proofread by: Karen at Barren Acres Editing
Formatted by: Bravia Books
Cover photo by: Ellen Christy Intimate Portraits
Cover Model: Travis Roten
Cover Design by: Frank Manson and Ellen Christy Intimate Portraits

Printed in the United States of America

Trigger Warnings

Age Gap
Murder
Alcohol Abuse
Physical Abuse
Childhood trauma
Death of a spouse
Kidnapping
Sex trafficking
Sexual assault

To everyone who is afraid to open their heart and let someone in...
It's so much better on the other side.

Prologue

Ethan and I walk into the hospital room to find Freddy sitting where we left him yesterday, slumped over the side of her bed. He hasn't changed his clothes or combed his hair since we brought Amelia here three days ago.

It feels like yesterday when I was sitting in the same spot with Ethan after he was shot during a gunfight at the shelter.

Ethan walks over and touches Freddy's shoulder, and he startles awake. His bloodshot eyes focus on us, then look up at Amelia.

I've never seen this side of Freddy before. He's always so stoic and rarely shows any emotion. Happy or sad. He's all business, all the time. His six-foot-five-inch mountain of muscle makes him the tallest of the group. He has the same olive skin as his brother, Nico, with dark hair and eyes. His stern, square jaw is always clean-shaven, but this morning, its dark stubble matches the circles under his eyes.

"Hey, man… how's she doing?" Ethan asks softly. Freddy stands and gives him a bro hug, then turns to me. I pull him in tight for the real hug I know he needs right now, even if he won't admit it. I try to be strong for him, but seeing my frail friend lying in a hospital bed is killing me.

"She's still unconscious. There's been no change."

"You need to get out of this room for a little while. Let Lola sit with her," Ethan suggests.

I touch Freddy's arm and smile. "I'll watch her like you watched Ethan for me. She's going to be all right." He nods, and I take his place by the side of her bed.

They leave the room, and I look over my best friend. The left side of her face is covered with bruises. Her eye is still swollen shut, and the cut on her bottom lip is dry and cracked. The bruises around her neck are shaped like fingers. Today, they are starting to change colors. Her left arm is wrapped in bandages from her surgery to put a few pins in her arm. When the swelling goes down, she'll get a cast. I can't see under the blankets, but Ruck said she has a few cracked ribs and her back has a lot of cuts and bruises on it, as if she was dragged across the ground. I straighten her blanket and sit in Freddy's chair.

"Amelia, it's Lola. I'm here, sweetie," I say, taking her hand in mine. *What did that maniac do to you? Why won't you wake up?*

A younger brunette nurse enters the room to check her vitals.

"Why doesn't Mr. Acosta have one of those chairs that turns into a bed?" I ask.

"I think it was moved to a different room," she answers, checking the monitors and writing in the chart.

"Can you please find him one? He needs to get some rest."

"We offered him one, but he said he didn't want it."

"*I* want him to have one."

My stern Mafia wife voice doesn't come out to play very often, but when she does, she means business. This situation definitely calls for it because Freddy can't sit in this uncomfortable chair for days on end.

"Can you please find him one?" The nurse just stares at me. "Now!"

Her eyes grow wide. "Yes, Mrs. Martinelli."

"Thank you."

Freddy and Ethan have known each other since high school, but they've grown closer over the past few years. Freddy has become his trusted confidant and second-in-command.

Freddy's father did a real number on him after his mother and sister died in a horrendous car accident. Mario Acosta turned him into his own personal punching bag. Freddy took everything he dished out to protect his younger brother, Nico. But when he was seventeen, his father punched Nico and threw him into a wall. It flipped a switch inside Freddy, and they physically fought. He struck his father in the head with a lamp, causing him to fall into the fireplace hearth, and he died.

Soon after, Freddy and Nico showed up on Ethan's doorstep, asking to see Antonio Martinelli. They made a deal with the devil that night. Antonio agreed to dispose of the body and make sure Nico wasn't put into foster care. In exchange, both boys would come to work for The Organization the day after they graduated from high school, indefinitely.

Freddy worked his way up through the ranks from a soldier doing Antonio's dirty work to being Ethan's second-in-command. He runs all of the illegal operations for The Organization, while Ethan handles day-to-day operations, investments, and the legal businesses. Ethan holds the title of Don Supreme and ultimately has the final say in all matters.

On the way to the hospital, we stopped by Freddy's house and packed him a change of clothes and some toiletries. Ethan borrowed the key to the doctor's locker room from Ruck so Freddy could take a shower. Hopefully, he can get him to eat something too.

Ruck is short for Ruckowski. He's a former Navy SEAL and the doctor for The Organization. He's highly skilled and has seen just about everything. We have a small clinic at the shelter, but Amelia's injuries were too extensive. Ruck decided to bring her directly to our wing at Johnsonville Hospital.

Amelia was my assistant when I worked at Kingsley and Masters Advertising. She was a giggling twenty-one-year-old ray of sunshine when she started working for me. Always looking for romance and rainbows. Always searching for the good in everyone.

She's petite at five foot four with long blond hair and bright blue eyes. It's easy to make her blush, and I don't think I've ever heard her say a negative word the whole time I've known her.

Freddy and Amelia met the night of the masked ball. They hit it off immediately and have been together ever since. He's the old man of our group at the ripe old age of thirty-six, while Amelia is the baby at twenty-four. The age difference doesn't seem to bother either of them. They balance each other perfectly.

I opened The Battered Women's Shelter of Johnsonville not long after Ethan and I were married. Amelia left the advertising world to come work with me. She basically runs the place now. She has fresh new ideas that keep the residents learning and growing. She creates a positive atmosphere of love and acceptance. She's encouraging and patient with them on their journey to independence from their abuser. She has matured into a savvy businesswoman, all the while maintaining her cheerful outlook on life.

According to Amelia, Freddy has had a hard time letting her in. He has never told her that he loves her, and they've been together for more than two years now.

"How can you stay with him if he won't talk to you, Amelia?"

She scowls at me. "We do actually have conversations. He just hasn't said those three little words yet."

"But you love him?"

"With all my heart." She always gets all swoony when she talks about the grumpy Mafia boss.

"Why don't you tell him you love him?"

"I don't want him to say it because I said it first. I want him to say it because he means it."

"What if he never says it?"

"I'll have to learn to deal with it, I guess."

"I don't know, Amelia. You might be holding out for something that never comes."

"I have to give him the time he needs to work through whatever is holding him back."

~

By the time Ethan and Freddy return to Amelia's room, there's a convertible sleeping chair beside the bed, and Freddy looks somewhat refreshed.

"How are you feeling?" When I take his hand, he flinches. Looking down, I see his knuckles are bloody.

"What happened?" I ask, scowling at Ethan.

"There was a disagreement between Freddy and the shower wall." I frown at Ethan. He was supposed to be taking care of him.

"Are you all right?"

"I need her to wake up. I need to tell her—" His words get stuck in his throat. I can tell this is breaking him, but he never lets a tear fall.

I rub my hand on his forearm. Gently, I say, "She's going to wake up."

"She has to."

"Have you talked to her?" I ask. His brows crease.

"Talk to her? She's unconscious."

"I know, but maybe your voice will help guide her back to you." He shrugs and resumes his place by her side. He takes her hand and carefully kisses her palm before placing it on his cheek.

"I don't think I can live without her, Lola." His voice is a whisper.

"Don't talk like that," I snap. I clear my throat and calmly speak again. "Only positive words now."

"Call us if you need anything. Day or night," Ethan says.

"Thanks, man."

"You're family, Freddy. We'll always have your back. Whatever you need."

~

I warned Amelia repeatedly about the Mafia life and the danger it can bring to the women these men love. I learned my lesson when Buddy kidnapped me and almost raped me. But she always thought she wasn't important enough for anything to ever happen to her.

"You need to keep an eye on your surroundings at all times. And, for God's sake, listen to your security team," I lecture.

"You're overreacting, Lola. Who would want me? I'm nobody."

Well, they decided she was somebody. Freddy's somebody. And now look at her, lying in this damn hospital bed, unconscious.

Chapter 1
Freddy

t's been three of the longest days of my life. The door to Amelia's hospital room opens, and Ruck walks inside.

"How are you doin'?" he asks with compassion.

"I'm okay."

"I'm going to check Amelia's vitals, then we're going to run some more tests."

"Whatever you need."

"You look like shit."

"Thanks, man. What kind of tests?"

"We're going to do a chest X-ray and a CT scan to check her pneumothorax. We need to make sure the air is being absorbed and there are no complications with the lung. I also want to do another MRI and verify there's no brain swelling or damage. Why don't you go take a shower?"

"I did that while Ethan and Lola were here." He knows that because he gave us the keys.

"Oh, well, then you should try to get some sleep."

"I'll try, but all I can think about is Amelia, and what she went through at the hands of that monster."

Ruck comes over and puts his hand on my shoulder. "You

got her back, man. That's all that matters."

"I know but…"

"That's all that matters." His voice is calm but stern. I nod in understanding. Transport knocks and comes to take her to radiology.

"She'll be gone for a few hours. I'm turning off the light. Sleep."

I lower the back of the chair into a sleeping position and use my jacket to cover my arms. As I lie there in the darkness, my mind wanders back to when I was ten. Nico was seven, and our little sister, Laura, was five.

We just got off the Tilt-A-Whirl ride at the county fair. Laura looks a little green, but she's laughing, so I guess she's okay. Momma takes her by the hand and leads us to the midway, where the games are.

Laura looks up at all the stuffed animals. "Momma, can Freddy win me a teddy bear? Please…" she whines.

Momma turns to me. "Do you think you can win her a toy?"

"I can try."

"Yay!" Laura squeals, clapping her hands and jumping up and down. "Darts. Play the dart game, Freddy."

"Settle down now. Freddy will try. But no promises," Momma says in her soothing voice.

"He can do it. I know he can," Laura announces firmly.

I take the five-dollar bill from Momma and move over to the dart game. You get three darts for two dollars. You have to hit two balloons to win a prize. I take the darts in my hand and feel the weight of them in my palm. When I throw the first dart, it misses.

"It's okay, Freddy. You can do it," Laura says quietly, patting me on the arm.

I toss the second dart, and it pops a red balloon. Laura jumps at the sound and then claps.

"Yay!" she squeals.

I aim and let the last dart fly. It pops a blue balloon.

"You did it!" she yells. The guy behind the counter hands

her a little stuffed skunk, and she scrunches up her nose. It wasn't what she was expecting.

"How do you win the teddy bear?" I ask the guy behind the counter.

"If you win again, then you can upgrade to the teddy bear." I look at Momma, and she nods in approval, and I use the change from the five to play again. Momma pulls Laura back away from me so I can concentrate. I let the first dart go, and it hits another blue balloon. My gut twists in a knot because I really want to win a teddy bear for Laura. I like to put a smile on her little face. When I let the second dart fly, it misses. This is my last chance. I hold my breath, aim the dart where I want it to hit, and let it fly. Pop! It hits the red balloon. Everyone yells. The sound of her laughter fills me with warmth.

"Tell the man what you want," I say, pointing at the prizes. My chest fills with pride, knowing I put that smile on her face. Laura points at the teddy bear, and he hands it to her. She hands the little skunk back, pulls the bear into her tiny arms, and hugs it fiercely. She crooks her finger for me to come down to her level, and I do.

She places a sweet little kiss on my cheek.

"I love you, Freddy."

"I love you too, Squirt. Come on, let's go home." She puts her tiny hand in mine, and we head for the exit. One of Momma's friends stops us and takes our picture.

I reach into my back pocket and pull out my wallet. Inside is a copy of the picture we took that day. Using the flashlight on my phone, I look at the photograph of Momma, Nico, Laura, and me. Laura's cheeks are smiling so wide she looks like she might explode. She holds a bag of pink cotton candy in one hand and the teddy bear in the other. I run my finger over the faces of that sweet, innocent family. I miss them all so much. I put the rumpled picture back into my wallet and roll over onto my other side.

The police officer stands at the front door when I swing it open. I stop dead in my tracks.

"Is your parent home?" he asks. His voice is deep and stern. I yell over my shoulder for my dad, and he comes to meet us in the doorway.

"Officer. How can I help you?"

"Can we speak in private, please?" the officer asks, looking down at me.

"Yes, of course." My father goes out on the porch and pulls the door closed. I try to listen, but the words are muffled through the door. Dad comes back inside. His face is as white as a sheet of paper, and tears hang in his eyes. He walks to the living room and sits down on the couch.

"Dad, what's wrong?"

"Where's your brother?

"Upstairs."

"Go get him."

"Dad, what's wrong?"

"Do as I say, Freddy!" he yells. I turn and run up the stairs for Nico. Pulling him down the stairs with me, we sit on the couch.

"There was an accident," Dad says, looking at his hands in his lap.

"Accident," I repeat under my breath.

"Momma and Laura were hurt very badly." Nico immediately begins to cry.

"Let's go to the hospital to see them," I say, standing from my seat. He takes me by the arm and pulls me to sit back down.

"No, Freddy. We can't go see them. Because they're not at the hospital."

I know what those words mean, but I don't think Nico does. I need to hear him say the words.

"No, Dad. They're not..."

"Yes, Freddy. They're dead."

Dad doesn't say another word. He walks upstairs to his bedroom and closes the door. He doesn't come out to put us to bed. He doesn't take us in his arms and comfort us. He just shuts down. Lost in his own grief, he doesn't have room for ours. It's as if he has forgotten we exist. I pull Nico under my arm and hold him as his cries fill the room.

I get my little brother ready for bed and climb in beside him. He cuddles up to me and cries himself to sleep. But I can't sleep. I can't believe they're gone. I won't believe it `until I see them with my own eyes. They were here a few hours ago. Momma hugged me goodbye. I keep running the last words she spoke to me through my mind.

"Keep an eye on Nico. I need to take Laura to an impromptu dance practice tonight. The instructor decided they needed one more practice before the recital. We won't be gone too long."

"Okay."

"I love you," she says, kissing the top of my head.

"I love you too Momma." I wave and watch as the car drives down our street. That was the last time I saw them alive.

❧

Two Days Later

There are so many people at the funeral. Everyone loved my momma. She was kind and loving to all the neighborhood kids. She helped out at our school and was in the stands for our sporting events. The guests stand in line to talk to our dad while Nico and I sit in chairs off to the side. The smell of the flowers fills the air, and soft music plays in the background.

Momma's wearing the pink dress she wore to Aunt Susan's wedding. She looks so pretty. Her gray casket is lined with a shiny white material. Laura's casket sits next in line. It's smaller than Momma's. Hers is white with a pink material inside. Pink was her favorite color. The teddy bear I won for her is tucked under her arm. She looks like she's sleeping.

When all the visitors have left the room, it's just Dad and us. I stand beside the casket and stare at Momma. I know she's gone because she was so cold when I touched her. Tears fill my eyes as I walk over to Laura's casket one last time. She looks peaceful, and I know she's not afraid because Momma is with her in heaven. Nico grabs my hand, and we stare at Laura. After a short while, Dad comes up behind us. He squeezes our shoulders and walks us outside.

We watch as they put the caskets into the back of two big black cars. We follow behind in a fancy black car. I look out the back window and see a long line of cars following us. It wouldn't do any good to ask Dad questions because he won't answer. He's not even crying anymore. His head just hangs forward, and he picks the skin on the sides of his fingers.

Dad holds each of us by the hand as we walk into a tent and sit in chairs in front of the closed caskets. The reverend says a prayer, and a song plays from his cell phone. "You Are My Sunshine." Laura used to sing it all the time. The guests file out, and before long, there's no one left but us. We sit there and sit there and sit there. It feels like he's never going to take us home. The funeral man pushes a button, and the caskets begin to lower into the big hole in the ground. I'm scared. Is he going to push us inside too? Is he going to jump in himself? I want to leave, but I don't say it.

When the machines stop running, Dad stands. So do Nico and I. He turns, and we follow him to the waiting car. We all slide into the back seat. As the car pulls away, I try to turn my head to look back, but he squeezes my leg hard, and I face forward. Never returning to their gravesite again.

Chapter 2
Freddy

I'm jerked awake when the lights in the room blaze on. Transport is bringing Amelia back from radiology. When they move the bed back into place, I look at Ruck for answers.

"There's no sign of brain damage. All the scans looked good."

"Then why isn't she awake?" I plead.

"She's been through a terrible trauma, Freddy. We won't know the long-term effects of her injuries until she wakes up. It's only been a few days. Her body needs a chance to recuperate." The memory of Ethan's doctors telling Lola the same thing floods my mind. Ethan lay in this same room for weeks before he woke up.

"Be thankful she wasn't hurt worse."

"Worse?" I yell and rise from my chair. "What the hell is worse than this?" Throwing my arms out, I point at Amelia.

"We need to give her more time. She needs to heal."

"I'm so fucking frustrated. I need her to wake up. I need to tell her—"

"Talk to her, now. Tell her what you want to say. They say a person can hear what's happening around them even when they're unconscious."

"What do I talk about?"

"The weather. Who the fuck cares? Your voice can be calming and healing. Talk to her. Sing her a song." I stare at him in disbelief.

"I'm not fucking singing to her," I grumble.

"I know. Tell her a story. No one else is in here. It's just the two of you."

"I don't know." I run my hands through my hair in frustration.

"It can't hurt, man. Try it." I give him a nod, and he leaves the room. I pull my chair closer to the bed and take her hand in mine.

"Talk to you. Tell you a story. What kind of story? You asked me to tell you about my family, and I didn't want to talk about it. Now is as good a time as any. I guess I'll start at the beginning.

"Life was good before we lost Momma and Laura. We were kids, doing stupid stuff. Playing baseball, ghosts in the graveyard at dusk, and riding our bikes over homemade ramps in the middle of the church parking lot. Just kids being kids. Then they died, and everything went to shit. Dad was never the same. The only time he talked to us was when he was yelling. And the only time he was yelling was when he was drunk. At first, he would go to work at the car lot, come home, and have a drink. It transitioned into him coming home and having a few drinks. Then he started stopping off at the bar for a few drinks on his way home. By the time I was twelve and Nico was nine, the hitting started."

I'm alone at the kitchen table doing my homework. I try to keep Nico out of the house after we eat dinner, just in case Dad comes home early. Sure enough, tonight, he stumbles into the kitchen, drunk.

"Why the fuck didn't you do the laundry?"

"I had to feed Nico, and I had homework to do."

"I need a shirt to wear to work tomorrow."

"I'll do it after my homework."

"You'll do it now!"

I'd better do what he says, or I'll get hit, so I stand from the table and walk into the laundry room.

"Where is that little shit?" He stops at the base of the stairs and yells, "Nico!"

"He's not here. I sent him to Mark's house to do his homework."

"Why would you do that?" he rages, shoving me to the floor. Then he grabs me by the shirt and lifts me off the floor, throwing me into the wall. He pins me to the wall by my throat. I can smell the alcohol on his breath. I gasp for air as I try to explain.

"He needs help with math, and Mark can help him," I croak, bracing myself for the hit I know is coming.

Slap!

"You should've helped him."

"I'm not good at math." He stares at me like I'm speaking another language. He lets out a huff and pushes me away in disgust. "Get the fucking laundry done. Now!" He heads for the living room to lie down on the couch and watch the news.

It won't be long before he'll be asleep. I got off easy tonight.

"By the time I turned fourteen, he would be gone for days at a time. He lost his job at the car lot when he stopped showing up for work. He was still paying the bills, so he had to be working somewhere, but we never knew where.

"Every day, I made sure Nico was clean, fed, and ready for school. When we came home from school, we did all the chores and our homework. I learned very quickly that the less I gave Dad to be mad about, the better life was for us. I did my best to protect Nico. Momma would've wanted it that way.

"By my sophomore year, I started staying after school a few days a week. Dad was coming home later and later, if he would even come home at all, so he had no idea what I was doing. He wouldn't let me play sports. He said it would take up too much of my time. But he never told me I couldn't stay after school and hang out in the weight room with the guys. So I would lift weights for an hour and then run all the way home. As long as I was back home, and dinner was ready by the time he got there, he was none the wiser.

When Dad was drunk, I could usually distract him or re-direct the conversation away from Nico, but sometimes there was nothing I could do."

"Shit. Dad's home early. Nico, go to your room and hide. Be quiet. I'm going to tell him you're not home."

But before Nico got to the fourth step, Dad was standing at the bottom of the stairs yelling. "Where do you think you're going?"

"To my room. I have homework to do."

"Get the fuck back here." He points at the floor in front of his feet. Nico looks at me and back at our dad. I nod, and he descends the stairs. Stopping in front of Dad, he keeps his eyes lowered.

"Look at me when I talk to you, boy!" Nico raises his hood-ed eyes to him.

"I got a call from your school this morning. They had to bother me at work to tell me you didn't have any lunch money left in your account. Why don't you have any lunch money, Nico?" Nico shrugs. The kid is twelve years old. He shouldn't have to worry about lunch money.

"Answer me! What did you spend your lunch money on?"

Nico looks at him, confused. "Lunch."

"Lunch. I gave you twenty dollars to put in your lunch account last month. What did you spend it on?"

Again, Nico's brows scrunch in confusion. "Lunch. I put the money into my account, just like you told me to. Now it's gone. I used it to buy lunch."

I want to tell Dad that twenty dollars doesn't last forever and he has to give Nico money every month, but I keep my mouth shut. Dad knows he has to give us lunch money every month. He's the adult. But here he is, picking a fight with a twelve-year-old.

He grabs Nico by the arm and shakes him.

"What did you spend the money on, boy?" I run up behind

Dad and push Nico out of his hold. Dad punches me in the face, and my head snaps to the side.

"Go upstairs, Nico!" I shout. He hesitates, but I yell again, "GO!"

When Dad was done giving me a black eye, four bruised ribs, and a multitude of scrapes on my back from sliding down the brick wall by the fireplace, he finally went to bed. Leaving me in a heap on the floor. Nico sneaks down the stairs and helps me to bed.

"I hate him, Nico," I say through gritted teeth.

"I know. Me too, but what can we do about it? He's our dad."

"I don't know yet. But I'll figure something out."

Reliving these old memories has been more tiring than I thought it would be. I fix Amelia's blankets, place a chaste kiss on her lips, and turn off the light. I try to get comfortable and relax in the tiny chair bed thingy. Praying tomorrow she'll wake up.

Chapter 3
Freddy

The following morning, I wake up to the sounds of the nurse taking Amelia's vitals.

"Good morning, Mr. Acosta."

"Good morning." I stretch on my tiny bed before I try to sit up. "How is she?" I yawn.

"She's stable, sir. The doctor will be in around ten. He had a meeting to attend."

"Thank you."

The nurse writes on the whiteboard and exits, closing the door behind her with a click. I change my bed back into a chair and move it closer to her bed. I use the restroom, then wash my face and brush my teeth. Taking a bottle of water from my bag, I sit back down in my usual spot.

"Good morning, sweetheart." I kiss her forehead and brush her hair from her face. I take her hand in mine and hold her cool palm against my warm cheek.

"I guess you want more stories before you'll wake up for me." I kiss her hand. "Let's see, where did I leave off? Oh yeah, the night he beat me up. I think I was around fifteen when that happened, and Nico would've been… twelve. After that night,

Dad started leaving for longer periods of time. He never told us where he was going or when he would be back. He would leave money on the counter for food, and he was gone.

"Life was calmer when he wasn't around. Can't say I ever missed his ass. Nico and I kept our heads down and tried to stay out of trouble. We didn't want anyone to find out how much Dad was gone. We were afraid someone would call social services, and they would split us up. We became model students, and boy, was it boring."

Nico and I are sitting at the kitchen table.

"I'm so bored!" Nico whines.

"Do your homework."

"All my homework's done. Can't we go somewhere? Do something?"

"What do you want to do?" I ask, raising a brow to him.

"Let's go outside and throw the ball around."

I let out a huff, closing my book. "I guess that can't hurt anything."

We get our gloves and the baseball out of the garage and head for the backyard.

"Do you think Dad will ever get back to normal?" Nico asks, tossing me the ball.

"I don't know, dude. It's been six years since the accident. You would think he could've got his shit together by now." I toss it back.

"Where do you think he goes when he leaves?" Nico asks.

"I have no idea. He's probably passed out in a gutter somewhere."

"Then where does the money come from?" He lobs the ball my way.

"Nico! Why are you asking me all these questions? I know the same information you do, dude."

"I just wish we had some answers."

"We may never know the answers. All I care about is that you and I don't get separated. We're a good team. We need to keep it that way," I say.

"Hey, do you think Dad will teach you how to drive?" The ball flies over my shoulder and bounces off the fence. I stoop down to retrieve it.

"It doesn't matter. Joe's going to teach me. You know, in case of emergency." I smirk.

"You better not get caught, or he'll skin you alive, literally."

"He won't catch me. I run home every day. I'm too fast for him." We laugh. "Have you had enough sunshine and exercise yet?"

Nico rests the ball in the center of his glove and pulls it from his hand. Reaching for my glove, he says, "I guess. Let's get something to eat. Do you think we have enough money left for pizza?"

"You put the stuff away, and I'll go check."

"Nico and I have always gotten along well. I liked being his big brother. I liked having someone to take care of. Someone who depended on me. He didn't do drugs and had all his teachers wrapped around his little finger, so he never got into trouble. All the trouble was left for me, I guess."

My friend Joe and I are sitting in the parking lot on Monday after school. He's a senior, and I'm a junior. We met in the weight room and started talking about driving. He agreed to let me drive his car if I helped him with his civics homework. I had no idea Joe drove a classic car. It's a 1970 blue-and-white Chevelle.

"This car is so fuckin' cool," I say, sliding into the driver's seat. My hands caress the steering wheel.

"Man, you look like you're gonna have sex with her."

"I would if I could. She's a beauty. Thanks for letting me do this."

"I know your dad's been gone a lot. It's no problem. Just be careful with her."

"Oh, I'll be gentle."

"You can circle the parking lot once," Joe says.

"Ah, come on, man. Five times," I plead.

"Nah, dude, you've never driven before. Twice."

"Four times."

"Three, and that's my final offer. Take it or leave it."

"I'll take it."

"All right, start her up."

I turn the key, and the engine roars to life. The rumble makes my dick hard.

"Now, put your foot on the brake and put her in drive." I do as I'm told.

"Look over your shoulder for traffic, ease off the brake, and give her a little gas." There are no other cars around. I have no worries about hitting anything, so I let off the brake and ease into the gas as he instructs. The power comes through the seat and into my ass as I give her a little rev, and we begin to move around the parking lot.

"Good, you're doing good. Now, when you need to turn, hit the brake and turn the wheel." We glide around the parking lot once, twice, and finally, three times. I hate that it's over already, but it was an amazing first experience.

"Park her over there," Joe says, pointing to a space. I whipped her in between the lines and put her in park.

"That was amazing. Thank you so much."

"You did great for your first time. When you get your permit, maybe I'll let you drive us home."

"Really?"

"Sure."

"Fuck yeah! Thanks, Joe. I gotta head home before my old man finds out I didn't ride the bus." I open the door and grab my backpack from the back seat.

"Why don't you let me drive you home? It'll be faster."

"You don't mind?" He shakes his head. "That would be great, thanks."

Joe lets me out on the street before mine, and I walk the rest of the way. When I turn the corner, I can see my house. Before I know what's happening, a car pulls up beside me. Someone rolls down the window and yells at me.

"Hey!" Fuck. I don't even have to look to know it's my dad.

There's a sickening feeling in the pit of my stomach, and I think I'm about to lose my lunch. I try to be cool. Like it's no big deal that I'm walking down the street instead of riding the bus.

"Hey, Dad." My voice wavers with fear.

"Get in this goddamn car right now!" I can hear the blood whooshing in my ears as I climb into the car. I'm a dead man.

"How was your trip?" I ask casually.

"Trip?"

"Yeah, you've been gone for a few weeks. I figured you were on a business trip." His eyebrows scrunch up in the middle.

"Why the fuck aren't you on the bus?"

"I missed it." The lie falls from my lips before my brain thinks it through. "You missed it?"

"Yeah. Mr. Smith, my biology teacher, let us out a few minutes too late, and I missed the bus."

"Why didn't you call me?"

"My friend offered me a ride, so I took it." He pulls into the driveway and puts the car into park.

"You're lying," he snarls.

"What?"

"I said you're lying." His angry tone makes my knees weak.

"N...No, I'm not." I stammer.

His fist shoots across the car and connects with the side of my head. I think I see stars for a second.

"Now. Wanna try it again, boy?"

"I caught a ride home with Joe."

"But why?"

"I missed the..." My sentence is interrupted by another fist to the face.

"Why?" comes from my trembling lips.

"Why what?" he asks.

"Why are you hitting me?"

I'm sixteen years old. I've been lifting weights. I'm stronger than I've ever been. I'm almost the same height he is now. Could I take him? I'm not sure. I'll only get one shot at it, and if I don't succeed, he'll beat me within an inch of my life. What would happen to Nico? Without me, Dad would eat him alive. I can't do anything unless I'm positive I can follow through. I try to talk my way out of it.

"I told you my teacher let us out late."

"Just stop fucking talking. I was there."

"Huh?"

"I got back in town and thought I would pick you and Nico up and take you out for pizza. I was in the bus lot, watching the buses load. But you never got on. When I turned to go back into the school to find out where you were, I saw you getting into the driver's side of that boy's car in the back parking lot."

Now I know I'm going to throw up.

"Dad, I can explain."

"Oh really? You wanna explain to me why you were driving some kid's car around the parking lot when your ass was supposed to be on the school bus? Not to mention the fact you don't even have a fucking driving permit yet. How many other times have you disobeyed my orders?"

"Dad..." He doesn't give me a chance to explain. He gets out of the car, slams the door, stomps to the front porch, and lets himself into the house. I carry my ass in behind him and prepare for the worst.

"You're sixteen now, so you think you don't have to follow my rules?"

"I never said that."

"What would've happened to Nico if you weren't home by the time he got here? He would've been all alone. He's only nine years old."

What the hell is he talking about?

"Dad, Nico is thirteen." Dad looks at me like I've lost my mind. He doesn't even know how old his own kid is. "He's a teenager. He can stay by himself for a few hours."

He rubs his hand down his face. Is he really this clueless?

"I want you home right after school, every day, dammit!"

"Yes, sir. But..."

"Don't you fuckin' but me, boy!"

"Can I go to the football game on Friday night?"

"So, you can hang out with your friend who drives the Chevelle?"

"Yes, and some of my buddies."

"No."

"But..." As soon as the word comes out of my mouth, his fist collides with my stomach, and all my breath leaves my body.

"What did I tell you about saying that word to me?" I'm doubled over in pain. Son of a bitch, it hurts.

"Not to say it again," I rasp.

"That's right. Now, get in the kitchen and make something for dinner."

"There isn't very much in the kitchen left to cook."

"What did you spend all the money I left you on?" He was gone a fuckin' month. What does he think I spent it on?

"We used it for food, Dad, that's all, I swear."

He slaps me across the face. "Bullshit!"

Nico comes in the front door, and we hear it click closed.

"Freddy, you home?" My eyes connect with Dad's. He lifts his eyebrow and waits for me to answer. "Yeah, dude, we're in the kitchen."

"We?" Nico's words cut off as he enters the kitchen and sees Dad standing there. "Hey, Dad."

"Hey. Do you feel like pizza?" Dad asks.

Chapter 4
Freddy

"I should probably tell you about the night I killed my father. I was seventeen, and Nico was fourteen. I had walked to the store to get some stuff to make dinner. When I came home, Nico was lying on the floor."

"Get up! You worthless piece of shit!" I hear my dad yell as I come in the back door.

"What the fuck are you doing?" I drop the grocery bags to the floor and run to Nico's side.

"Are you okay?" He shakes his head as I pull him up to sit. The look on his face breaks me. His eyes are wide, and he's scared to death. In this moment, my brain no longer recognizes the man in front of me as my father. He's just a body I need to break. I grab Mario by the shirt and throw him against the wall.

"You son of a bitch! It wasn't enough for you to beat the shit out of me for the last seven years, but now you think you're going to do it to Nico too! I'm sick of you taking everything out on us. It wasn't our fault Momma and Laura died. But you've punished us every single day since for it. You're the piece of shit." Mario struggles in my grasp, but I hold him firmly to the wall.

"You don't know what the hell you're talking about. I provide for this family." He gasps, trying to suck in a breath.

"This family?" I laugh. "You're delusional. You stopped being part of this family when you shut us out after the funeral."

"I put a roof over your heads and food in your bellies."

"Being a family is so much more than that, and you know it."

"What did you want from me? To throw the ball around in the backyard and have barbecues on Sunday afternoon?"

"We just wanted you to be here."

"I had work to do."

"What kind of work? We don't even know where you go when you leave us alone for weeks on end."

"It's none of your fucking business what I do. I'm the adult, and you're the child."

"Child... child? I haven't been a child since I was ten years old! I had to take care of Nico because you sure as hell weren't here to do it."

"You're an ungrateful brat, just like your brother," he barks. Something in me snaps, and I punch him in the face. Right. Left. Right. The exhilaration I feel makes me want to do it more. He pushes me, and I stumble back. I grab for the only thing I can reach, the lamp from the end table. I swing, and it connects with his head, and he wobbles backward. He looks me in the eyes as he stumbles, and it feels like he takes part of my soul with him as he falls to the ground. The thud sends a chill down my spine as his head makes contact with the fireplace, and he rolls to the floor.

"Holy shit," Nico hisses as he comes to stand beside me. "Do you think he's...dead?"

We approach the body together. I use my foot to kick Mario's boot. Nothin'.

I roll him over. Nothin'.

I shake him and say his name several times. Nothin'.

I place two fingers on his neck and check for a pulse. Nothin'.

"I think he's dead, Nico."

"Oh my God," he says on an exhale.

"He can't hurt us anymore."

"What do we do now?"

I'm almost afraid to look into Nico's eyes for fear I'll see sadness. Sadness for the man who has abused us for years, but when I look up, I don't. I think I almost see...relief.

"It was an accident," I say, standing in front of him, pleading my case.

"I'm glad you did it." His voice is cold.

"What?"

"I'm glad he's gone."

"I need to think. We need a plan." I run my hands through my hair and scrub them down my face.

"They're going to take me away and put me in a foster home somewhere, aren't they? I don't want to go live with someone else, Freddy." Nico begins to panic. I take him by the shoulders and force him to look at me. I can't have him spiraling out of control.

"No one is going anywhere. No one is going to split us up. We're family, and we take care of each other." I pull him in for a quick hug. "Let's think." I pace around the room, and then it hits me. Antonio Martinelli. He can help us.

"Get your shoes on, let's go."

I take the keys to Dad's car and drive us to the Martinelli mansion.

Chapter 5
Freddy

We're standing on the front porch of the Martinelli mansion, drenched from the pouring rain, begging the butler to let us see Mr. Martinelli. He tells us it's too late, and we need to make an appointment tomorrow.

"You don't understand. This is urgent," I plead.

"What's going on down there?" Mr. Martinelli's voice rings out as he descends the staircase. "It's a little late for you boys to be out on a night like this, isn't it?"

"Yes, sir."

"What can I do for you?"

"Is there somewhere we can talk in... private?" He waves off the butler and leads us into his office.

Nico and I sit in the big burgundy chairs in front of his desk. I should be terrified. This is the most powerful mobster in our town, but I'm not. I feel powerful in my own skin right now. I just killed my father. I need to do what I always do and take care of Nico and me.

"My father had a little...accident."

"What do you mean by accident, Freddy?"

"He's dead."

"What happened?"

"My father's not a good man, Mr. Martinelli. He's been beating us since our mother's death. Tonight, he attacked my brother. We had words, and we fought. I hit him with a lamp. He fell into the fireplace, dead."

"Why did you boys come to me?"

"Because you're the most powerful man we know, sir, and I can't lose my brother to the foster care system. I can take care of him myself. I have been for years. I thought maybe we could make a deal." "What kind of a deal?" He props his steepled hands under his chin and waits.

"I turn eighteen in four months. If you help me get rid of the body and fix it so I can keep my brother, I'll quit school and come to work for you." He sits back in his chair. His gaze is hard and unblinking.

After a few moments, he speaks. "Here's what I can do for you, boys. I'll have my cleaning crew take care of the body. I'll have my lawyer draw up papers giving you full custody of Nico when you turn eighteen. Keep your heads down and don't call any attention to yourselves. Freddy, you stay in school and graduate. Then, you'll come to work for me, indefinitely." I feel a sense of relief flood through my body. Finally, all of our problems are solved. Dad can't hurt us anymore, and we get to stay together.

"Thank you, Mr. Martinelli. You won't regret it. I'll work hard—"

He cuts me off. "But..."

"But?"

"When Nico graduates, he comes to work for me also, indefinitely."

My eyes shoot to Nico's. He raises a brow at me, and without hesitation, his hand shoots out, and he says, "Deal."

*"Good, good. Now give me the address where the body is."
You two can stay here tonight. I don't want you going back there until the place has been cleaned."*

"Yes, sir. Thank you, sir."

"The next day, Nico and I went to school like nothing ever happened. When we arrived at the house after school, it was spotless, but there was an overwhelming chemical smell. We went on with our lives for the next four months, as if nothing had ever happened.

"Mr. Martinelli, well, I guess I can call him Antonio now that he's dead. Antonio helped me get a driver's license, paid all the bills, and watched me graduate in May. The next day, I went to work for The Organization.

"Antonio took me under his wing and taught me to be a good and faithful soldier. He started me out as a bouncer at Scarlett's. I wasn't old enough to buy or sell alcohol legally, but I could provide security. I saw a lot of crazy shit working there. Drunks, drugs, and hookers filled the place every night.

"The deeper I got into The Organization, the more I tried to distance myself from Nico. I was getting into shadier shit with Antonio and needed Nico to be safe. I wanted him to be normal as long as he could. I didn't hold him back from anything he wanted to do or try. He played sports and had friends, two things I was never allowed to do. I even taught him to drive and bought him a car his senior year. It was a 2015 Octane Red Hellcat. It was the first big thing I purchased with the money I made working for Antonio. I'm sure he got a lot of pussy in that car."

It's the night of the big game. If they win, they'll go to the championship. I'm standing against the side of the fieldhouse watching. I haven't missed a game yet. Our team is down by three. Their quarterback, Craig Fields, snaps the ball. Nico rushes forward, plows through a linebacker, and lunges at Craig. The ball pops out. Nico snags it and takes off running. I watch him sprint his way to the winning touchdown. He spikes the ball, and his team surrounds him. They lift him onto their shoulders and prance around the field. They're off to the championship. I'm so fucking proud of him.

"He always was a good kid with a lot of common sense. He knew when to keep his mouth shut and keep his head down and stay out of trouble. I always wondered if I did the right thing introducing him to this world."

⌒

First day of school, Nico's senior year.

"Ya know," I say awkwardly. "If you've changed your mind and want to go to college or something instead of working for The Organization, I can try to make a new deal with the boss."

"Why would you say that?"

"You were only fourteen when we made that deal, Nico."

"So?"

"So. You were just a kid when you made a decision that would affect your entire life."

"I knew what I was doing."

"I just don't want you to be sorry."

"Listen. I know what I agreed to. I might have only been a kid, but I know what you did for me all those years with Dad. I know how you kept me out of the line of fire, protected me, and took all those hits instead of me. I don't want to go anywhere else, man. You're all I have. I want to do this...with you."

"There's just a lot of...death. Are you going to be okay with seeing it? Inflicting it?"

"Mr. Martinelli kept us together. We promised to be loyal to him, and I'll keep my promise. I'll learn to do whatever needs to be done."

"If you're sure this is what you want, then I'm going to train you."

"Train me?"

"I'll teach you how to fight, track, shoot, kill, and all about the rules."

"Rules?"

"Yes, Mr. Martinelli has strict rules."

"What kind of rules?"

"Never. I mean never show any emotions. He doesn't like it.

Especially, if you don't approve of something he's doing, don't ever let your face show it."

"Okay, what else?"

"Never ask him why. Never raise your voice to him. Never speak unless spoken to."

"I can do all those."

"And never. I mean never flinch when he's taking care of business."

"What do I do?"

"Look straight ahead. Don't eyeball him or look at the ground. Just stare straight ahead, no emotions."

"Got it. Straight ahead."

"There are more, but we'll go over all them before you start."

"Thanks, bro."

"I put Nico through the paces all year. There was boxing, weightlifting, self-defense, bare-knuckle fighting, wrestling, target practice, knife play, and guns. Lots of guns. Any gun you can imagine, Nico can take it apart, put it back together again, and shoot it like a marksman. He took my place at Scarlett's the day after graduation and hasn't looked back since. I moved on to more scrupulous jobs for Antonio. He knew I was completely loyal to him, and he trusted me with more and more responsibility as the years went by."

Chapter 6
Freddy

"Good morning, sweetheart," I say to Amelia, even though I know she's not going to answer me back.

The nurses come several times a day to take her vitals and blood, clean her up, and run tests. In between, I talk and talk and talk. I'm running out of things to say, not to mention the fact I feel like a total idiot sitting here talking to myself. Maybe I'm not saying what she wants to hear?

"Amelia, can you hear me? Can you open your eyes for me, baby?" I ask her the same questions multiple times a day, but there's never a response. Ruck comes in to check on her.

"Hey, man." He picks up her chart and checks the information the nurses have added since yesterday.

"Hey."

"When was the last time you got out of this room?"

"I don't know, why?"

"Because you need to take care of yourself so you can be strong for Amelia when she wakes up."

"I'm doing just fine. *When* is my girl going to wake up?" I snap.

"You know I would make it happen if I could, but it's all

up to her." I stand with my hands clenched in fists by my side.

"You have to fucking do something, Ruck!" His eyes connect with mine, and he takes a calming breath before he speaks.

"We're doing all we can right now. You know that. She needs time."

"Time. Time. That's what everyone keeps saying. Can't she heal with her eyes open and talking to me?" Ruck walks over to me and grabs me by both shoulders, forcing me to look at him.

"She'll wake up when she's ready. Are you talking to her like I suggested?" My death glare could burn a hole through his face.

"Yes," I say through gritted teeth. "I've talked myself blue in the face, man. She never moves." I pace around the room.

"It's only been a few days."

"A few more days, a few more days. It's been a fucking week!"

"We can pull back her pain meds, but it may cause her to be in a lot of pain. Do you want that?"

"No," I say, defeated.

"Look. Let's give her a few... I mean a little more time. If nothing changes, I'll lower her pain meds, and we'll see what happens."

"Fine." I blow out a breath. "I guess I'll think of some more things to talk about."

"Take care of yourself," Ruck says as he walks out the door.

"Did you hear that, sweetheart. You have a little more time to listen to me word vomit, and then you'll need to wake up." I get another water bottle and take my usual seat.

I rub my head. Trying to think of something I haven't talked about yet. I know.

"Remember the night we met?"

Chapter 7
Freddy

"**Y**ou were dressed in that red dress with all the sparkles on it. It fit so tight across your ass. I can still hear your giggle when I asked you to dance."

Ethan saunters across the dance floor and stops in front of a woman dressed in a sapphire blue dress. She has long dark hair, and her mask covers her entire face. Beside her stands the most beautiful creature I've ever laid my eyes on. Her blond hair falls in a soft braid down her back, and she has an ass that just won't quit. Her jeweled red mask only covers her eyes and nose, so I can see her rosy cheeks and her plump red lips. Ethan holds out his hand and leads his lady to the dance floor, so I do the same.

"Would you care to dance?" I ask, and a soft giggle comes from her candy-apple-red lips.

"Yes, I would. Thank you." I tower over her small frame, standing six foot five to her five-foot-something. I might split this girl in two if I fuck her too hard.

I take her by the hand and lead her to the dance floor, staying in proximity to Ethan and his lady for security reasons. We sway to the music for a short time before Ethan's eyes connect with mine. He nods his head, and the two of them are gone. I know where he's headed. To the secret room to hook up with the woman in the blue dress. That's all he does anymore is hook up with random strangers or hookers to try to fuck Lola out of his system. He even paid for girls for Nico and me one night while we waited to take care of business. I'm not sure he'll ever be able to move on from Lola.

"What's your name?" I ask.

"Amelia." Her voice is light and friendly. "What's your name, Big Guy?"

"Freddy." That name, Big Guy, makes me chuckle.

"Nice to meet you, Freddy." When the slow songs are over, I lead us back to the table. I hold the chair out for her, and we sit.

"You're really tall," she says.

"Thank you? And you're really short." Could I sound more stupid?

"I think I'll call you Big Guy."

"Why not Freddy?"

"Because when I called you Big Guy before, you smiled. You have a nice smile." I'm not sure what to do with this information. I don't smile. I have an image to uphold. I can't show weakness. Just my presence should put the fear of God into people. But I smiled for this girl and didn't even realize I did.

"How old are you?" I ask.

"Twenty-two. How old are you?"

"Thirty-four." I'm too old for this sweet little thing, but God, she's stunning.

"What do you do for a living?" she asks.

"I'm in...uh...security."

"So you're the other guy's security?"

"You could say that, sure. What do you do?"

"I work for an advertising agency."

"Nice."

"You know they're back there fucking, right?" Her candor surprises the shit out of me, and any nervousness I had before just left the building.

"Yeah, I figured as much."

"The only reason she would come tonight was because I told her there were secret rooms she could get fucked in." She leans in closer to me. "She's trying to forget her ex."

"Him too. Do you have an ex you're trying to forget Amelia?" My voice is smooth.

"No. I've never had an ex-boyfriend I needed to forget."

"Never?"

"No. Don't get me wrong. I date, but I don't sleep around."

I've never met anyone like this woman. She's so innocent and sweet, and yet she tells you exactly what she thinks.

"Good to know." The servers walk by with champagne flutes on a tray. Amelia takes one and points as if asking me if I want some. I wave it off because technically I am working.

"I love the little bubbles." She giggles that sweet sound again. Can she really be this happy?

The slow songs come on again, and we return to our spot on the dance floor. The champagne seems to be helping her relax. She's not as tense in my arms this time. I love the way my arms wrap around her. Pulling her in close, I breathe in her vanilla shampoo and realize her head fits perfectly beneath my chin. She sighs, and I have a strong desire to never let her go. She's making my body feel drugged with relaxation and calm. No woman has ever made me feel this way before.

"Amelia."

"Hmm."

"Can I kiss you?"

"I'd like that."

I lean down and press my lips to hers. When I pull away, a gentle smile spreads across her lips, and she sighs.

"Ya know, if you're going to keep calling me Big Guy, I'm going to start calling you Poppy."

"Why Poppy?"

"Because poppies are used to make drugs like opium and morphine. And you make me feel high." Her eyes grow wide, but this time, there are no giggles.

"Kiss me again," she coos. And I do as I'm told.

It's been about an hour, and the boss is walking toward us, with the woman in the blue dress leading the way. He sits at the table while she motions for Amelia to follow her to the ladies' room.

A few minutes later, Amelia returns to the table alone.

"I need to leave. I'm so sorry."

"Sure. No problem."

I want to yell, "Wait, don't go! I was just getting to know you." But I keep my cool.

"Can I have your phone number?" she asks. This woman is not shy at all. I stand and take out my phone. We exchange numbers, and I watch as the red dress walks away.

"That was a great evening. I've never felt like that with anyone before. Only you. I'll never forget the first night we slept together. We went to Lowell's after work. You had that surf and turf you like. You looked so professional in your suit with your hair pulled up in a tight bun. It makes me hard just thinking about it."

I walk her to her door after dinner.

"Do you want to come in?" she asks, wide-eyed and pointing over her shoulder with her thumb.

"I can stay for a little while, I guess."

She ushers me into her quaint studio apartment.

"This is nice, but it's really small."

"I don't need a lot of space. I'm small." She makes me laugh. "Have a seat." I take off my suit jacket, drape it over the arm of the tiny, flowered love seat, and sit. This couch is like a toy to me. I decide to be a smart-ass. I lie down and stretch out my legs, but my body hangs over two feet on each end.

"Um, Amelia. Your couch is too small for me." I laugh. She brings two bottles of water over, and she sits down on my stomach.

"Don't make fun of me." She pouts and crosses her arms over her chest.

"I'm not making fun of you, baby. I'm making fun of your so-called couch. It's like a big chair to me." She stands, and I move to sit up, and she plops down beside me. A glimmer of a smile crosses her lips. She knows I was only teasing.

"I've never had a man in my apartment before, let alone a giant."

"You haven't had a man in your apartment? Yeah, right," I say sarcastically, opening my water and taking a sip.

"I haven't...ever." She lifts an eyebrow at me in challenge.

"Well, I'm happy to be your first, then." I put my arm around her, and we sink back into the soft couch. "Does my age bother you?"

"Should it?"

"I hope not. Unless..."

"Unless what?"

"Unless you have some unresolved daddy issues?"

"Are you trying to be my daddy, Freddy?" she purrs.

"I can be your daddy if you want me to be, baby." I waggle my eyebrows at her.

We've gone out a few times, and I really like her. I've never taken my time with a woman. I fuck and leave. There are no feelings that way, but Amelia is different. Amelia is good and kind and fun to be around. I enjoy talking to her. She's intelligent and has a great mind for business.

I can't keep being around her with a dick of steel though. The only relief I've had has been my own fist in the shower. I need to touch her skin and feel her naked body against mine. I want to feel her pussy tighten around my cock when she comes.

"Freddy," she says, shaking me out of my daydream.

"What? Huh?"

"We need to talk." Oh crap. Here it comes. She's dumping me already, and I never even got to touch her.

"What's up?" I try to play it cool.

"I've never..." Dumped somebody as fast as I'm about to dump you.

"You've never what, baby?"

"I haven't..." Wanted to run away from anyone as fast as I do you.

"What's wrong?" I ask as she wrings her hands, looking nervous.

"I've never had sex." The words fly out of her mouth, and she covers her face with her hands. Leaning forward, she puts her elbows on her knees. Is she embarrassed?

"Amelia. The night we met, you said you don't sleep around. I just thought it meant you're really picky."

"Well, I am picky, that's why I've never done it. I haven't found the right person I wanted to share something so intimate with."

"Oh."

"I'm sorry. I should've told you sooner. You probably don't want to..."

"No, I didn't say that. I've just never been with a virgin before. I'm not a small man, Poppy. I don't want to hurt you."

Reaching out, I touch her back, trying to give her some form of comfort. I've had my fill of all kinds of women, hookers included, but usually they were just quick fucks to scratch an itch. I want more from her than just a meaningless fuck. I care about her.

"Amelia, I..."

"It's okay. Just forget it. I'll walk you out." She stands and heads for the door.

"Amelia, I..."

"No one wants to be with a twenty-two-year-old virgin. Thanks for the nice evening."

I hate her sad tone. Who wouldn't want to be with this wonderful woman?

"Amelia! You're not listening to me."

I stand, and in two strides, I have her body pinned against the front door. A whoosh of air leaves her lips.

"I don't want to leave," I say quietly, my forehead resting against hers.

"You don't?" Those big blue pools look up at me, and my chest clenches.

"I like being with you, and if you want to wait." I swallow hard. "I can wait."

"Wait?"

"I want it to be right for you. A woman's first time is supposed to be... special." Even I know that.

"I don't want to wait."

"You don't?" Thank fuck.

"No. I just wanted to be honest with you. I needed you to know I have zero experience. I mean, it's not like I don't know stuff, but it doesn't mean I've actually done stuff. I mean, there's a lot of stuff I want to do, but..." I stop her incessant talking by slamming my lips to hers. I lessen my grip on her body and use my fingers to remove the pins from the bun in her hair.

"Can you please stop calling it stuff," I murmur between kisses. I run my fingers through her hair, and it falls freely around her shoulders in soft waves.

"Okay," she coos.

"Are you sure you want to do this...tonight?"

"Yes. I like you, Big Guy."

"I like you too, Poppy. But you have to talk to me. I don't want to hurt you."

"I will. I promise." Her eyes are hooded as they look up at me. I swipe my tongue over her plump lips, and a little hum escapes her chest.

"Why don't you show me your bedroom?"

She giggles and leads me down a short hallway.

This room is just as small as the living room, and it looks like a flower shop exploded in it. Next time, we'll have to go to my apartment. I have a Wyoming king-sized bed, and it's equipped for whatever kinky play we can come up with.

"Can I touch you?"

"Yes," she purrs.

"I want to touch every inch of your skin. I want to know what you taste like." I hold her face in my hands and look deep into those ocean-blue eyes. I swipe my thumbs across her cheeks, and a sweet smile appears. God, she's so young. What the hell am I doing?

"Yes, please."

I lean over and place soft kisses on her lips, her forehead, her cheeks, and the tip of her nose. Out comes her shy little giggle, and my dick twitches. I nuzzle into her neck as I pull her body to mine and breathe her in while I run my hands over her back.

"Are you on the pill?"

"The shot."

"I'm clean. I was tested last week," I say. I hate this conversation, but I know it's necessary. "Condom?"

"No. I've heard they make your first time uncomfortable. And I think I'll be uncomfortable enough taking that big dick of yours."

"How do you know how big my dick is? You haven't seen it," I say with a curious grin.

"No, but I've felt it on my back when you've been behind me. That thing is massive."

"Well, I don't know about massive, but it will definitely fill that sweet pussy of yours."

"May I?" I ask as I reach the top button of her shirt.

"Yes."

Slowly, I unbutton each shiny button of her blouse. I slide the sides open and take in her soft skin, begging to be touched. My finger traces the edge of her nude lace bra, and her breath hitches. I remove her shirt and let it fall softly to the floor. I stand in awe as I take in the sight of her.

"What's wrong?" she whispers.

"Nothing's wrong. You're just so…beautiful."

Her cheeks blush, and she casts her eyes downward. Using my finger, I lift her chin. "Please, don't look away from me."

"Freddy."

"Shh. I got you, Poppy."

With a sweeping motion from my tongue, her mouth opens, and her tongue meets mine. My large hands roam over her ass searching for the zipper to her skirt. When I find it on the side, she shimmies it down her hips, and she's left in nothing but her bra and panties. I lower myself to my knees. Her breasts are at eye level now. I unhook her bra, and it falls away. Cupping her breasts in my hands, I knead them and roll her pert nipples between my thumbs and forefingers. When I suck one into my mouth, her head falls back, and she arches her back. I push her tits together while my mouth moves from one breast to the other, licking, sucking, nibbling. She runs her fingers through my hair, and the feeling sends chills down my spine. I stare up into her blown pupils and lower her panties down her legs.

I want to worship this woman. I want to bury my face between her legs and make her body feel sensations she's only ever dreamed of.

I stand and lift her into my arms and lay her on the bed. Her tiny bed will have to do for tonight.

"I have to get you ready for me, baby." She nods, and she lies back on the pillows for me.

"Spread your legs for me." She obeys, and my cock begs to be set free. I readjust myself and remind my cock that I need to take it slow. I can't hurt her. I remove my shirt and crawl between her legs.

With one hand on each thigh to open her wider for me, I lick and nip my way over her skin.

"Freddy," she gasps.

"I told you I want to learn every inch of this sweet body. Patience, Poppy." She groans.

I hold her exactly where I want her. One hand splayed across her stomach, while I run a finger through her folds.

"You're so fucking wet for me already, Amelia."

"Uh-huh."

I flatten my tongue and lick her from bottom to top, and her legs tremble.

"Your pussy is the sweetest thing I've ever tasted." She lifts her hips to me for more. "What do you need, sweetheart? Use your words."

"I need more."

"More what?"

"I need your mouth on me. Suck my clit." She doesn't have to tell me twice. My lips surround her clit, and I suck. Not releasing the pressure while I place little flicks with my tongue on her sensitive bud. Her head thrashes from side to side, and I can't take my eyes off her. She's so responsive to my every touch. I turn the finger I have inside her clockwise, and she bears down on it. I place a second finger inside her slick pussy, and I feel her muscles flutter around me.

"Oh fuck, Freddy. I'm going to—"

"Come all over my face, Poppy." My words push her over the edge, and her torso lifts off the bed.

"I... I..." She tries to speak, but she's lost in the pleasure. Her body tenses, and her legs clamp around my head as her orgasm rolls over her.

When her aftershocks have quelled, I sit back on my heels.

"Are you okay?" I ask softly, stroking her thighs.

"Yes. No one's ever made me come like that before."

"We're just getting started." I give her a wink and stand from the bed. I remove my belt in one swift movement, and her breath hitches. I drop my slacks and boxer briefs to the floor, and my dick is released from its confines. I watch her face when her gaze lands on me.

A smirk crosses her lips before she asks tentatively, "Can I touch it?"

I'm at a loss for words. Fuck, yeah, you can touch it! I decide to keep my mouth shut and walk to the side of the bed where she meets me. She holds out her hand, and I place it in her palm. My length stretches up her forearm.

"Oh my God. That'll never fit inside me."

"You'll be fine, sweetheart."

"Can I taste it?"

"Amelia, I'm trying to be patient tonight, but I think you're trying to kill me."

"Please," she whines. *"I've never tasted one before."*

"Stick out your tongue," I say, the words getting stuck in my throat. She does as she's told, and I move my cock to her mouth. Keep it together, man. Don't embarrass yourself.

Her tongue slides over the crown, and I swear my knees go weak. She wraps her lips around it and sucks. The sensation is enough to make me burst, but I get a grip and push her back like the pussy I am.

"Okay, okay. This evening is going to end a hell of a lot differently if you keep that up." She smiles and lies back on the pillows.

"Thank you," she says sweetly, licking her lips.

I climb between her legs, holding my weight up on my forearms. I lower my face to hers.

"I'm gonna go slow. You tell me if you need me to stop or move or whatever, okay?"

"Okay."

Reaching for my cock, I rub the tip over her pussy. Her sweet cream mixes with my precum as our soft skin slides together.

"Ready?" I notch my tip at her entrance.

"Ready."

I slide in just about an inch and hold it there. She moves her hips around my girth until I'm seated just inside her warm center. I push in a little more, and her body tenses.

"Freddy, oh shit." Her wide eyes look down at me.

"Am I hurting you?"

"A little." Before I can retreat, she slides her hands around my neck. *"It's not a bad hurt. It's more of an 'I'm stretched beyond belief' kind of hurt."*

"Take a deep breath and relax for me, Poppy." She breathes in and out. Her eyes soften, and they connect with mine once again.

"I'm okay. I'm ready."

"I'm going to go a little deeper." I press forward another inch. Her eyes close, and her mouth flies open, but no words come out.

"Amelia, look at me." She opens her eyes and focuses on me. "I got you, baby girl. Breathe." She takes in a cleansing breath and slowly exhales. "You're gripping my cock so tight. I don't know if I can go any deeper." She takes a few more breaths, and the clenching begins to subside. I slowly push in once, twice, and by the third push, I'm fully seated inside her warm, soft pussy. I hold my position for a moment, giving her a chance to get used to the fullness.

"Are you okay?" I ask as I use my hand to massage her tight shoulders. "You have to relax, Amelia. I promise it'll be worth it."

"I'm trying. I'm just scared."

"Why are you scared?" She shrugs and shakes her head. "Don't you trust me?"

"Yes, I trust you, or I wouldn't be here with you now." Her soft eyes connect to mine.

"The hard part is over, only the pleasure remains." I kiss her plump lips and pull my cock out of her channel and slowly slide back in with one slow stroke. Her muscles relax around me, and her hands slide around the back of my neck and into my hair. Her nails slide along my scalp, and when she scratches, chills cover my skin.

"More," she purrs.

"Wrap your legs around me." She does, and I begin to move a little faster.

"Freddy, I don't think I can come. I'm so full."

"Yes, you can. Get out of your head. Close your eyes."

I watch as those big baby blues close on my command.

"Now, concentrate on how well we fit together. Feel each thrust. Does it feel good?"

"Yes," she moans.

I move a finger to her clit and begin to rub her in circles. My body hovers above hers as I watch my dick sliding in and out of her. My cock swells even more at the visual, and she moans my name.

"Amelia, play with your clit. I need both of my hands to grip your hips." She doesn't hesitate. Her hand slides between us,

controlling her pleasure. I grab her hips and lift her legs to my shoulders, changing the angle of penetration.

"Oh, Freddy!" Her eyes fly open.

"Are you good?"

"More than good. That feels amazing." I can't help but smile as I thrust my cock in over and over. Her fingers circle her clit with the same pace as my cock slamming into her. It doesn't take long before her head thrashes from side to side and her body contracts around my cock.

"Fuck, Amelia, your pussy has a death grip on me." She's so fucking tight.

"I-I-I'm sorry," she says softly with hooded eyes. I dip down and kiss her plump lips.

"No, I fucking love how tight you are." A content smile plays over her lips. It doesn't take long for my balls to tighten, and I join her with my release.

I plant my forearms on either side of her head, and I pepper her with soft kisses.

"You are fucking amazing. Thank you for letting me share this first with you," I hum.

"I hope there will be more firsts with you, Freddy."

I pull her into my arms and bury my face in her neck.

"Plan on it."

This feeling in my chest is overwhelming. Sex has never been like this before. I feel...

"I think I knew that night, you were it for me. I never felt so complete. I never wanted to leave the safety of your tiny little bed ever again. I wanted to hide you away. To keep you all to myself, where I knew you were safe. But I didn't keep you safe, did I?"

"Just tell me what you want," I say to Boris Petrov over the phone.

"I want all the assets from The Organization."

"You're out of your fucking mind." I laugh. "They're all under Ethan's name, and you had Sasha kill him. Remember? What else?"

"I want you dead."

"You don't scare me, motherfucker. Try again."

"I should scare you, comrade, because I have your lovely lady in my dungeon right now."

"Sasha's not my lady."

"Oh, not Sasha...Amelia."

"You're lying."

"No, I'm not. Listen."

A small whimpering sound comes from the other end of the line.

"Freddy?"

"Amelia?"

"That was the first time in my life I was totally out of control. I wanted to destroy everyone and everything that got in my way of finding you. Sasha told me how strong you were. How you talked back to Bruce. How he hit you, and I wanted to kill that motherfucker all over again."

We're searching Petrov's house for Amelia. When I turn the corner into the kitchen, Bruce is holding Sasha off the floor by her neck. Her eyes are closed, and I'm not sure if she's even still alive. I pick a plate up from the table and hit him in the back of the head with it. He drops Sasha's limp body to the floor, and he redirects his anger to me.

We exchange jabs. He tries to get me in a headlock, but I duck out and hit him with a thigh punch. We square off again. I use my advantage to strike first and use the heel of my hand to drive up into his chin and push his nose into his head. Then I use his chest as my punching bag.

His knee comes up and hits me in the groin, and I get a sucker punch to the ribs. My left comes up with an uppercut and then a right cross to the jaw. He backs away from me like he's trying to catch his breath.

"Is that bitch downstairs yours?"

"Did you fucking touch her?" I growl.

"Petrov promised me her pretty cunt first."

"She has nothing to do with any of this!"

"Tough shit. I can't wait to taste her sweet pussy." His words make my brain snap, and rage flows through my fists. I grab him by the shoulders and throw him to the floor, where I begin to pummel his face. I close my eyes and see my father hitting Nico. I imagine Amelia bloody and broken. Over and over, I beat him with my fists. I feel the warm blood splatter on my face when someone taps me on the shoulder.

"Boss... Boss! BOSS!" I hold my fist suspended above his bloody face. "I think he gets the point." Shaking off the need to hit him one more time, I stand, take out my gun, and aim it at his head.

"This is for Veronica."

Bang.

∽

"And when you screamed from the basement of the devil's lair, I couldn't get to you fast enough."

∽

We're standing in the kitchen watching Bruce die when I hear Poppy screaming. I'm going to kill this motherfucker. I fly down the stairs and take off running. I throw the door open, and there stands Petrov, holding Amelia in front of him by a fistful of her long blond hair. The barrel of his gun points at her temple.

"Don't take another step or I'll blow her brains out all over the wall." I know what kind of man Boris Petrov is. Killing her would be nothing to him, so I stay where I am.

"Let her go, Boris," Sasha barks. His black eyes shift to

her. "You don't want Amelia. You want me. Let her go, and I'll do whatever you want."

Boris pulls back harder on Amelia's hair, and she cries out. Tears stream down her face. My fists clench at my sides. I have to keep my cool, or he'll kill her.

"Put your guns down...NOW!" he bellows. We all look at one another and lower our weapons to the floor.

"Kick them away!" We each use our foot to kick them out of the way.

"There. See...? We did what you asked. Now let her go and take me instead," Sasha says. Petrov looks around the room.

"This is family business," Boris spits and pushes Amelia in my direction. She stumbles forward, but I catch her.

"Take your bitch and get the hell out of here. Don't ever come back." I turn to look at Sasha, and she nods toward the door. I lift Amelia into my arms, and she clings to my chest.

When we're safely in the car, I rest her on my lap and smother her with kisses.

"This can never happen again, Amelia. I can't lose you."

"I-I-I wasn't paying attention. It happened so fast," Amelia sputters out between tears.

"I know, baby. It wasn't your fault. I didn't prepare you. But I'm going to teach you to shoot and defend yourself. I want you to carry a gun and have a full security detail. You're going to let me protect you now."

"Yes. Yes. I'll listen. I promise."

"But everything I taught you and the security I surrounded you with still couldn't protect you from this, could it? When someone is out to get you, they'll stop at nothing to follow through. I would keep you locked up in your room if I could, but I know you would be miserable. But this, all of this, was my fault. I'm so sorry."

Another day filled with stories has passed, and Amelia still hasn't woken up.

Chapter 8
Freddy

Today started out the same as all the others. Nurses, doctors, vitals, IVs, and meds—repeat. I'm in my usual spot, and we're finally alone once more.

"Poppy. Can you hear me, sweetheart?" My voice sounds more frustrated today because I'm at the end of my rope. How long do they expect us to live this way?

"I need you to open your eyes for me *today*, sweetheart."

I try to decide what to talk about, and all I feel is regret. Regret he took her from me. Regret he hurt her because of me. Regret it took me so long to find her. All I was thinking about was myself and how saying those three little words would make *me* feel.

If I said it... it would make me look weak.

If I said it... you might say you don't love me back.

If I said it... you'd think I'm not enough.

If I said it... it would make this all become too...real.

In my selfishness, I couldn't see that loving you...

Made me stronger.

Gave me purpose.

Made me want to be a better man.

Made me feel alive for the first time in my life.
"Come back, Amelia."

Chapter 9
Freddy

Something is wrong. Amelia's heart monitor is rising.

"Amelia?" I tap her cheek. "Amelia, wake up, baby." But she's not waking up. Instead, all the monitors are screaming now.

The nurses flood the room and push me aside. The chair I've been sitting in for days hits the wall with a loud bang.

"Amelia!" I try to move closer, but a nurse holds me back. "What the hell's happening?"

"Mr. Acosta, you need to leave." She pushes on my chest, but I won't budge.

"I'm not fucking leaving her!"

"Call a code blue!" another nurse yells.

"Please, sir, you need to let us help her."

"I can't leave her. She needs me." My voice quivers.

Ruck runs into the room. "What the hell happened? Freddy? Someone get him the hell out of here!"

The nurse uses all her strength to turn me around, then gives me a hard shove. My feet begin to move, but the noises surround me.

"Her pressure's dropping…"

"She's in V-fib!"

"I need the paddles! Get me the fucking paddles!" Ruck shouts.

The door closes, and I'm standing in the quiet hall. It's a stark contrast to the chaos in her room.

The nurse points at the chair. "We'll take good care of her," she says, patting my shoulder before turning to go back inside the room.

For a moment, the door swings open, and the chaos is released into the hall. And then it's quickly gone again. Only the muffled sounds coming through the crack in the door remain.

I drop down into the chair and rest my elbows on my knees. My head is buried in my hands, while my heart thumps wildly in my chest.

"This can't be happening. Not now. I was so fucking selfish. I waited too long. This is all my fault."

The seconds tick by slowly. They're filled with worry and self-loathing until…I realize I don't hear any muffled noises seeping from under the door. I lift my head and try to listen. No voices are yelling for this or that. No chaos. Just uncomfortable…heavy…silence.

"No. No. No. No. No. This can't be happening."

I jump from the chair, ready to bust my way into her room. As I reach for the door, it swings open, and Ruck stands in front of me. He places his hands on my chest and pushes me back out into the hall.

"What the hell happened?"

"She had a cardiac event."

"What does that mean?"

"Her heart stopped."

"What? Why?" Panic fills my body. This can't be happening. I feel an unfamiliar wetness in the corners of my eyes. "Get back in there and do something!"

"We did all we could do, Freddy."

"No. This can't be happening." My hands find my hair again

and pull until the pain matches the feeling in my chest. "He got exactly what he wanted. He took Amelia from me."

I try to move away from Ruck, but he grabs me hard by the shoulders and forces me to look at him.

"Freddy…"

I shake my head. "No. She can't be…"

Chapter 10
Freddy

Two Months Ago

The sun streams through our bedroom window. What a way to start the day, with my beautiful Poppy stretched out over my chest. I run my finger through her long blond hair. I wake her up by twirling a lock of hair around my finger and giving it a little tug.

"Good morning, sweetheart. Time to wake up."

A groan comes from her chest. "Do we have to?"

"Yeah. I have meetings today I can't miss. We'll sleep in tomorrow."

"Promise?"

I kiss her on the top of the head. "I promise." I groan and leave the warmth of our bed. Tucking the covers around her, I say, "You lie here and get a few more minutes while I take a shower."

"Thank you." She rolls over and covers her head with the blanket.

I can't believe this woman is mine. I've smiled more these past two years than I have in my entire life.

I turn on the shower and brush my teeth while the water heats. Surely, she knows how I feel about her by now. Why do I have to say it out loud? I've tried to tell her several times, but the words get caught in my throat, and they won't come out.

I step into the hot shower and let the water pour over my face. It's dangerous to have a woman in your life when so many want to take them from you. Every important role model in my life has lost the woman he loved, and look how it changed them.

My parents were in love. They were happy when I was growing up. We were a family and did things together. We were…normal. But when Momma died, Dad changed so drastically that I didn't recognize him anymore. He built his wall and shut us out.

Look what happened to Boris Petrov when he lost the mother of his child. He became a killing machine. He could torture and mangle men, sex traffic women, and kill innocent people and never blink an eye. He became a maniac.

I can never forget how Antonio changed after his wife, Lucia, passed away. He killed five men with his bare hands, forced a team to follow Guilia all around the world, kidnapped Lola, forced her to break up with Ethan, and eventually drove him into the life he never wanted.

I open the shower door and grab my towel to dry off. Why seek out the woman of your dreams only for them to be taken away from you? I never thought I would have a chance in my lifetime to care about someone the way I do for Amelia. I need her. I want her in my life. I'll just have to keep her safe whether she likes it or not. Because I don't think I could ever live without her.

I leave the bathroom in just a towel around my waist. Hair dripping wet. Amelia is lying on her stomach. I crawl on top of her, pull back the comforter, and shake my wet hair onto her naked body.

"What are you doing! You're getting me all wet!" she squeals.

"You need to get your ass up." I kiss her on the cheek. "C'mon, we need to go."

"I'm coming. I'm coming." She stands from the bed and heads for the bathroom. I smack her ass, and she yelps. Rubbing her ass cheek, she smiles at me as she begins to close the door behind her. "I thought you were the adult in this relationship?"

"Nah, I'm just a kid at heart."

We both exit our small house forty-five minutes later.

"I'm going to spend the day at the shelter. Lola and I are having pizza brought in for the residents as a treat. I should still be home by five," Amelia chimes.

"I don't know when I'll be home. I have to touch base with the cleaning crew and meet with the Irish. If I'm not home in time for dinner, you go ahead and eat without me. I'll get something when I get home."

"Okay, if you're sure?"

"I'll try to text you."

"Be careful today, Big Guy."

"Always, Poppy."

With one quick kiss, she settles into the back of the SUV, and Marco drives them away.

We got rid of our apartments and moved into this small house on the edge of town. I bought it after Petrov took her. I had to keep her safe. I also have a full security team keeping tabs on her every move. When she's not with me, she's with them. She's never tried to go off on her own. We've spent a long time discussing her safety and what I do for a living. I think she understands how important it is for her to have security around her at all times.

Running illegal operations for The Martinelli Organization means I now have many potential enemies I never had before. I have a good relationship with the other families, but you never know when one will go rogue and try to take something that doesn't belong to them.

There are men out there who would take Amelia, just to get to me. Even after our discussions, she still thinks no one would want to hurt her. She only sees the good in people. That's all well and good for her, but that's a naïve way of thinking in my line of work. I'll do everything I can to keep her safe.

I've installed trackers in all the vehicles, on her phone, and in her shoes and purses. I've done everything except put a tracker in her neck. All she knows about is the security team. When I told her an internal tracker would be the most effective way to find her in case of an emergency, she laughed and said no. I will never let down my guard when it comes to her.

$$\backsim$$

Amelia

Lola and I had the security team pick up pizza for the residents as a treat. This place isn't supposed to exist for their own safety. We can't just have food delivered. We take a few slices back to my office and sit at my table to eat.

"How did you feel when you first got a security team?" I ask.

"I didn't like it. But after Buddy kidnapped me, I knew I needed one for Ethan's sanity."

"For Ethan's sanity?"

"Yeah, if he didn't know where I was at all times, he would lose his mind. There was this one time I went into the bank vault, and he lost the signal. It sent some kind of alarm to his phone, and he freaked out. He was sending in the troops until I came out of the safe and the signal popped back on."

"Freddy and I aren't married though. I don't think it's necessary."

"Don't ever let him hear you say that."

"Why?"

"Another thing I've learned about Ethan is that he can't function unless he knows I'm safe. Freddy was a crazed lunatic when Petrov took you, so I'm sure he has a little touch of possessive Neanderthal in him too. Do you doubt the way Freddy feels about you?"

"No. I mean, yes. I mean, I don't know. He still hasn't told me he loves me yet."

"Still?"

"I know he cares about me, but he hasn't said the words."

"I'm gonna kick his ass!"

"No, Lola. God no. Don't say a word, please."

"You can tell he loves you, Amelia, by the way he treats you."

"I know, that's what I meant to say."

"It's been more than two years since you met, for fuck's sake. What the hell is his problem?" She takes a big bite of her pizza.

"Sometimes I think he's going to say it, but then he gets all quiet on me and leaves the room. Sometimes I just need to hear him say it, ya know?"

"Yeah, I get it. Do you doubt your feelings for him?"

"When you and I first talked about it, it didn't bother me so much. We got along great, and we always have so much fun. I thought he just needed some time to figure his shit out. To get over whatever was haunting him."

"But?"

"But I'm still waiting. When I try to talk to him about feelings, it always ends in an argument. I don't want to fight."

"I asked you what you would do if he never said it."

"And I thought it didn't matter to me, but now I think maybe I was wrong. I'm starting to need to hear him say it more and more each day."

"You need to talk to him, Amelia."

"I know. You're right. Maybe I will tonight."

Our day continues as usual, with stacks of paperwork and time spent with the residents. I try to sort out what I want to say to Freddy tonight on my ride home.

I don't want to start an argument, but I need to make him

understand how much this means to me. I need him to explain to me why he can't say the words. Who hurt him so badly that he can't allow himself to love me?

"Miss Amelia," Marco calls out, snapping me back to reality.

"I'm sorry, yes, Marco."

"We're here." I look out the window to see he's parked in front of the house. He comes around and opens my door. He helps me step out and walks me inside. He clears the house before he stands by the door to leave.

"Thank you, Marco."

"Are you sure you're all right, Miss Amelia?"

"Yes, yes, I'm fine. I'll see you tomorrow."

I shut the door and lock it. Freddy's not home yet. Checking my phone, he hasn't texted me either. I take a shower and eat some ramen noodles and get into bed to watch Netflix. Around eleven o'clock, he finally makes it home.

The bedroom door opens, and Freddy whispers, "Amelia, baby, are you awake?"

"Yeah. Just watching a show."

"How was your day?" he asks thoughtfully. He closes the door behind him with a click.

"Good. We had pizza, and I got a lot of work done. How was yours?"

"Long. My meeting with the Irish took us past six, and I still hadn't finished the payroll yet. I didn't want the guys to wait to get their money, so I stayed. I'm sorry it's so late." He removes his clothes as he's talking and climbs into bed in just his black boxer briefs. He takes me in his arms, and I cuddle into his chest.

"This is the best part of my day," he moans. *I'm afraid I'm about to ruin it.*

"Freddy, we need to talk." I run my palm over the muscles on his chest.

"What about, Poppy?"

"I need to know how you feel about me." His whole body goes rigid beneath my touch.

"You know how I feel about you. You're the most amazing woman I've ever—"

"That's not what I mean."

"What do you want me to say?"

"Do you like me?"

"Amelia, that's a dumb question. You know I *like* you." The words sound condescending as soon as they come out of his mouth. He pushes the blankets back and gets out of bed.

"Why can't you tell me?"

"I show you every day how much you mean to me."

"You do, but why can't you use your words?"

"Why do I have to *tell* you, if you can feel it?"

"Some days, I really need to hear it, Freddy. I didn't think I did, but I do. I got rid of my apartment to live with you. You have a security team following me everywhere I go. You have to know where I am every minute of every day. But you can't tell me how you feel?" He scrubs his hands through his hair and paces around the room.

"Why do we fuckin' have to do this now, Amelia? We're tired. We've both had a long day. Let's just go to sleep and talk about it tomorrow."

"You always do that."

"What?"

"Change the subject."

"Fuck, Amelia." He pauses and then quietly says, "I've never said the words before, okay?"

"Why?"

"I don't know how."

"You don't know how to say three little words?" I'm trying to stay in control, but I'm becoming impatient with his answers.

"Everything changes when you say those three little words."

"Yes, it would change everything. I would finally know how you feel about me."

"Other things change, Amelia. You don't understand."

"Make me understand, then. Make me understand why you don't love me enough to say it?" I scoot up and lean against the headboard. Folding my arms, I stare at him. My heart thumps in my chest, waiting for a response.

"Like… like…" he stammers.

"Like what? Like we would be happy?" He raises a brow at me. "Oh my God. That's it."

"That's what?"

"You can't let yourself be happy, can you?" I say cautiously.

"When you're happy, someone always takes it all away." His voice grows quieter.

"Oh, Freddy."

"I said those words to Momma and Laura, and they left."

I try to be as sympathetic as I can when I say, "They didn't leave you, Freddy…they died."

He stares me down just the same. All at once, it all snaps into place.

"Oh my God. You think just because you love me… I'll die?" I throw back the covers and walk toward him. Sadness surrounds us.

He lowers his eyes to the floor. "As long as I don't say it, nothing bad will happen."

"Freddy." I place my hand on his chest. "Think of all the happiness you're missing because you can't open your heart and let love in."

"It's not my heart I'm worried about, Amelia… It's you. I can't lose you too." His hand palms my cheek.

"You won't lose me, Freddy." We look into each other's eyes. Neither one of us wants to break the silence. But Freddy finally does.

"I can't say it." He shakes his head and backs away from me. "If you need me to say it, then maybe we need to rethink this."

I feel like I'm going to be sick. He would rather break up with me than tell me he loves me.

I take a deep breath and square my shoulders, calling his bluff. "Maybe we should." I glare at him. He hurt me, and I want to hurt him back. His eyes grow wide, and I feel my heart breaking. "I think I would like to take some time and get away for a while." I step away from him and move into the closet. I pull out a suitcase and place it on the end of the bed.

"Where do you want to go? I'll set it up for you." He picks up his phone from the dresser and holds it, ready to type. "When do you want to leave? It'll take me a little bit to set up the security team…" His words are businesslike. I pull clothes off their hangers and place them in the suitcase. He doesn't understand.

"No, Freddy. I'm going away. Alone. To think. No Marco. No security team. Just me. Alone." I open the dresser drawers, take out a handful of panties and socks, and place them in the bag.

"No fucking way, Amelia. You have to have at least one bodyguard with you."

"No one will want me if I'm not yours anymore, so I'll be safe." My voice is a little too snippy. I head into the bathroom and come out with a handful of items, tossing them into the bag.

"I didn't say I don't want you, Poppy. Please, you misunderstood me."

"Oh, I understand completely. You love me, but you won't tell me you love me, and if that bothers me, then we should break up."

"Break up? I didn't say break up." He's sounding panicky.

"Yes, you did."

"Fuck, Amelia, nothing's coming out right. Please," he begs. I put my hand up to stop the words coming out of his mouth.

"I'll be fine. I'm a big girl. You taught me well." I place my handgun on top of my clothes and zip up my bag. He watches me without a word as I pull on his black hoodie and my sweatpants and slide my feet into my sneakers.

"I need my car keys, Freddy," I say, holding out my hand.

"I don't want you to go, Amelia."

I swallow down my emotions and glare at him. "I need some time alone. Now give me my keys." I refuse to back down. He lets out a huff, then walks out of the bedroom and down the hallway to his office. Opening his desk drawer, he pulls out my car keys and places them in my hand.

"Amelia, please…"

"Goodbye, Freddy."

I take a deep breath and walk out the front door, letting the door slam behind me.

Chapter 11
Freddy

I watch as the blip on the screen comes to a stop at the Brighton Hotel downtown. She doesn't know I have a tracker on her car, but if she leaves it and gets on a plane or bus, I'll have to switch to the one on her phone. I make the call.

"Marco, take Phil, and the two of you keep an eye on Amelia, but don't let her see you."

"Yes, Boss." She can have her so-called freedom, but I need to know she's safe.

Amelia

I sit in my lonely hotel room, trying to figure out what the hell I just did. How did everything get so out of hand? So what if he can't say those three little words? I know he loves me. Why do I need to hear them so badly? Maybe I do have Daddy issues.

My dad left when I was seven. He wasn't a bad man. He never hurt my mom or us. He just didn't love us enough to stay. He left my mom to raise my older brother and me alone. She was a single mom who did her best. We had a good life. There just wasn't a dad in it. I pick up my cell and call Lola.

"Hey, Lo."

"What's up?"

"I was just wondering if I could borrow your cabin in Big Bear for a few days?"

"Amelia? Are you all right?"

"I need to get away for a while, to think," I say, trying to stifle my tears.

"To think? I'm coming over there."

"I'm not home. I'm at a hotel."

"Hotel! What the fuck did he do, Amelia?"

"I finally had 'the talk' with him. He'll never be able to tell me he loves me." My voice breaks.

"Why the fuck not? He loves you, and you know it."

"I know, but not enough to say it. He told me we might need to rethink our relationship if I can't live with him not being able to say it. So I left."

"You left. Tell Marco to bring you here."

"No, Lola. I took my car, and I left. No security. I need to be alone."

"You know he isn't going to let you *just be alone*. He'll have someone tailing you."

"How do I get away from them?"

"Amelia, it's the mob. You don't just get away from them."

"Please, Lola, you have to help me." Tears roll down my cheeks, and I bat them away. "I need to think, and I can't do it with Freddy controlling everything I do. How would you get away?"

"I'll do what I can to help, but Ethan will be pissed at me."

"I'm sorry. Maybe I shouldn't have bothered you with this."

"No, I'm glad you told me, Amelia. That's what friends are for."

The line is quiet for a moment, and it sounds like she's walking. I hear a door shut, and she begins in a hushed voice.

"Here's what you need to do. When you get off the phone with me, you'll need to turn it off and don't turn it back on again until you're ready to speak to Freddy."

"Why?"

"Because I'm sure there's a software tracker in it. There's probably a GPS tracker in your shoes, your purse, and your car too."

"What the hell?"

"Get used to it, Amelia. They need to know where you are at all times to be sane. I told you this."

"I didn't think he would do those things to me."

"Go down to the gift shop and buy some new shoes. Leave the ones you brought with you behind. You'll need to rent a car and tell them you want to pick it up in the alley behind the hotel."

"Okay."

"Make sure you stop and pick up some food and supplies before you get to the cabin so you don't have to leave again. There's a little store about a mile or so before you get there. The couple who owns it are very sweet. I'll tell them to put whatever you want on my tab, so he can't trace your credit card transaction."

"Lola. This sounds so…"

"Crazy. I know. But if you want to get away, you have to do as I say."

"I will."

"The caretaker lives in the cabin next door. He keeps a spare key for us. I'll tell him you're coming."

"Anything else I need to know?"

"Yeah, there are no cameras, internet, or phone service up there. It's off-grid except for electricity and water. There's wood in the garage for the fireplace if you want to start a fire. Lock yourself in. You should be safe up there. Let's say…three days."

"Okay. I have my gun with me."

"Smart girl. There are weapons in every room. Look in the drawers and under the tables."

"Thanks, Lola."

"Love you, girl. Be careful. Call me in three days."

"Love you too. I will."

I go to the gift shop and buy a new pair of shoes. Then stop by the front desk and use their phone to arrange for the rental car to leave first thing in the morning. I go back to my room, make a list of things to pick up at the little store, and try to get some sleep.

Chapter 12
Freddy

Ethan busts into my office the first thing in the morning.

"What the fuck is wrong with you, man?" he shouts. I jump up from my desk, gun drawn.

"Good God, Ethan, I could've blown your fucking head off." I look at my watch. It's before eight, so Lori, my assistant, isn't in the office yet.

"Lori wasn't at her desk."

"What the fuck did I do to you?" I place my gun back in its holster and sit down behind my desk.

"You idiot. You let Amelia just walk out with no security?"

"I have Marco and Phil following her."

"Really? Where is she right now?" I've got it under control. I don't understand what he's so mad about. I bring up the app on my phone and hold it up to him.

"She's at the Brighten Hotel downtown."

"No, she's not."

"What do you mean, she's not?"

"She's…not…there. Who do you have watching her?"

"Marco and Phil."

"Call them."

I dial Marco. My heart starts to race in my chest. I begin pacing the room.

"Hey, Boss," Marco says calmly.

"Don't you fucking 'hey, Boss, me. Where the fuck is Amelia?"

"In her hotel room. We're sitting in the parking garage looking at her car."

"Looking at her car. You dumbass. She's gone."

"No, Boss, she…"

"Go make sure, but I have it on good authority she checked out, and she's gone."

"But how?"

"GO!" I hang up on him and turn back to Ethan.

"How do you know she's gone? And where the fuck is she?"

"Lola."

"Ah, so she's at your house?" I breathe a sigh of relief and sit down behind my desk.

"No. Lola helped her get away."

"She what?" The thumping in my chest is back again. This roller coaster of emotions is going to give me a heart attack.

"She won't tell me where she sent her, just that she wants to be alone for a few days to think because you can't tell her you love her. You idiot." He sits in the chair across from my desk.

"This is ridiculous. Now everybody knows our business."

"Not everybody. Just Lola and me. Now, tell me, what the hell is your problem?"

I lean back and rub my hands down my face.

"Wait. I have a tracker on her phone," I say, swiping on my phone to bring it up.

"She turned it off," Ethan informs.

"You just know everything today, don't you?"

"What about her shoes and purse?""All left behind. You didn't answer my question. Why can't you tell Amelia you love her?"

"I can't say it, Ethan."

"Don't you mean it?"

"Yes. God, yes. I fucking mean it."

"Then why, man? Why would you hurt her like this?"

"If I tell her. If I say it out loud to her. Bad things will happen."

"Where did you hear shit like that from? Don't you know life only gets *better* after you say it?"

"No, it won't. Not for me."

"Why the fuck not?"

"Because everyone I've ever said it to has… died."

"You think if you tell Amelia you love her, she'll die?"

"Yeah."

"Look, man, the world doesn't work that way. Remember how much Sasha worried about falling in love with Gary?"

"Yeah."

"Have you seen Gary lately? He's very much alive and kickin'."

"It's not the same." He just stares at me like I'm insane.

"Why the fuck not?"

"Because this is me."

A loud belly laugh rolls from Ethan. "You're fuckin' crazy, man." He sits back in the chair.

"How do I find her?"

"Lola told me she promised her three days alone. Then she'll tell me where she is, and I'll tell you, and you can go get her."

"Thanks, man."

I don't know if I can handle three days of not knowing where the hell Amelia is, but now is as good a time as any to work through my shit.

The next day, I take my BMW M8 Gran Coupe out for a long drive, and I end up at the cemetery where Momma and Laura are buried. I stopped and picked up flowers along the way, then laid them on their gravestone.

"Hi, Momma. I'm sorry I've never visited before. Being without you both just hurts so much." I sit down on the grass in front of their headstone. "I don't know where to start."

I run my fingers over Laura's name. "Hey, Squirt. I miss you." I feel a stinging in the corners of my eyes. I take a deep breath and shove the emotions back down.

I look around the cemetery to see if anyone's going to see this thirty-six-year-old giant—that's what Amelia calls me—talking to a gravestone. But I'm all alone.

"Things were really bad after you left. After you…died." I think of Amelia's words. "Dad was never home, and when he was, things weren't good. I killed him, raised Nico on my own, and now we both work for the mob." Shit, that sounds ridiculous hearing it out loud.

"I've met a girl. No, I've met a woman. Her name is Amelia. She's amazing. She's kind and sweet. She makes me laugh. She makes me a better man every day." I wring my hands in my lap. "You would really like her. But I can't tell her how I feel. I can't say the words she needs to hear. I'm… a-afraid. But I can't live without her either. What do I do?" I lean my elbows on my legs and bury my head in my hands.

I hear a faint shh sound and whip my head up to see who's there. I don't see anyone in the cemetery at all. But I can't seem to shake off the feeling that I'm not alone.

"I'm afraid she'll leave me like you did. Like Laura did. Shit, even like Dad did. I can't talk to Nico about it. He's on his honeymoon with Guilia, and I don't want to bring him down." My hands go to my face again. I sit in silence until I hear the faint little shh sound again.

"Momma?"

I hear the sound again. My head is on a swivel, looking in every direction. I stand to my feet with my hand on my gun, but I still see no one. *Have I lost my fucking mind?*

"I'm gonna go for now, Momma. I miss you. You too, Squirt. I know you're both all right because you're together."

I climb back into my car and head for the house. That night, I had a dream about my mom.

She looks ethereal in her light pink dress as she walks, no dances, across the field ahead of me. Her dress flows loosely around her body in the warm breeze. Her cheeks are flushed pink, and her short auburn hair is in waves around her face, like she always used to wear it. She has the happiest smile on her face as I run toward her. My arms are outstretched, trying to reach the hand she holds out to me. But I can't get close enough to her. She keeps walking away from me and turning back to smile.

"Wait for me. Take me with you," I call out to her.

I see Amelia in the distance. Momma is walking toward her. She holds her arms out until they grasp hands, and I come to a screeching halt at the edge of a cliff. I can't reach them. They both float just ahead of me, smiling and waving. I want to go with them. I want to step out and see if I can float too.

"Take me with you," I beg. I reach my hands out to them and take a step...

I'm jolted awake when I fall to the floor beside my bed. Sweat covers my skin. I sit up and look around the room. *What the hell was that?*

⸺

The dream stays with me all day while I try to figure out what it meant. Does it mean Amelia is going to die and go with Momma? Does it mean I'm going to die trying to get to her? Does it mean Momma wants me to be with Amelia? My mind whirls with theory after theory. I need Amelia. I need to talk to her. I dial Lola.

"Hi, Freddy," Lola answers.

"Tell me where she is, Lola," I demand.

"I don't know what you're talking about," she says coolly.

"Ethan told me you know where she is. Now, tell me."

I hear her hand muffle the receiver as she begins to yell at him. "I'll never tell you anything again, Rocco Ethan Martinelli!"

Ethan's words are muted, but I think I hear him say, "I had to tell him, Lola. He's my friend. I couldn't keep it from him."

"I can't tell you, Freddy. I promised her three days, and it's only been two."

"Call her. Tell her I need to see her. Tell her I can't live without her. Please, Lola," I beg.

"I can't call her."

"Why not?"

"I told her to turn her phone off until she's ready to talk."

"You're telling me there isn't a phone wherever the hell she is?"

"Nope."

"Fuck, Lola, what did you do?"

"I can call a neighbor and have him go check on her and tell her to call."

"Okay. That sounds better. Thank you."

"I'll call you back in a little while."

I pace around the room, waiting for Lola to call me back. It's been almost an hour and still no call, when there's a knock on my door.

"Who is it?"

"Ethan." *What the fuck?* I open the door and let him in.

"Hey. Did Lola get ahold of Amelia?"

"She called the neighbor and asked him to go over there." Ethan steps inside, and I close the door behind him.

"And?"

"She's not there."

"What the fucking hell? Tell me where she is right now so I can go get her!"

"Lola sent her to our cabin in Big Bear. She picked up the keys from the caretaker two days ago."

"And?"

"When he went to check on her, the place had been ransacked. She's gone."

"Gone?" Panic fills my chest. Someone's taken her. "He found the rental car in the garage, a grocery bag with the contents of her purse in it, and her dead phone on the coffee table."

"C'mon, we gotta go." I grab my keys and head for the door.

"Freddy. She's not there."

"Check the cameras."

"No cameras. It's a place to unplug and get away from the world. No one knew she was there but Lola."

"Well, someone else fucking knew because they took her!"

"There was a message."

"A message? Why didn't you say that before? What did it say?"

"'She's mine now, Freddy.'"

"What?"

"The message read 'she's mine now, Freddy.'" The room spins, and I can't breathe. "Someone must've followed her to the cabin."

"Someone took her. Because of me. Just like I said they would."

"C'mon, man, snap out of it. We'll find her." His hand clamps down tightly on my shoulder.

"How?"

"I'll send some guys up to the cabin. Maybe they can find some tracks or something."

"You told me there are no cameras up there."

"Someone took her for a reason. They'll contact you. Then we'll find them and fucking kill them for taking her," Ethan rages.

My knees are weak, and I need to sit.

"We don't know if they took her today or if they've had her for two days. She could be anywhere."

"We'll find her."

"No, we won't. She's gone." Just like in my dream.

Chapter 13
Amelia

My eyes are heavy, and I have a thumping headache.

"Where am I?"

The last thing I remember is standing at the stove making soup. I try to move my body, but I can only stretch so far. My arms are bound behind my back.

It's pitch dark. Are my eyes even open? I blink several times, and I can't see the outline of anything. I kick my feet, but they hit something hard. I can hear the rev of an engine, and the ground beneath me bumps and shakes. I feel like I'm going to be sick. I swallow down the bile and take some deep breaths.

"Somebody. Help me." I try to yell, but my throat is raw and burns.

"Help me, please." I'm so tired. Just that tiny bit of exertion has exhausted me, and I fall back to sleep.

I'm startled awake by the feeling of being jostled, and I'm dropped with a loud metallic bang. I open my eyes, but my vision is blurry. The darkness is briefly replaced by scalding sunshine as my cage is slid up a ramp into a plane. *My cage!*

I'm in a fucking cage. The cage slides into place with a clank, and darkness falls once more as I'm shut inside a new vehicle.

My restraints are gone, but my cage is so small I can only sit or lie down. What the hell is happening? Where am I? Where are they taking me? Who's doing this? I really need to pee.

"Hello? Anybody?" I whisper-yell.

"Hello?" a faint female voice says.

"Hello? Who's there?" I ask again.

"Monika. Can you help me?" I try to look around, but I can't see where her voice is coming from.

"My name is Amelia. Where are you?"

"I'm over here by the wall. Can you see me?"

"No. Can you see me?"

"No. I'm scared."

"Monika. Is there anybody else with you?"

I hear the groggy sounds of another voice. "Here. I'm here."

"What's your name?"

"Carrie. Where am I? I need to pee."

"Me too," Monika says.

"Carrie, I'm Amelia. I think we're in the cargo hold of an airplane. You're going to have to hold it."

"Where are we going?" Carrie's weak voice asks.

"I don't know. Did you talk to anyone or see anyone else?"

"No," Monika says.

"No," Carrie echoes.

The engines start to rev. We're going to die in here if it's not climate-controlled and if it doesn't have oxygen. Why would they go to all the trouble taking us, if they're going to kill us in the belly of a plane? The engine noise is deafening as the plane shudders and jerks forward. It won't do any good to try to talk now because we won't be able to hear each other. I lie back down in my cage, hoping I don't freeze to death or suffocate.

When the plane takes off, my stomach lurches again and vomit wants to escape, but I keep swallowing it down. My cage slips a few inches, and I thank God the door is shut. I hear the creaking of wood rubbing together on both sides of me.

Once the plane levels off, I survey my situation like Freddy taught me and try to find a way out. I trace along the steel bars, looking for the door. I find a padlock hanging on the side. I'm stuck in here for the foreseeable future. I push my hand out into the darkness, and I'm stopped quickly by a wall of wood on three sides. I lie in the fetal position and try to hold in my urine, but I feel like I'm going to explode.

It's cold in here but not freezing, so at least they keep their captives from dying of hypothermia. I lie in the darkness, trying to remember what Freddy taught me. Don't go to a secondary location. *So much for that one.* I'm sure I'm on a third or fourth location by now.

It feels like we've been in the air for at least an hour, maybe more, and I can't hold my bladder any longer. I move to the opposite end of the cage and pee in the corner. This is the most embarrassing thing I've ever done, but I can't take it any longer. If they're going to keep us in a cage, they should've let us pee first.

The others must've had the same idea because the smell of ammonia fills the plane. My stomach growls, and I'm so thirsty.

⸺

We touch down with a bounce and come to a stop. There are voices outside, and the big door opens and turns into a ramp. The light filtering in hurts my eyes.

"Oh fuck! What's that smell?" a male voice asks.

"Didn't you take them to piss before loading them up?" another man says.

"No, they were all asleep." *All? How many of us are there?*

"Dumbass. The boss is gonna blow a gasket. Now we have to clean them up."

My cage slides down the short ramp. A heavy chain falls on top, and I scream. Two men attach the chain, and a crane hoists me into the air. I squeal as I lie flat on the bottom of the cage as it swings in the breeze. My cage is loaded onto the back of a flatbed truck. The desert heat is already causing me to sweat.

I take in my surroundings. I watch as five more cages are loaded onto the flatbed. I count eight guards. The land is flat and dry. All the plants look dead or dying, and there are mountains far off in the distance.

My eyes connect with two girls. Their eyes are wide and pupils dilated. I put my finger to my lips, telling them not to speak. We're all scared, and some girls are sobbing, but we can't afford to provoke them.

"Get me out of here!" a female yells from the other side of the truck.

"Shut up, bitch," the big, burly man snaps. He hits the bars with something metal, and it makes a loud pinging sound.

"You can't keep us in here," she argues.

"Watch me." Burly Man stops beside a shorter man. "There's always one with a big mouth," he says, and they laugh.

"We're just going to have to teach this one to behave," the other man says. This won't be good. The girl speaks up again.

"Hey! I need to pee!" she yells.

"I told you to shut the fuck up!" Burly Man struts over to her cage and hits her with something.

"Ow!" she cries out.

"That'll shut you up," he says, walking away. Hitting little girls makes him feel like such a big man. I hear her crying. I want to comfort her, but this is survival now.

The cages are tied down with straps, and I hear the truck rumble to life. We begin to move down the runway. I can see the plane. It has a skydiver painted on the side. The men left behind are unloading long black crates and putting them on another flatbed truck. We roll to a stop at the end of the runway and make a hard left turn onto a dirt road.

Dust swirls around the cages, causing me to cough. I curl into a ball and try to cover my head so I can breathe. Thank goodness we don't travel very far.

We stop in front of a long gray metal building. Burly Man releases the lock on my cage. I push myself as far back inside as I can, but he reaches in and yanks me out by my shirt. My bare feet drop to the hard ground, and another man grabs both of my arms and handcuffs them together behind my back.

"Holy hell, they smell awful," the shorter man says, letting out a gagging sound.

"That's your fault, asshole," Burly Man says.

They release the other girls from their cages and handcuff them as well. There's lots of crying and sniffling, heads hanging low, and slouched shoulders. I don't have anything left in me to cry, so I try to pay attention to everything.

They walk the six of us into the building. We each have a male partner holding us in line.

I look over all the girls. They're all young, maybe fifteen or so. I'm the oldest one here. Why would they want me? I see the girl who I think opened her mouth on the trailer, and she has a big red mark across the side of her face.

The room they take us to is open and made of concrete. Showerheads line the back wall. The guards remove our handcuffs, and the girls huddle together.

"Strip!" Burly Man yells. He's met with wide eyes and hesitation from all of us. "You're going to shower and get into clean clothes. If you do as you're told, we'll get you something to eat," his deep, harsh voice barks orders at us.

"Can we have some privacy, please?" a little blond girl says.

"No. You lost all your privacy when we took you. Now, strip!" I nod to the other girls and move to go first. I think we need to comply, at least for the time being, until we can figure out a way out of here. If we anger them, they'll only hurt us.

I still have on the same clothes I had on when I was making soup—baby-blue sleep shorts and one of Freddy's giant T-shirts. I drop my sleep shorts and my panties to the floor, and the shirt still covers my body. Burley Man nudges me with the barrel of his rifle to remove my shirt. I glare back at him and reach for the hem of my shirt. I take a deep breath and raise it over my head. I cover my breasts with one arm and squeeze my legs together. He nudges me toward the shower, and I move forward.

"Wash your hair and your body and get the hell out." I eyeball him again, but I don't say a word. The water is freezing. I wet my hair and reach for the shampoo. I lather my hair and start to rinse. My teeth are chattering from the cold water pelting my body. When I have all the bubbles rinsed clean, my hair feels like straw, but I reach for the soap next. I clean the urine smell from my body and rinse. Raising my chin to him when I turn off the water, he tosses me a towel. I wrap it around my body and follow him into the next space.

Each of the girls follows my lead. Some in tears, some defiant, but we all make it through our showers unscathed.

We line up again. This time, we're all dressed in baggy T-shirts and shorts, no panties or bra, and neon-yellow flip-flops are on our feet. The men use a rope to tie us together around our waists and lead us to a long table.

"Sit." Burley Man barks. We all hike a leg over and sit together on one side of a long table.

When the men turn their backs, I lean in close to the girl on my right and whisper, "I'm Amelia."

"Monika." She's one of the girls I talked to on the plane. I lean to my left just a smidge and do the same with her. "I'm Amelia."

"Sandy." I turn my head and look at each of them. I motion for them to push their shoulders back and hold up their chins. Hoping the others follow our lead because I'm not going down without a fight.

Two men bring us cold soup, crackers, and bottles of water. We're all starving, so we eat it without a fuss.

An older man comes to stand in front of us.

"I'm sure you're wondering why you're here. You belong to us now. You'll do as you're told, and my men will take good care of you." Turning to look at the girl with the hand mark on her face, he says, "But if you don't do as we say, you'll suffer the consequences."

"What are you going to do with us?" I ask respectfully.

"Why, we're going to sell you to the highest bidder, of course." All the girls gasp, and some start to cry again.

"When?"

"Three weeks."

Three weeks for Freddy to find me. Three weeks to find a way out of here. Three weeks to protect these girls.

Chapter 14
Amelia

We've been separated into individual cells in the basement of the warehouse. A small window above one of the cells is the only light we have. We each have a small, dirty mattress, a blanket, and a pot with a lid in the corner to do our business in. It's humiliating, and these girls did nothing to deserve this. They were just in the wrong place at the wrong time.

I still don't understand what they want from me. I'm too old to sell to the highest bidder at the ripe old age of twenty-five. Men who buy women want them young so they won't fight, and they can mold them to do their bidding. That's not me.

Burly Man comes into the room at dusk with some bagels and bottles of water.

"This is all you get today, so make it last."

"When do we get to leave? I wanna go home," the girl with the mark on her face whines.

"You're here to stay until the boss takes you to auction."

"I want to go home!" she yells.

"I thought you got the point last time, you little bitch. Do I have to come in there and school you again?"

"No." I speak up. "She understands." The girl's eyes meet mine, and I shake my head, trying to get her to stop talking.

"Maybe I need to teach you a lesson instead?" He moves to stand in front of my cell, and I take a step backward out of his reach.

"I understand," I say.

"Then shut the fuck up." The man backs out of the room and locks the heavy door to the outside world behind him with a loud bang.

"What's your name?" I ask the big-mouthed girl.

"Beth."

"You need to stop antagonizing him, Beth. He can hurt you very badly."

"I don't need you telling me what to do, lady. I can take care of myself."

"We need to figure out a way to get out of here," I say. All the girls move forward to the door of their cell.

"My name is Amelia. I know you're all scared, but we can't give up. We can find a way out of here." Beth waves me off and goes to sit on her mattress. I don't have time to deal with her when I can try to help the others.

"What's your name?" I ask the young girl in the cell across from me.

"Jennifer. Jen," she says quietly.

"We can't provoke them. It's obvious they're going to feed us and give us water. They can't sell you if you're dead or sickly. So we need to keep our eyes and ears open."

"Lady? Do you see a way out of here?" Beth asks, holding her arms out wide.

"No, not yet. But..."

"They're bigger than us. They're stronger than us. We'll never be able to get away from them. I choose to fight. Who's with me?" Beth looks at the other girls, but they just stare at her wide-eyed. All of them turn to look at me instead. Beth turns her back to us once again in a huff.

"There *will* be a time to fight, but it's not right now."

We all sit at the edge of our cells and eat. I try to get them to talk to me and get them to relax.

"Where are you all from?"

"Chicago," Monika replies.

"St. Louis," Sandy chimes.

"Little Rock," Carrie answers.

"Louisville," Jen says quietly. I turn to look at Beth, but she just shakes her head.

"I'm from Johnsonville," I say. They must take girls from all over the country and bring them here, so no one notices any pattern. I wish I knew where *here* was. If we got on a plane back home and flew for an hour, we could be just about any-where—Chicago, Denver, Virginia, Texas, California. Who knows where we are. I need to figure that out first.

"What do you like to do? Are you in a club? Band, choir, drama…"

"I miss my phone," Sandy whines.

"Yeah, I miss my phone too." If I had my phone, Freddy could track us.

"I'm in choir," Carrie says softly.

"Me too," Monika adds. Maybe those two can bond over music.

"What about you, Amelia. What do you do?" Carrie asks.

"I help run a battered women's shelter back home. We help women get back on their feet after being in bad situations."

"That's why you're trying to help us," Beth snips. "You're a people pleaser." Her tone makes me want to smack her too.

"There's nothing wrong with wanting to help people, Beth."

"I know people like you. You're always happy. Always smiling and wanting to help."

"And you're always miserable and hateful. I choose to be happy and help others."

"How old is everyone?" I turn back to the others.

"Fourteen," Carrie says.

"Me too," Jen chimes.

"Fifteen," Monika and Sandy say in unison.

Beth doesn't answer. Maybe her defiance makes her look older, but I think she's probably sixteen.

⌒

The next day, Burly Man brings us all a sandwich and water. Beth just can't keep her mouth shut. The rest of the girls sit on their mattresses, their backs against the wall, trying not to be seen, but Beth stands at the door to her cell.

"Let me out of here. Don't you know who my father is?" she barks as she pulls on the door, making it clatter.

"I've heard just about enough from you, bitch," he says, quickly crossing the short distance to her cell. I refuse to come to her rescue again. She's choosing to behave this way, and I can't help her.

"I want to talk to your boss." She stands with her hands on her hips. The picture of an entitled brat if I've ever seen one. Who is this girl?

"Not gonna happen, princess."

"I want…" She doesn't get a chance to finish her sentence before he grabs her by the hair and slams her face into the cold, hard steel.

"Ow! Stop it!" she yells as she tries to squirm out of his hold. He grips her face with his other hand and pinches her cheeks together like a fish.

"Now, you're going to fuckin' listen to me. This is your last chance. The only reason I haven't beaten the shit out of you already is because the boss said no marks. But I'm sure he'll make an exception when I tell him what kind of a pain in the ass you are." He throws her body away from the bars, and she falls to the concrete floor. He slams the main door as he leaves, and the whole room shakes from the noise. I stand and go to the front of my cell.

"Are you all right?"

"Leave me alone." Her voice cracks. She crawls over and lies down on her mattress and turns her back to us.

"Who's your father, Beth?" Monika asks.

"Wouldn't you like to know," Beth spits.

"Well, you made it sound like he's some big deal. Who is he?"

"If you must know, his name is Ronan McAnally." She turns to look at us.

"Who the hell's that?" Sandy says.

"He's the CEO of the Anton Corp in New York City. He's a very powerful man. He'll be looking for me. He won't let them get away with this. He knows the Irish Mafia." The Irish Mafia? I wonder if that's who Freddy met with the other day?

"Where did they take you from?" I ask.

"I was shopping at a mall in Newark."

"So they didn't necessarily know who your father was. You could've just been any other pretty girl."

"I guess."

I turn and look at the other girls. "Are any of your fathers rich and powerful men?"

"Not mine. He runs a car wash," Carrie answers.

"Mine works in a bakery," Monika replies.

"My dad is a businessman, but I don't think he knows any-one in the Mafia," Jen says.

"What about you, Sandy?" I ask.

"My dad's dead."

"I'm sorry, honey."

"My mom's a banker though."

"I don't think we're connected in any way. They just randomly picked up a girl whose father happens to know the mob."

Chapter 15
Amelia

Two days have gone by, and the only time we were out of the cells was to shower this morning. My hair is a mess. They keep us clean but don't allow us to brush our teeth or comb our hair. When Burly Man locks me in my cell, I ask, "Would it be possible to let us brush our teeth and comb our hair?" He glares at me, and I take a step backward out of his reach.

"I'll bring you a brush. You can share it."

"Thank you."

He comes back later with a brush with no handle. It's been sanded round and smooth. I guess he thought we might make a weapon out of it somehow. But it will do the job just the same. We each take a turn running it through our hair. The only thing keeping me going is my thoughts of Freddy.

It's Saturday afternoon, and we're riding in Freddy's 1970 Chevelle. The roar of the engine makes my body tingle. It sounds powerful. The muscle car suits him. The windows are rolled down, and my hair blows wildly around my face. I'm glad I wore my pink tank top and blue jean shorts. It's going to be another hot summer day.

"I love this car," I say, using my scrunchie to lasso my hair into a ponytail.

"I learned how to drive in this car."

"You did? Did your dad teach you?"

"No. My friend Joe taught me."

"Did he sell it to you?"

"Yeah, a few years after I started working for The Organization. I saved enough money and made him an offer he couldn't pass up."

"It makes me feel untamed and wild," I say.

"That's how a muscle car is supposed to make you feel, baby. Alive and free."

"Where are you taking me?"

"You'll see."

"Freddy Acosta, are you kidnapping me?"

"Baby, if I were going to kidnap you, I would be taking you to my bed."

"Freddy." I giggle.

He's been driving farther and farther away from the city. We're on some winding country roads that I didn't even know existed around here. He makes a right turn onto a gravel lane and comes to a stop at the head of a large field and parks the car.

"We're here." I look around, and all I can see is a field of green grass and a forest off in the distance. He gets out of the car and comes around to open my door.

"Where exactly is here?"

"Home." I stand from the car and look around again, but I don't see a house or any buildings.

"I don't see a house." I squint, trying to see what he's looking at.

"I bought the land, silly. It's all mine." His eyes are shining brightly as he smiles down at me. He seems to be truly... happy. My big Mafia boyfriend doesn't let a lot of emotions shine through, but right now, when it's just the two of us, he's beaming with pride.

"You bought it?"

"I closed on it last week. Twenty acres of land in the middle of nowhere, and it's all mine. I'm going to build a house and escape the world here someday."

"What do you mean, escape the world?"

"I don't want to run illegal operations forever. I've given the last eighteen years of my life to The Organization. Someday, I hope my debt will be paid, and I'll be free to sit on the back porch and watch the grass grow, if I want to." He wraps his arms around me from behind and pulls me close. He rests his chin on the top of my head. His normally tense muscles begin to slowly relax around me.

"It's so peaceful out here," I say.

"Can you imagine how deep you could sleep out here? No noise from the city. No bright lights. Just crickets and frogs. C'mon, I have another surprise for you." He pulls me by the hand. My stomach jumps. Oh God, is he going to propose? Why did my brain go there? We walk around to the trunk of the car, and he pops it open.

"What do you think?" he asks, pointing into the trunk.

"It looks like a trunk full of... camping equipment." My heart sinks. Disappointment fills my belly.

"I thought we could spend the night out here tonight. Just you and me under the stars."

"Oh. Okay. Yeah. I guess," I babble. He proceeds to empty the trunk. There's a big heavy bag, an air mattress, a cooler, a backpack, and a grocery bag with hot dogs, buns, and marshmallows, among other things.

"We aren't really going to sleep out in the open with the bugs and animals and stuff, are we?"

He lifts the big bag and nudges it. *"I brought a tent to sleep in, silly."* Thank God. I'm not the outdoorsy type. He seems so excited, and I want him to be happy. I guess I can muddle through anything for one night for him.

"What can I do to help?"

"Let's set up camp first, and then we can go for a walk."

"Sounds like a plan."

We put up the tent together. He pumps up the air mattress, and I make the bed. He clears a space for a small campfire, and I empty the backpack. He thought of everything, right down to the sticks to cook the marshmallows on.

"You know, I'm not really much of a wilderness girl. But this is kinda fun."

"See, I knew you would like it out here as much as I do." He takes a deep breath of the country air, and his shoulders relax.

"When are you planning on building this house of yours?"

"I guess when we can agree on a floor plan."

"We?"

"Well, you don't think I'm going to live all the way out here by myself, do you?"

"What?"

"You're my girl, aren't you?"

"You know I am." I feel warm all over.

"I want you to live out here with me."

"Oh."

"Amelia, I could never live out here without you." He places a soft peck on the tip of my nose.

"But, Freddy..."

He reaches into the cooler and pulls out the package of hot dogs. He flicks open his switchblade and, in one fluid motion, slices through the plastic.

"Yes, baby." He looks at me with a hopeful expression. Like a child waiting for Santa. I know he loves me. He wants me to live out here with him, for God's sake. I can't ruin this night for him by starting that conversation again.

"Did you bring the mustard?" I ask, letting out a breath.

"Did I bring the mustard?" He chuckles boastfully. He pulls it out and hands it to me. "Of course, I brought the mustard. I know that's all my girl will eat on her hot dogs." He remembered that?

We jab the hot dogs onto the sticks and hold them over the fire. The coals glow hot, and the juices from mine catch it on fire. Though a little burnt, it was still the best hot dog I've ever eaten.

When the fire starts to die down, I pull out the bag of marsh-mallows. "Time to burn some marshmallows," I announce, holding them up.

"Burn them?" Freddy turns up his nose and sneers.

"Yeah. They're only good if you burn them a little."

"You're crazy, woman."

"I'll show you." I take two out of the bag and stab them with my stick. Freddy takes two out and places them on his stick. I chuckle under my breath as we hold them out over the coals. This huge man holds his marshmallows delicately over the fire, away from the flames, and they slowly start to turn the perfect shade of light brown.

I dance my stick right in a flame and wait until it catches fire. I pull it back out, count to three out loud, and blow them out. Freddy looks at me like I've lost my damn mind.

"Oh my God, it tastes so good," I say as I stuff one marsh-mallow into my mouth and savor its sweetness. My eyes roll back in my head, and I moan with delight. He's paying more attention to me eating than he is his precious marshmallows. I point at his stick. My mouth is still full of sweet gooey mess, but I try to yell.

"Freddy! Fire!" His head snaps to where I'm pointing.

"Dammit." He blows them out and starts to yank them off the stick.

"NO!" I yell. "Don't throw them away. I'll eat them." He blows on them until he's sure they won't burn me. He takes one between his fingertips and raises it to my waiting mouth. I stick out my tongue and wait. His gaze on me is feral. He places the marshmallow on my waiting tongue, and I pull it back into my mouth. Swirling the melty goodness around, I hum like I could come from the taste.

He looks like a man possessed. He takes the second marsh-mallow between his fingers, and he holds it up to me. I stick out my tongue like before. He leans in closer and holds out the gooey goodness, but this time, he throws it in the flames, and his mouth crashes down on mine. Our tongues, teeth, and lips collide in a feverish kiss. His tongue takes over my mouth. Long licks mimic how he uses his tongue when he eats my pussy, and I feel wet between my legs. As I pull him tighter to me, my name comes from his panting lips.

"Amelia."

"Yes, Freddy." I'm sure he's ready to go inside the tent.

"Let's go for a walk," he says as he pulls away from me. My whole body deflates. What the fuck? Two seconds ago, he was devouring my mouth, and now he wants to go for a walk? I don't get it. I shake my head to clear my thoughts.

"Yeah, sure, whatever." I brush the blackened crumbs from my shorts and stand. He takes me by the hand, and we begin walking through the field. The sun is setting, and the air smells clean and fresh. A soft breeze blows the grass around, tickling my ankles.

"Where are we going? It'll be dark soon."

"I wanted to show you the spot I think will be perfect for the house."

"Oh, okay." He pulls me into his side, and his strong arm holds me close as we walk.

About fifty yards from the campsite, he stops. His head turns from side to side as if he's looking for something.

"Here. Right here," he says. He steps back from me and holds out his arms. "We can sit on the back porch right here and watch the sunset. I turn and look in his direction, and I can see the sun beginning to dip behind the trees.

"It's perfect, Freddy," I croon. He releases my hand to walk around, telling me his plan.

"Over here, I thought we could put the kitchen. It can have classic white cabinets, marble countertops, and black fixtures, or we can go for a more country feel with dark cabinets and light floors. Whatever you want, you decide. Then over here would be the living room with a floor-to-ceiling stone fireplace, big heavy furniture, and a bearskin rug. He walks down a little

farther and says, "This area could be the primary bedroom. Big enough for an Alaskan king bed that will fit the dogs and us.

"Dogs? When are we home long enough to take care of dogs?"

"Gotta git a big dog er two out yonder on the land, little darlin'," he says with a country twang that makes me laugh. Who is this man, and what did he do with Freddy?

"Are you going to turn into a cowboy, Freddy Acosta?"

"I might. We can get some cows and some chickens and a horse or two..."

"Hold up. Do you know anything about taking care of those kinds of animals?"

"Well, no. But we could learn."

"We!"

"You could plant a garden and some fruit trees over there," he says, pointing off to the left. "Oh, Amelia, it would be like our own little slice of heaven."

"It sounds like a lot of work to me."

"We can hire some people to help. It'll be fine."

"If you say so. How many bedrooms is this house going to have?"

"Let's see. We need the primary bedroom, of course, a room or two for when we have guests, and a library for all your smutty books."

"Oh stop." I push on his chest. "I don't have enough books to fill a library."

"I'll buy you whatever books you want to fill it with."

"Do you see any rooms for kids in this dream of yours?" He stops in his tracks. Oh shit. What have I done?

"Kids? I never thought about kids."

"Do you want kids someday, Freddy?" An image of this mountain of a man covered with children makes me chuckle.

"No. Yes. Maybe. I don't know. Do you...want kids?"

"Maybe, someday." His mood softens as he takes my hand and changes the subject, telling me more about his dreams for the new house.

"You can have a walk-in closet as big as a room here, and this would be our primary bathroom. Radiant-heated floors, towel warmers, and a huge soaker tub big enough for both of us to fit in comfortably."

"What about a shower? Can we have one of those with lots of showerheads that you can fit like six people in?"

"You sure can. And how about a bench I can lean you over while I fuck you?"

Chapter 16
Amelia

"I think I'm going to go mad," Sandy says as I'm shaken out of my daydream into my crude reality.

"I want to go home," Carrie says quietly.

"Do you think they would let us go outside?" Monika suggests. "Maybe if you ask them, Amelia?"

"Why me?"

"They listen to you."

"Oh really?"

"Maybe it's because you're older."

"Gee, thanks."

A different man comes to bring us sandwiches for lunch. He has reddish-brown hair, and he's not as large as the other man. I hope he's not as mean either.

"Would it be possible to let us go outside to get some sun?" His brows wrinkle. I wonder if he speaks English.

"I'll ask." At least he didn't cut me off and just say no.

A couple of hours later, he comes in with six men.

"We set up a place for you to get some air. But don't think about doing anything stupid because there's nowhere for you to run out here."

"We won't. Thank you." They cuff our hands behind our backs and lead us to a small fenced-in area on the backside of the warehouse. Scanning my surroundings, I make a mental note of all the structures on the property.

There's a smaller building opposite this one. It's one story and has lots of doors like a motel. Maybe the guards live there. I count ten black Lincoln Aviators parked around the area, three motorcycles, and twenty-two men with guns. They're walking across rooftops and around the perimeter. We're definitely in the desert because everything is covered in a layer of dust, and the ground is hard and cracked.

"See, I told you they'd listen to you," Monika says. The girls walk around the little area and stretch their legs. I sit back on the long bench, lean my head back against the chain-link fence, and let the sun warm my face.

My thoughts lead back to Freddy and our night under the stars.

We return to camp, and I sit down by the fire. Freddy is at the back of the car rummaging through the trunk. He takes out a heavy blanket and spreads it out on the grass and sits on it.

"Amelia."

"Yeah?"

"Wanna come join me?" He crooks his finger in a come-hither motion and pats his hand on the blanket. Lying on our backs, we gaze up at the night sky.

"The stars are so bright out here," he says softly.

"They're stunning," I chirp. He rolls onto his side and faces me. I'm not going to get too excited this time because he might have something else he wants to drag me off to see. His fingers circle the buttons on my blouse, and my breath hitches.

"Thank you for sharing this with me," I whisper.

"I want to share everything with you, Poppy."

"Freddy, I..."

"Shh. Let me make you feel good under the stars." His mouth meets mine, and his woodsy scent fills my nostrils. His soft and sensual kisses glide down my neck to my shoulder and land at the top of my chest.

"*I need you naked in the moonlight, Amelia.*" *I sit up, and he helps me lift my tank over my head and tosses it to the edge of the blanket. He reaches around and unhooks my bra, and I slide it down my arms. The cool evening breeze makes my nipples harden into tight buds. I shimmy out of my shorts and panties and lie back down on the blanket.*

"*You look so beautiful.*" *Embarrassment washes over me as his eyes slide over my naked body. I try to cover myself with my hands, but Freddy catches them in his.*

"*I've told you before not to hide yourself from me, Amelia. I want to see all of you.*"

"*But someone could see us out here,*" *I whisper as if someone is listening to us.*

"*We're miles away from anyone. And besides, do you think I'd let another man see what belongs to me?*"

"*No. I guess not.*"

"*That's right. Because you're mine.*"

"*No other man's lips will ever kiss these lips, but mine.*" Kiss.

"*No other man's hands will ever touch your warm skin, but mine.*" Kiss.

"*No other man's tongue will ever taste this luscious pussy, but mine.*" Kiss.

His words flood my center with anticipation. I do as I'm told and move my hands to rest by my sides.

"*The way the moon bounces off your skin makes you look like an angel lying here waiting for me.*"

"*Freddy.*" *My voice comes out needy.*

His pupils are blown, and he looks like he could pounce on me at any moment, but he's holding back. He always holds back part of himself from me. I want all of him. All the gentle and all the dangerous.

"*Freddy, please.*"

"*You don't have to beg, baby. I'll give you whatever you want. Tell me what you need.*"

"*I-I-I don't want you to make love to me.*" *My words cause his brows to furrow, and he tries to pull away from me.*

"What?" He acts like I just slapped him.

My hands grab his wrists. "I don't want you to make love to me tonight, Freddy. I want you to fuck me. I want you to use me and take me like you never have before." His eyes are wide in disbelief, and he leans back into me.

"Amelia. You don't mean that."

"Yes, I do. You're always so gentle with me."

"You were a virgin, Amelia." His tone is like a teacher reprimanding a student.

"Were, Freddy. That's the keyword here."

"I want to treat you with the respect you deserve. I want to treat you like a queen."

"And I appreciate that, Big Guy, but there's a time and a place for gentle, and I'm asking you for something different tonight."

"You're not ready for all the fucked-up things I could do to your body, Poppy. All the things I want to do to you."

"It's been six months since the first night in my apartment."

"Amelia." He tries to dismiss me, but I carry on. "I can feel you holding back on me. Do you know how much it hurts me to know you aren't being your true self with me? To know there are things you won't do with me... to me." He scrubs his hand down his face and sits back on his haunches. "I want to try new things with you. I want to be daring and wild."

"What do you want me to do, baby? Tell me."

"I want you to talk dirty to me and manhandle me. I want you to treat me like one of those whores you used to fuck. I want it to be rough and unforgiving. I want to feel you in my pussy days later. I want..."

"I don't think you would like it like that, Poppy." He shakes his head.

"Don't tell me what I'd like and wouldn't like!" I can't help my frustration at his dismissive tone.

"I don't want to hurt you."

I take a deep breath and calm myself. "I know you would never hurt me. Not on purpose."

"But what if I get carried away and do something you don't

like? Or worse, what if I hurt you?"

I lean up on my elbows and look him in the eye. "You won't."

"Amelia, where's all this coming from?"

"I'm afraid if I can't give you what you need...you'll go somewhere else to get it."

"Amelia, baby, I wouldn't..."

"You need to be sexually fulfilled too, Freddy. I want to help you live out your fantasies."

"But you are my fantasy, Poppy."

"Then maybe I need you to help me live out mine."

"What if my fantasies are darker than yours?"

"Then we'll figure it out. I'm not a fragile piece of glass, Big Guy." My hand cups his cheek.

"Amelia—"

I cut him off before he can talk me out of it, and I stand my ground. "You asked me what I wanted. This is it. We'll use a safe word. I promise I'll use it if it gets to be too much." His eyes darken, and his body overtakes mine as he smothers me in lust-filled kisses, while his large hands roam over my body, rubbing and squeezing my flesh.

"Is that a yes? You'll do it?"

"Yes. Fucking, yes. Amelia. What's your safe word?"

"How about...marshmallow?"

"Remembering you eating those damn marshmallows just makes me hard. It has to be something to make me stop whatever I'm doing."

"Hmm. Starlight."

"Fine, starlight."

I rub my legs together, trying to find some friction. I need him to touch me. To release this need building in my core.

"Are you my needy little slut?"

"Yes," I hiss. "Fuck me, Freddy."

"Oh, I'll fuck this cunt until you scream my name, but first I get to play. On your knees." He stands and rolls a big log over to the edge of the blanket. He takes his shirt and lays it across it to protect my skin.

"Use the log for balance and lean over."

I do as I'm told and wiggle my ass in front of him playfully. He slaps my ass, and I yelp. I can't stifle a naughty giggle. Before I know what's happening, Freddy is on his back, and his head is sliding between my legs.

"Sit, Poppy." A flutter fills my chest.

"I can't sit on you. How will you breathe?"

"Do as I say. Now. Sit!" His demand makes my stomach clench. I lower my pussy near his face and hover.

"Sit the fuck down, Amelia!" he demands. He grabs my thighs and forces my sex onto his face. His tongue slides through my pussy, and I moan. He explores every inch of me, running the tip of his tongue around my opening before plunging it deep inside. The sensation almost has me coming already.

"Holy shit. That feels amazing," I hiss. His head nods. There's a twinkle in his eyes as he looks up at me, and I swear he's grinning. One hand slides up my ass and pulls me down even closer, as his mouth consumes my pussy, and he feasts on my needy sex.

I lean back, and my hands grip his thighs to steady myself. I throw my head back in pleasure as his hands move to my breasts, kneading and pinching them. It sounds wet and sloppy as I close my eyes and allow my body to soak in all the sensations he's giving me. He slaps the side of one breast and then the other, reminding me of what I asked for tonight.

"Eyes on me, slut." The way he draws out the word slut intensifies the heat. My hips rock, and I grind down onto his mouth as I chase my orgasm.

"That's it. Grind that pussy on my tongue. Take what you fucking need." He pulls me back down on his glorious mouth. I lean forward onto the log, and there's a smack to my right ass cheek. Another to my left, and my orgasm washes through me. My body shakes as incoherent cries leave my lips.

"You're such a good little slut for me, Poppy." I look down into his dark eyes, and a mischievous smile crosses his face as he slides out from beneath me. I turn and sit on the blanket.

His face glistens in the moonlight, covered with my release, before it crashes to mine in a hungry kiss.

"You make me so fuckin' hard."

"Prove it," I purr. I swear I hear a growl come from his chest.

"I'm gonna fuck this sweet cunt of yours until you collapse from exhaustion." That's the Freddy I was looking for. "Chest on the ground, ass in the air." His orders make my body ache with anticipation. "That's right. Up in the air. Just like that. Mmm. I want to see every inch of this wet pussy." He slides a finger through my folds and puts it in his mouth. "It's mine. All fucking mine."

I arch my back a little farther. I am his. Only his.

"You liked it when I spanked your sweet ass, didn't you, Poppy?"

"Uh-huh." Smack.

"Let's try that again, shall we? You liked it when I spanked your sweet ass, didn't you, Poppy?"

"Yes…sir."

"That's better." Smack. *He soothes my flesh with his large hand.*

"You think you'll like it when I take you hard and rough?" Smack.

"Oh. Y-Y-Yes, sir." It's hard to have a complete thought when he's circling my ass cheek with his palm.

"You want my cock buried deep in your needy cunt?" Smack.

"Oh God. Yes, please." My hips push back against him, looking for more. Lust grips my body as his words continue to drive me wild.

"Your pretty ass likes to be punished, doesn't it?" Smack.

"Yes, sir."

Smack. Smack.

"Please, sir."

"Please, what, Poppy? Tell me what you need."

"Your cock. I-I-I need your cock inside me."

A finger makes its way to my puckered hole, and my breath hitches.

"I'm going to take you here one day, Poppy. Would you like that?"

"Y-Y-Yes, sir," I say, hiding my face. Did I just agree to that?

"What did I say about hiding from me!" His hand comes down on my ass harder this time.

"Aw, fuck. I'm sorry, sorry, sir." I try to push my hair out of my face, but he swats my hand away, and he collects all my hair into his fist and holds it tight.

"That's better," he says.

His large hand cups my pussy, and I grind down on him, seeking the friction I desperately desire. When his thumb makes contact with my swollen clit and two fingers slide inside me, I can't control what my body does any longer. I come hard and fast. Crying out in pleasure.

"That's my needy little slut," he speaks low against my ear. His hot breath burning a path along my neck.

"Now be a good girl and sit on the blanket. My brain hears his command, but my mouth can't make words. My body does as it's told, and he moves to stand above me. He looks menacing, towering above me. "Take it out," he growls deep and heady.

No hesitation here. I go straight to work undoing his belt. I can feel his eyes on me as I pull the belt slowly through each loop and toss it aside. Adjusting myself onto my knees so I can reach better, I unbutton his jeans and pull down his zipper. Pushing his pants over his ass and down his legs, I look up at him through my sooty lashes for approval.

He nods, but his expression is still dark, as I run my fingers across the waistband of his boxer briefs and slide them down. His cock springs free, and I lick my lips. My mouth waters, imagining him in my mouth, but I wait for instructions.

"Open up." My mouth eagerly opens. He grasps his hard cock and feeds the crown of it into my mouth. "You know what I need, Poppy." I nod and wrap my right hand around his shaft and take over control of his cock.

His hands slide across my scalp, and he clutches my hair between his fingers. Their hold is firm but not painful. I flatten my tongue and lick the underside of his cock while I suck him into my throat. Sliding my left hand to his balls, I roll them in my palm, and a moan leaves his throat. I'm so turned on by having this powerful man at my mercy that I can feel the wetness slide down my thighs. I want to please him so bad. I suck his cock deeper into my throat, and I swallow around him.

"Enough!" *he shouts, and I release him from my mouth with a pop.*

"Did I do something wrong?"

"Fuck no. I want to fill your pussy with my cum, not your greedy mouth." *Oh fuck.*

"On your knees." *I scramble quickly at his order.* "Head down, ass up." *I get into position.* "You're going to be a good little slut and take all of me." *I nod.*

He notches his crown at my slick entrance and rubs his tip through my folds and growls, "Sucking my cock made you so fucking wet, didn't it, slut?"

I nod.

"Say it!"

"Sucking your cock made me wet, sir."

"Your cream is running down your legs. You're so needy for this cock."

His hand runs up my spine and lands in my hair.

"Fuck, baby. I love wrapping your hair around my fist when I fuck you," *he says as he winds the ponytail he made around his fist and pulls it taut at the same time he pushes his cock deep inside my center. We both moan in pleasure at the sensation of him finally taking me.*

He doesn't pause. He doesn't wait until I adjust to his size. He's not Mr. Manners tonight. He pounds into my pussy. His strokes confuse me at first, but I quickly learn the rhythm. Long stroke, short stroke, long stroke, short stroke. The rocking motion lulls me into a false sense of security before his hand comes down on my ass.

"More," I pant.

He pulls my head back farther, and my chest lifts off the blanket, as he turns his thrusts loose on my pussy. They're harder, deeper, faster than ever before.

"That's it. Fuck. Right there. You can take it, baby."

"Freddy. Oh shit."

"You feel so fucking good creaming all over my cock."

He pulls me back to meet his chest. His strong arm holds me in place while he pulls my head to the side, and his tongue slides up my neck. It's filthy and so fucking hot. When the callused pad of his thumb finds my clit, I explode with pleasure. My cries of euphoria fill the night air as his body becomes rigid. He stills as he fills me with his cum as promised.

He lowers his forehead to my neck and gives a contented sigh before he lays me down on the blanket. I fall into slumber, wrapped safely in his arms, under a sea of stars. Exhaustion claims me, just like he said it would.

Chapter 17
Amelia

"Hey!" a familiar voice grates in my ears, and my smile is wiped from my lips. Burley Man towers above me, and my body is on alert. He has five men with him to escort us back to the basement.

"I'm not sure who you talked into bringing you out here, but playtime is over." He grips my arm roughly and pulls me to my feet. One by one, they lead us across the compound toward the warehouse.

"Boy, it sure is hot here," I say.

"The desert usually is hot." He snickers. *He thinks he's so smart.*

"How can we be in the desert when there are mountains over there?"

"Those are the Sierra Madre, idiot."

"Oh." *Thank you, dumbass, you just told me we're in Texas or Mexico.*

"Don't get any ideas about running, lady. If the snakes don't get you out here, the coyotes will."

They lock us into our cells, and we take our spots on our little mattresses. Some of the girls fall straight to sleep, but I can't. I lie here looking up at the ceiling, remembering making plans for the house. Our home.

We stand at the edge of the jobsite, watching the concrete truck feed the slurry into the frames for the basement and the safe room. The big drum rotates, and a loud hum fills the air.

"Are you ready to pick the details for your kitchen?" Freddy asks.

"My kitchen? It's your house. You pick."

"I told you, Amelia, this is our *home."*

"I haven't put in any money. It's your *home."*

"You don't have to put in any money. I have plenty of money to build you whatever the hell you want."

"It's still your house."

"I knew you would say that. So…" He pulls a folded sheet of paper from his back pocket. "I got you this." He holds it out to me.

"What's this?"

"Read it." I do as he says.

"This deed, made and entered into on this day, blah blah blah, between the parties of the first part, Jamison and Marilynn Jennings and party of the second part, Frederick Acosta and Amelia Peters. My breath hitches. "Freddy, what did you do?"

"I put your name on the deed. Now this house and the twenty acres of land belongs to us."

"But —"

"No buts, Amelia. It's our home. I don't care about the money. I want you here with me."

"Oh my God. Thank you, but you didn't need to do this." I hug him around the neck.

"If it helps you feel like this is your home too, then yes, I did need to do it." He picks me up and twirls me around. "Now, how do you want your kitchen designed, Ms. Peters?

"I want the dream you described to me the first night you brought me out here." I turn to look at him. "The white cabinets with black handles, black pendant lights hanging from the ceiling, the massive island and the quartz countertops."

"You mean marble countertops."

"I thought quartz would be better because they're easier to maintain."

"But marble has an upscale feel, and since the island will be so large, it will provide a seamless design."

"I guess you're right. Marble countertops, it is."

"What kind of flooring would you like?"

"Something that won't git all scratched up by them thar dogs we're gittin'," I say in my best country accent.

"Really?" A big smile fills his cheeks. *I'm not used to seeing Freddy Acosta smile this much. It makes my chest warm, and I want it to happen more often.*

"Yeah, why not. Let's go for it. But not until the house is finished," I clarify.

"Deal. You'll see, they'll be great for protection from the critters and varmints that come out of the forest.

"Critters? Varmints? What kind of critters and varmints are we talking about here?"

"You know like possums, ground hogs, rabbits... bears."

"There aren't any bears out here." I smack his chest playfully. *"Are there?"*

"Well, I haven't seen one, but that doesn't mean there aren't any out here. A dog or two will keep them at bay."

"I hope so."

A smile covers my face as I roll onto my side and try to check on the girls. Moonlight streams into the room through the tiny window above Beth's head, and I can see them all lying on their mattresses. I can't tell if their eyes are open or not, but I hope they're all fast asleep. I fall back into my thoughts of Freddy.

"Where are we going?" I ask as we climb into the new pickup truck he bought for the property.

"I thought we would go out to the house and see what they got done today." I'm always up for checking out the house, so I hurry and climb into the truck.

We pull up twenty minutes later. It looks like they've installed some of the windows, and the roof is done. The structure is wrapped in white paper, and it's ready for the masons to install the brick. There still isn't a front or garage door, but a big sheet of plastic is stapled across them to help keep the elements out. Freddy comes to my door and helps me out of the truck.

"Looks like they've gotten a lot done since we were here last time," I say.

"Yeah, it looks good. Let's go in." We walk up the path and onto the front porch. He pulls back the heavy plastic, and I duck my head as I enter the foyer. He gestures for me to take a left into the kitchen.

"Wow, they've installed the cabinets, and look, the island is going to be huge," I say.

"I'll be able to lay you out on top of it and eat your pussy every night when I get home."

"Every night?" I cuddle into his side.

"Whatever my girl wants."

"This is where the stove will be, and the refrigerator, oh, and the dishwasher," I point out as I walk around the space.

"Look, Amelia," Freddy says, and I turn to face him. He's standing between the studs with his hands braced on either side.

"What are you doing, silly?"

"This will be the last time we can walk between the walls. When we come back, all the drywall will be installed. Come here, so you can say you walked inside the walls too." I think he's a goofball, but I join him. When I step between the two-by-fours, I see a faint glow of a fire burning behind him.

"Oh my gosh, Freddy. What the heck is—" The stone fireplace has been completed, and it reaches all the way to the ceiling. There's a heavy blanket with tons of pillows spread out in front of the hearth. Champagne is chilling, and a charcuterie board sits on a wooden crate off to the left, while candlelight fills the space.

"But how?" I ask, floating into the room.

"The masons got the fireplace done a few days ago. As soon

as they gave the word it was safe, I told them I wanted to make a fire and spend the night. Lori, my assistant, set up everything while I was picking you up."

"I love it. I need to thank her." I stand on my tiptoes and gesture for him to come closer. He wraps me in a bear hug and lifts me off the ground. He peppers me with kisses as he carries me over to the makeshift bed.

"Have a seat. I'll be right back."

I take off my shoes and get comfy on the pillows in front of the crackling fireplace while he opens the champagne and fills our glasses. Handing them to me, he goes back for the charcuterie board and sets it between us.

"You thought of everything," I say, handing him his glass after he joins me on the floor.

"Well, not everything."

"What do you mean?"

"Well, there are no toilets out here yet. So we'll have to go outside to use the bathroom."

"Ugh. I didn't think about that. I'd better not drink too much champagne then," I say with a laugh.

"We'll figure it out."

We sit and nibble on snacks, pointing out things around the room that are different since our last visit. When we're done, Freddy moves everything out of the way, and he lies down on the pillows and motions for me to cuddle in his arms. I pull the blanket up over us, and we watch the fire.

"This is perfect," I say.

"No, you're perfect."

Chapter 18
Amelia

The next day in the compound, the guards usher us back outside to the fenced-in area. I don't have a watch, but I hope they give us an hour or more to soak up the sunshine. We're hot and sweaty, but that's better than being in the dark, dank basement.

When the guards return to escort us back, I get the sense Burly Man would make us march if he thought he would get away with it. We walk past the Spanish-style home on the right, and I notice a heavyset man with jet black hair sitting on the balcony. The older man stands and yells down to us.

"Is your name Amelia?" With wide eyes, I nod. *How does he know my name?*

"Why the fuck is she with those girls?"

"Boss?" Burly Man asks, confusion etched on his face.

"She wasn't supposed to go to the basement, you idiot! She was supposed to come to the house." *Holy shit.*

"Boss?"

"How long has she been down there, and no one's told me?" he blares.

"Three days."

"Get her the fuck up here."

Panic surges through the girls, and they start to drag their feet.

"No. You can't take her," Beth, of all people, says. Burly Man slaps her, and her head whips to the side.

"I want to stay with the girls," I plead. He grips my arm and turns me toward the house.

"The boss says he wants to see you." He's addressing this man the same way Freddy's men address him. Could he be in the Mafia also?

"It's going to be okay, girls. I'll be fine. You go back to the basement and do as you're told." Their eyes are teeming with fear, and Carrie starts to cry.

"Get them to the basement," Burly Man barks at the other men.

"Who is this man?" I ask as he marches me to the house. "What does he want with me?" He refuses to answer. He leads me into the house and deposits me on the couch in front of the older man.

"Take those fucking handcuffs off her!"

"Boss?"

"If you question me again, Lenny, I'll kill you myself."

"Yes, Boss."

Lenny? His name is Lenny. Just like in that show with Lenny and Squiggy. I show no expression when all I want to do is laugh. Lenny removes the handcuffs, and I sit on the edge of the couch at attention.

"So. You're Amelia." I keep my gaze forward as he walks back and forth. He's looking me over like I'm one of his troops or something.

"Yes, sir."

"Do you know who I am?"

"No, sir."

"Does he talk about me?"

"Sir?"

"Freddy. Does he talk about me?"

"No, sir."

"You really don't know who the fuck I am?"

"No, sir." I shake my head.

"My name is Mario." He looks at me like I am supposed to know who he is, but I don't.

"Do you know who I am now, Amelia?"

"No, sir. I don't know anyone named Mario."

"I'm Freddy's father."

"Freddy's father is dead."

"Stupid girl. I'm standing right in front of you, very much alive."

Chapter 19
Freddy

It's been the longest five days of my whole damn life. The team Ethan sent to the cabin found at least three sets of footprints, but it was such a mess they couldn't be sure whether there were more. Vehicle tracks led away from the cabin and turned right onto the main road.

They said it looked like she was making soup because the stockpot was sitting on the stove and there were cut-up vegetables on the counter. I'm trying my best to do what Ethan told me to do and wait by the phone, but it's killing me. I've been lifting weights and running on the treadmill to burn off my frustration, but nothing seems to work.

I can't concentrate on business because my mind is consumed with Amelia. What is she going through? Where did they take her? Who the hell has her? Why did they take her from me? What the fuck do they want? Will they ever let me have her back? Will I ever get to kiss her lips again? Have they hurt her? Are they going to hurt her? FUCK! I feel so useless. I'm forced to sit here like a dumbass waiting for whoever took my girl to contact me.

There's a knock on my door. I open it, but no one is standing there. I push open the screen door and walk out onto the porch, but there's no one around. I turn to go back inside, and I can't breathe. A paper is stuck to the side of my house with a switchblade.

SHE IS MINE NOW.
I'M GOING TO MAKE HER PAY
FOR YOUR MISTAKES.

"What the fuck?" I pull the knife from the wall and snag the paper. I run to my office to check the cameras. Someone in a black hoodie and black jeans posted the note to the wall. Probably just someone's flunky, but I need to find them. I call Daniel.

"I need you to access my front door camera, right now!"

"On it, Boss. What am I looking for?" The sound of fingers striking the keys feverishly fills my ears.

"Guy, black hoodie, black jeans. Just a few minutes ago. He used a switchblade to send me a message on the wall beside the front door."

"Got him."

"Now, follow him. I want to know where he goes."

"Yes, Boss."

"He's on Highway 16 heading toward the Golden Giraffe."

"Get a team on the road and tell them I'm on my way." I hang up on Daniel, grab my keys, and run to my bike. Throwing on my helmet, I start the bike and head in the direction of the Golden Giraffe.

∽

I'm about two minutes out when Daniel calls.

"Go."

"Boss, the guys are holding him in a back room at the Golden Giraffe."

"Got it! I'm almost there."

∽

I stride into the room and grab the guy by the throat. I hoist him into the air and slam him against the far wall.

"Tell me where the fuck she is!" I rage.

"Who?"

"Amelia! Where is she?"

"I don't know any Amelia." My grip tightens on his throat. He gasps for air and tries to pry my hand away.

"Did you or did you not leave a note on the side of my house with this?" I hold the knife up to his throat.

"Y…Y…Yes," he stammers.

"Who sent you?"

"I…I…I don't know."

"Who paid you?"

"I don't know."

"You better start fucking talking before I kill your sorry motherfucking ass." I lower him, but hold him against the wall by his throat.

"Talk!"

"Some guy paid me a hundred bucks to do it."

"Who?"

"Just a guy out in front of the bar. He gave me the address, the note, and the knife. Told me to go to that house, stab the knife through the paper, and run like hell. That's what I did."

"What did he look like?"

"Tall. Blond hair. Beard."

"When did he approach you?"

"This morning."

"Time?"

"Ten." I dial Daniel.

"Check the cameras in front of the Golden Giraffe. This morning around ten. Look for a tall guy, blond hair, beard. Talking to our guy in the black hoodie."

"On it." I let go of the guy and push him into a chair. He inhales a shaky breath and rubs his throat.

"Don't you fucking move from that chair. We'll see what my guy says when he calls back."

Twenty minutes later, Daniel calls.

"Go."

"I know that guy. His name is Marty Johnson. He's in the Miller gang."

"Miller gang? Why would they take Amelia?"

"Track him. Give Phil the address. Tell him to go pick him up and take him to the warehouse. I'll bring this guy and meet them there."

"Yes, Boss."

⸺

Sitting in the warehouse waiting for Phil, I try to get more information from our guy.

"What's your name?"

"Jeremy."

"How did you get yourself into this mess, Jeremy?"

"I just wanted to make a few bucks. I never thought it would get me killed."

Phil and the team burst into the warehouse with the guy Jeremy described. He's struggling and arguing with them. They throw him down in the metal chair across from Jeremy.

"What the fuck am I doing here?" His words are angry, but I don't give a shit.

"This is Freddy Acosta. He wanted a few words with you," Phil says. The guy's eyes grow wide.

"I… I…I didn't do anything, Mr. Acosta, I swear." Now he looks like he could piss himself.

"What's your name?"

"Donald."

"Donald. Do you know my good friend Jeremy, here?"

"Yeah. I met him this morning."

"And what did you ask him to do for you this morning?" Beads of sweat run down the guy's face.

"I paid him a hundred dollars to make a delivery."

"Who gave you the order to do that?" I walk behind him.

His shoulders are shaking, but he's trying to keep it together. He sits up taller.

"A big guy. Said his name was Lenny, approached me on the street. Said he had a job I could do for him to make some extra bucks. He paid me five hundred dollars. He gave me the address, the note, and the knife."

"So you delegated the job to Jeremy?"

"Yes, sir."

"The Miller gang had nothing to do with it?"

"No, sir."

"Where can I find this guy, Lenny?"

"I don't know. I've never seen him before."

"What did he look like?"

"Huge guy, blond hair pulled back in a manbun."

"Where did you meet him exactly?"

"The corner of Main and Webster."

"What time?"

"Last night around eleven, outside the pool hall." I pull out my phone and dial Daniel.

"Daniel, I need you to see if you can find the guy Donnie here met last night at the corner of Main and Webster around eleven. Out in front of the pool hall."

"See if you can find out where he goes. Oh, and, Daniel?"

"Yes, Boss."

"Send the cleaning crew to the warehouse."

I leave Phil to take care of business, and I head back home. I fill Ethan in and wait for Daniel's call.

Chapter 20
Amelia

"Freddy told me he killed his father when he was seventeen," I say quietly.

"He *almost* killed me all those years ago, but Antonio saved me."

"Antonio?" My mind is reeling as he explains.

"He made a deal with the boys that night. He told them he would dispose of my body, and in return, they would have to work for him for the rest of their lives. When the cleaning crew came to the house, I was alive, but barely. When I regained consciousness, Antonio made me a deal."

"What kind of deal did he make *you*?" I ask.

"When I was well enough, he would move me down here. I would run the show, and he would reap the benefits. To the world, I would stay dead. He gave me a whole new identity, and I grew this into the largest illegal ammunition supplier this country has ever seen."

"Where is here?"

"Texas. The Chihuahuan Desert, to be more exact." He holds out his arms wide. "As you can see, I have succeeded and then some."

"What does 'and then some' mean?"

"When Antonio was murdered, everything here became mine. There was no trace of the business for Rocco to find because it was all off the books. I took it upon myself to add the girls." He casually waves his hand around.

"You mean the sex trafficking?"

"You don't have to make it sound so harsh, my dear."

"Your goon said you were going to auction us off to the highest bidder."

"Them. Not you."

"Why not me? Too old?" I fake a frown.

"No. You're mine." My stomach sinks. "I bring them here and find them new homes."

"They already have homes. You're just trying to justify the horrible thing you're doing."

"Whatever." He has no remorse for stealing these girls away from their families.

"Antonio wouldn't have approved of what you're doing."

"Antonio was weak," he snaps.

"Antonio Martinelli was a lot of things, but weak was not one of them. He drew the line at hurting women and children."

"Don't make him sound like such a fucking saint, because I assure you, he wasn't."

"Obviously not, because he told Freddy and Nico their father was dead, hid you away from the world, and guilted them into working for him for years."

"He was the master of the deal. I'll give him respect for that." The man actually smiles.

"What about the weapons?" I ask.

"What about them?"

"Who do you sell them to?"

"Any and everyone around the world. I'll take you on a little tour later."

"Those girls need to go home to their families."

"More will be coming to join them soon. They won't be lonely." His voice is so cold.

"What about me? What are you going to do with me?"

"Oh, my dear. I'm going to put you to good use."

"Use me for what?"

"I'm going to use your body in every way I can." He comes to stand behind me and runs his fingers through my hair. When he inhales deeply, my body shudders.

"Why me? What did I ever do to you?"

"You captured my son's heart, and I'm going to break it into a million pieces and shove it down his throat." *I would rather be sold as a sex slave than be anywhere near this disgusting pig.*

"Can I go back to the basement, please?"

"I told you that you're mine now, Amelia."

"I don't want to be yours."

He grabs me by the arm and pulls me from the couch. I struggle in his hold, and he slaps me across the face. He hauls me up the stairs and tosses me into the second room on the left.

"You'd better change your attitude, *little girl*. Or this will get a whole lot worse for you." He slams the door, and I hear the lock click and the deadbolt snap.

This room is more comfortable than the basement, but I would rather be sleeping on a dirty mattress on the concrete floor, as long as I was with the girls. At least I would know they weren't being harmed, and maybe we could find a way out.

This room has a full-size bed, and one single, uncovered light bulb hangs above it. There is one window, but it's too small to climb out of. When I push back the tattered curtain, I see there are bars on it. The attached bathroom doesn't have a mirror to break, but at least I don't have to piss in a can.

Throwing my arms up in disgust, I flop down on the bed and wait. What else is there to do in the middle of the desert all alone, but wait?

Chapter 21
Freddy

My phone rings.

"Yeah, Daniel."

"I found your blond guy with the manbun, Boss. He boarded a private plane in St. Louis, and then we lost him."

"Were you able to identify him?

"Yeah. His name is Lenny Pinson. He works for an arms dealer out of Italy."

"Italy? Troponi?"

"Yeah. Do you know him?"

"No, but Ethan does. Keep looking. I'll get back to you."

I dial Ethan.

"What'd you find out?" Ethan asks.

"The guy's name is Lenny Pinson. He works for Troponi, running arms."

"Really?" His voice singsongs. "Maybe I need to give my old friend a call."

"Thanks, Boss."

About an hour later, Ethan calls back.

"Hey."

"Lenny *used* to work for Troponi, but he skipped town after a deal went bad with the Russians. Enzo is looking for him too. I promised him we would deliver him, dead or alive."

"Holy shit."

"Enzo will help us in any way he can. Keep me posted."

"Will do. Thanks, Boss."

Chapter 22
Amelia

The door creaks open, and Mario pokes his head inside.

"Wanna take a walk?"

I don't move and say blandly, "Are you going to handcuff me?"

"I think we can do this without those, don't you? We're in the desert. There's nowhere to run, and my guards have instructions to shoot first and ask questions later."

"Great," I say sarcastically, rising from the bed to follow Mario.

We step off the front porch and walk back to the huge warehouse. It has to be at least two football fields long and half as wide.

"It's taken me almost twenty years to build this into the largest illegal ammunition stockpile in the US. People contact me from all over the world to buy my products." *Arrogant much?*

When we enter the warehouse, black crates are stacked on shelves from floor to ceiling, in rows and rows as far as the eye can see. I can only assume they're all filled with guns and ammunition. Two men stand beside a huge crate waiting.

"Open it," Mario barks. They do as they're ordered. When

the wooden lid is pried up and removed, I see a massive gun inside. No. It looks more like a rocket.

"Where did you get that from?" I ask.

"Stole it from the Albanians."

"Albanians. Aren't you afraid they'll find you and kill you for taking it?"

"I'm dead, remember? Besides, I've already sold it to the Russians." Holy shit. He really does sell all over the world.

"How much does something like this sell for?"

"Two million."

"Dollars?" I choke out. This explains how he can afford a small fleet of planes to transport women across the country.

"Why did you wait twenty years to tell Freddy you were alive?" I ask, hoping it doesn't set him off.

"I didn't tell him I was alive."

"Who does he think took me, then?"

"Hell if I know. I'll reveal myself to him when the time is right."

"What are you waiting for?"

"When it will hurt him the most." There's not one ounce of hesitation in his voice.

"And you're going to use me to hurt him?"

"Hell, yes."

"Well, I hate to break it to you, but we broke up." I try to bluff, crossing my arms over my chest. "Why do you think I was at the cabin in the woods all by myself? Sorry for your luck."

His demented laugh is loud and deep. "He'll come for you, Amelia. Stop kidding yourself. And when he does, he's going to watch as I destroy you. Then I'll kill him like he tried to kill me." A cold chill runs down my spine, and my knees grow unsteady. I take a deep breath and continue.

"But he's your son."

"He hasn't been my son since the night he left me for dead." He motions to the men. "Close it back up and get it ready for delivery."

"You deserved it for attacking Nico." We begin to walk down one of the aisles in the warehouse.

"You weren't there. You don't know shit. Don't act like you do."

"You're right. I only know what Freddy told me. I'm sure there's more to the story." Maybe if I can keep him talking, he'll see me as a human being instead of a pawn in his game.

"Damn straight there is. They were ungrateful little brats who didn't do as they were told. Everything I did was for them. I worked my ass off to keep a roof over their heads and food on the table after their mother… died." His voice breaks. "And they didn't appreciate any of it."

"You really loved her, didn't you?"

"Hell yeah, I loved her. She was the best thing that ever happened to me. When she and my sweet baby girl, Laura, were killed because of me. Well, let's just say I lost my shit."

"It was a car accident."

"Accident," he scoffs. "That's what the cops called it."

"Freddy told me your wife was driving your daughter to dance practice in the rain. And a semi-truck crossed the center line and hit them head-on. They died on impact."

"Oh, they died on impact all right, but it was no accident."

"What are you saying?"

"I worked at a fucking car lot back then. I made a decent living, but I wanted more for my family, so I borrowed some money from some very bad men. When I couldn't pay it back on time, they sent me a message."

"Oh my God! They killed them to get to you?" He eyeballs me. "I'm sorry. Who killed them?" I ask quieter.

"The Albanians."

"Albanians?" The air around us is tense, but I have to continue. "That's why you stole the weapon from them?"

"Among other things." We turn to the left and proceed down the next aisle.

"I don't understand?"

"You don't need to understand. I'm done talking."

"No, please. I know you don't have to tell me any of this, but I'm here now. Won't you please tell me how you got away from the Albanians?" He shoots me a look of disgust but answers my question.

"After Calliope and Laura were killed, I knew I had to do something, or they would kill the boys too, so I went to Antonio Martinelli and begged him to give me a job in exchange for calling off the Albanians."

"That's where you went to work after you lost the job at the car lot?"

"Yes."

"What did you do for him?"

"He sent me to other countries to take out targets of interest to him. I was new. No one knew who I was. They never saw me coming. I could get in and get out undetected."

"That's why you were gone for long periods of time." He nods.

"But those boys didn't appreciate anything I did for them." He picks lint off his shirt and lets out a huff.

"They didn't know what you were doing for them, because you didn't tell them. They thought you were lying in a ditch somewhere, drunk."

"Oh, I was drunk a lot of the time at first. I had to clean up my act to get the job with Antonio. He didn't allow anyone around him to be incapacitated and incapable of doing their job. So being drunk was not allowed on duty."

"You left the boys to fend for themselves."

"They were old enough to be by themselves."

"Ten is not old enough to be by themselves for days on end."

"I didn't start leaving them until Freddy was a teenager. Don't comment on things you don't know about. I did what I had to do. Besides, it taught them to be self-sufficient and strong."

"You beat them!"

"I beat them when they didn't do what they were told. Don't act like you know anything, Amelia. If I know my emotionally stunted son, he didn't tell you much."

Emotionally stunted? He doesn't know what he's talking about. Freddy is good to me. I know he loves me. He can't say those three words, but now I think I know why.

"I'd like to go back to my room, please."

"Oh, did I hit a nerve, little girl?"

"Don't call me that."

"I did." His condescending tone scrapes on my last nerve. "You're better off without him anyway."

"Now *you* don't know what you're talking about," I say, crossing my arms over my chest.

"Oh, don't I?"

"No! He's a good man. He treats me right. He lets me be myself and supports me in whatever goals I want to achieve."

"Why hasn't he married you yet, then?"

"Because…" The word catches in my throat.

"Because he doesn't have the ability to love anyone," he quips.

"He doesn't have to say the words for me to know how he feels about me."

"I knew he couldn't love you."

"He can't say the words because of what *you* did to him."

"You just told me everything I needed to know, little girl."

"What are you talking about?"

"He'll feel like it's all his fault you were taken. Because of the position he holds within The Organization. But he doesn't *love* you. He'll come for you out of obligation and guilt."

"I'm not his obligation."

"Sure, you are."

"We have a relationship. We respect and care for one another."

"Horse shit."

"I want to go back to my room." Tears burn my eyes.

"Does the truth hurt, Amelia?" His slimy voice fills my ears.

"No. I-I-I'm tired. I don't want to talk anymore." He gives me a little push toward one of the guards.

"Take her back to her room and lock her in. I have a message to send."

"Yes, Boss."

I'm escorted back to my room and shut in for the night. I can't believe a word he's saying. He's trying to break me. He's trying to make me think Freddy doesn't love me. He's trying to make me weak and doubtful. Freddy taught me that captors will try to break you down and tell you lies to get you to do what they want.

Freddy loves me. I know he does. He's going to find me. I have to stay strong until he gets here.

Chapter 23
Freddy

I have to get back to work, or I'm going to go insane. I have a meeting with the Irish. Something's happened, and he says he needs my help. Lori leads them into my office.

"Ronan. How have you been? Come in," I say, shaking his hand.

"Freddy, this is my second, Cormac O'Bryan," he says in his thick brogue.

"Cormac, good to meet you." I motion for them to have a seat.

"Ronan, what can I help with? It sounded urgent on the phone."

"Someone's taken my daughter," Ronan grinds his teeth.

"What?"

"She was at the mall in Newark. We found her on the security cameras carrying a pink bag out to her car. A white van pulls up beside her, and a big guy grabs her. He throws her inside, and she's gone. Just like that. My IT guys traced them to New York. But when the van enters the heart of the city, he loses them. We've exhausted all leads. I need your help."

"Of course, anything. I told you our alliance is important to The Organization. Tell me what you need, and it's yours."

"I'm trying to find this guy. I was wondering if you know who he is." Ronan pulls a folded sheet of paper from the breast pocket of his suit jacket and hands it to me. It's the picture of a familiar face.

"Lenny," I say on an exhale.

"Who?"

"His name is Lenny Pinson."

"Who does he work for?"

"He used to work for Troponi in Italy, but he took off after an arms deal with the Russians went south. There's something I need to tell you."

"If it has anything to do with finding my Elizabeth, tell me."

"My girlfriend was taken exactly two weeks ago from a cabin in Big Bear."

"What?"

"I couldn't be sure Lenny took her until now. Lenny paid someone to send me a message last week."

"What did it say?"

"She is mine now. I'm going to make her pay for your mistakes." I know it word for word because I see that damn note every time I close my eyes.

"Why haven't they tried to contact me about Elizabeth?"

"I don't know."

"I'll give them whatever they want. I just want my daughter back. She's all I care about."

"Are any of the other families' missing daughters that you know of? Maybe we're being targeted?"

"I haven't asked anyone else," he says.

"I'll have Holden make some calls to the other families. And I'll have Daniel see if there's any footage at the local airports on those days showing your daughter. Do you have a picture of her?" He texts me a few photos, and I forward them to Daniel.

"Whatever you need to get my daughter home, it's yours."

The next day, Daniel pays me a visit.

"What did you find?" He sets his laptop down on my desk. "Tell me what I'm looking at here, man."

"I used facial recognition and found Lenny at a hangar at JFK. He boarded a private jet to Chicago the day Beth McAnally was taken."

"Great work."

"And look at this. See right here…" He points at the screen. A large box is being loaded onto the flight.

"What's in the box?"

"It's not a box. It's a dog kennel."

"A dog kennel?"

"It's hard to tell the actual dimensions from the camera angle, but it could be just the right size to hold a teenager."

"Holy shit. They're moving girls around the country in dog crates?"

"They loaded two more crates onto the plane, and it took off again."

"Do you know where the plane landed?"

"St. Louis."

"St. Louis?"

"I have more."

"More. Okay, good. Go on." Daniel clicks the mouse, and another plane comes up on my screen.

"Where is this?"

"LAX, the day after Amelia arrived in Big Bear. Look real close." I lean in closer to the screen, and for a split second, I see a dog crate being loaded into a Cessna.

"Where's this plane going?

"St. Louis."

"Fuck."

"Got any more?"

"Yup."

"Of course, you do." *I don't know how Antonio ever got any work done without technology.*

"The Cessna lands in St. Louis. There's video of it taxiing

to a private hangar owned by, get this, Catch Me If You Can Enterprises."

"Who the hell is that?"

"I don't know yet."

"Track them down. I want to know who the fuck owns that hangar."

"Yes, Boss."

"What happened to the dog crates?"

"Whatever or whoever was inside them was moved to metal cages and were loaded into a C-212C. The graphics on the wings identify it as a skydiving plane."

"Who are these people? How did they get their hands on a fucking C-212C?"

"Military forces all over the world use that type of aircraft. They could've made a deal to get their hands on one. Weapons for a plane, easy trade. Or if their operation is big enough, they could've just bought one on the private market, fair and square. They're made in Indonesia and Spain."

"So whoever they are, they're dealing in women and weapons."

"Looks like it, Boss."

"Please tell me you found out where the plane landed?"

"Not yet."

"Isn't there a flight plan or something?"

"Usually, but it's been long enough that the information could've been scrubbed to cover their tracks. Oh, but I have one more thing."

"Please let it be a good thing," I say, rubbing my temples.

"It looks like Lenny was leading the mission." Daniel brings up another video. He zooms in on Lenny. His shoulder-length blond hair is out of its manbun and blowing in the wind. He must be about six foot two or three. He has tattoos running down both arms, but I can't make them out.

"Whoever he's working for trusts him to bring these women in from all over the country. Could you tell how many cages there were?"

"I don't know how many were already inside the fuselage before the plane arrived."

"How many cages can a plane like this hold?"

"Twenty to forty if they're stacked on top of each other, but that's just a guess. There were crates of ammo positioned between them. Probably so the women couldn't talk to each other."

"We have to catch these fuckers. I want a team staking out the hangar. I'm sure this wasn't their first rodeo. They'll be back."

"I'll have Holden take care of it. Give me a little more time and let me see if I can find out where it landed."

"What are you waiting for? Get moving."

"Yes, Boss."

Tonight, when I got home, I parked my bike in the garage, grabbed the mail from the mailbox, and entered through the front door. As soon as I'm inside, I can feel it. Something isn't right. My steps are quiet and calculated as I draw my gun from my side holster and make my way through the living room. As I turn the corner and enter the kitchen, there on the counter sits a manila envelope. Someone's been in my house.

I leave the envelope where it is for now and clear the rest of the house. When I know there's no one else here, I stride back to the kitchen and pick it up.

I carefully open the flap and pour its contents onto the counter. I can't believe what I'm seeing. Lying on my counter is a pile of blond hair. Amelia's blond hair.

"They cut your hair? What kind of sick fuck does something like that?"

A note falls out on top of the pile. Flipping it over, it reads:

I AM GOING TO MAKE YOU WATCH WHILE I DESTROY HER.

"Amelia. I'm so sorry, sweetheart," I say to the universe.

I scoop the pile of hair up and bring it to my face. It doesn't smell like her vanilla shampoo anymore. It smells of harsh chemicals and soap. I rub the strands of the hair between my fingers and think of the times we lay in bed, and I ran my fingers through her hair. Twisting a strand around my finger and giving it a little tug to wake her. The sound of her soft giggles. Or when I wrapped it around my fist when I fucked her under the stars.

"I'm gonna find you, baby. Hold on."

Chapter 24
Amelia

It's dusk, and I can see my reflection in the window. My long hair has been cut to the top of my shoulders, and I don't recognize the woman looking back at me. I tell myself my hair doesn't define me. It'll grow back. But it's still a loss just the same.

Thoughts of Mario entering my room last night run wild in my head.

"Get up!"

My eyes spring open, and I see his legs standing beside my bed. I look up at him through blurry eyes. He's wearing the same clothes he wore when we were in the warehouse last night. He's almost vibrating with anger.

"I said, GET UP!" he hisses as he throws back the covers and drags me from the bed.

"What's happening?"

"This is what's happening." He pulls out a large pair of shears and begins to cut my hair. "NO! Stop! What are you doing?"

He tightens his grip, causing pain to shoot through my scalp. I try to squirm, but it only makes it worse. He hands the clumps of hair to his lackey, who stuffs them into a plastic baggie.

"Why are you doing this?" My sobs fill the room.

"I told you I was going to send Freddy a message. Well, this is it."

"My hair?"

"Stop your bawling!"

What does he want from me? He woke me up out of a dead sleep, ripped me from my bed, and cut my hair off. Am I supposed to have a smile on my face? I try to muffle my sobs, but his big hand reaches out and slaps me just the same.

"Shut up!" Another slap comes, and I fall to the floor, clutching my face. I take in a ragged breath and try my best to stifle my cries.

I lift my hands to my hair. The cuts are ragged and messy. The cool air crosses my shoulders for the first time in years.

"You'll remember to do what you're told around here."

"I'm trying," I beg.

"You make Freddy weak, and I'll be able to get him to do whatever I want, if he thinks I'm hurting you."

Oh God. He played me yesterday: I thought I was asking him questions, getting information out of him. I knew he was giving me information too freely. He was really getting the information he wanted from me. He was trying to find out if Freddy cares for me so he can use it against him. What have I done? I'm so stupid. Mario leaves the room with the bag of my hair to do God knows what with it.

The deadbolt snaps, and Mario clears his throat. I can see his reflection in the window as he leans against the doorframe.

"It's time for dinner." He's calmer now. The madness is over.

"I'm not hungry," I say flatly.

"You're going to come downstairs and eat," he insists through gritted teeth. My body tenses as he begins to move into the room.

"I want to see the girls."

"That's not going to happen, Amelia."

"Please. They're just kids."

"Don't you worry. They've been behaving, Mommy."

"What are you going to do with my hair?""I'm sure Freddy is probably opening my little gift right about now."

"What did you do?"

"I sent him your hair with a little message."

"A message?"

"I told him you don't love him anymore, and you're mine. That you're going to live here with me forever or until I tire of your sweet cunt." His words make me flinch. He hasn't tried to take me that way, but I fear it's coming soon. He's closed the space between us, and I can feel his hot breath on the top of my shoulder. I flinch when I feel his hand on my ass. I clamp my eyes shut and pray he doesn't take this any further.

"Please. Don't do this." My voice quivers with fear as I stand stock-still while he palms my ass.

"I will have you, Amelia. All of you. But not yet."

Chapter 25
Freddy

Two days have passed since we found the hangar at the St. Louis airport. I told Holden to do a deep dive into the company and find out everything he can about them. My cell rings in my hand.

"Go."

"Boss, I don't understand it," Holden says.

"What don't you understand?"

"Antonio bought the hangar almost twenty years ago."

"Antonio? Why the hell would he call it Catch Me If You Can?"

"I don't know, but when he died, the hangar didn't become part of The Organization's assets. It became property of Oiram Atsoca Corp."

"Sounds foreign."

"I've searched, and I can't find them anywhere. If they're a foreign entity, we may never be able to track them down."

"Keep digging, Holden. My other line is ringing."

I pick it up, and it's Nico.

"Hey, brother, how's your honeymoon?"

"What the hell is going on back there?" His voice booms through the phone.

"I see you've heard."

"Fuck yeah, I heard. Lola and Gilly talk almost every day."

"I guess I didn't think about that."

"We'll be on the first plane outta here."

"No! Stay. Enjoy your honeymoon."

"I need to be there to support you. I can help."

"There's nothing you can do here. I won't ruin your honeymoon."

"Freddy, you're my brother. You gave up everything for me growing up. I *want* to help you," he pleads.

"You can help next week when you get home."

"What do we know?"

"We think Amelia and some other girls were taken from different locations across the US and put on a C-212C out of St. Louis. They flew south toward Texas, but Daniel lost them before they landed."

"Have they tried to contact you?"

"Yes. I got two messages."

"What kind of messages?"

"The first was a note posted on my house with a switchblade. It read, 'She is mine now. I'm going to make her pay for your mistakes.'"

"Fuck. What was the other message?"

"A bag of her hair."

"Did you say…hair?"

"Yeah."

"Was that it? How do you know it was hers?"

"There was a note."

"And…"

"It said 'I am going to make you watch while I destroy her.'"

"Damn. Whoever they are, they're definitely trying to use her to get to you."

"I'm going to rip this fucker apart when I find him."

"Who would want to do this to you? Have you pissed off the Russians or something?"

"No. Actually, Ivan and I have a good working relationship

right now. I don't know who the hell it is. I have to find her, Nico. I need to tell her…"

"I know, man…You love her."

"You know?"

"We all know, dumbass. Dad did a number on you, but you have to get past it. Tell her you love her so you can get on with all the good things in life."

"I will. The minute I find her."

"And you *will* find her. Keep me posted, brother."

"I will. See you next week."

"If you need anything before then, just call."

"I will."

Phil has been leading the team watching the hangar. He calls before my phone leaves my hand.

"Go."

"There's a crew at the hangar now. Four guys. Looks like they're preparing for a plane."

"Keep me posted." I start to hang up.

"Boss, wait."

"What?"

"There's a plane pulling in now. It looks like a C-212C, with a skydiver on the side."

"Tell me everything you see."

"They're dropping the ramp." The long pause is killing me. "Looks like there are metal cages and black boxes in it."

"That's them! Can you tell if there are people in the cages?"

"No. Whatever or whoever it is…they're not moving."

"Don't take your eyes off them while I call Daniel." I put down my cell and dial Daniel from my desk phone.

"There's a plane at the hangar. I want to know where it goes, so work your magic."

"On it, Boss."

"And get a team there to back up Phil and find out who owns that fucking plane!" I hang up and go back to Phil.

"Phil, what's happening now?"

"A Cessna just stopped in front of the hangar too."

"Did they offload any dog crates?"

"Two."

"Can you tell what's in them?"

He describes two men carrying each crate to the base of the C-212C's ramp, where a metal cage awaits. They take the top off the dog crate, remove the contents, and move it into the metal cage. They padlock the door to the cage and slide it up the ramp into place. They stack black boxes between the cages.

"Looks like a woman with long black hair is in one."

"How do you know that?"

"Her hair was blowing around when they lifted her out of the dog crate. I can't tell on the other one."

"Thanks, Phil. Backup is headed your way."

"Boss. Don't you want us to take them out and help those girls?"

"If we stop that plane, they'll just move somewhere else and start all over. Then we'll be back to square one. We don't have time for that. We have to find Amelia. Daniel will track the plane, and hopefully, it'll lead us to where they're keeping everyone. Then we can take out every last one of these fuckers who are taking our women."

"I understand."

Chapter 26
Amelia

We're sitting in the dining room eating dinner.

"You're just pushing your food around. You need to keep up your strength for the auction."

"I don't want to go to the auction," I mumble.

"You *will* go to the auction, and you *will* stand by my side. You *will* watch as I sell those girls to the highest bidder. And if you don't behave, I just might change my mind and sell you off too." His words make my stomach retch.

"Please, may I go see the girls? Just for a few minutes. I need to know they're okay."

He drops his fork to his plate with a loud clang. "Oh my God! Will you shut up about those girls!"

"They're young and alone," I beg.

"Another group of girls arrived a few hours ago. Now would you shut up about those girls."

"Please take me to them. Just this once. I swear I won't ask again."

"Maybe later."

"Please!"

By the look on his face, I know I've pushed him too far. I

cower, waiting for a smack. Instead, he takes in a deep breath before he speaks.

"What will you do for me, Amelia?" His words sound slimy.

"I, uh. I …"

"I know what you'll do for me. You'll suck my cock."

"No. I won't." The thought of this man's disgusting body part in my mouth makes me want to vomit.

"Then you won't see your girls," he says it matter-of-factly. He picks up his fork and continues to eat.

I'm pushing my food around my plate again when I hear the scream. The blood-curdling scream. My head snaps to Mario as panic sets in.

"Who was that?"

"Probably one of the new girls. You remember how your first day was, don't you? They have to learn who's boss."

"I'll do it."

"You'll do what?"

I swallow down the bile in my throat, square my shoulders, and lift my chin.

"I'll get you off. Just let me see them. Let me talk to them and make sure they're okay first, and then I'll do it." An evil grin spreads across his disgusting face.

"Fine, but finish your food first."

We finish our meal, and I put on my hideous yellow flip-flops. Mario has one of his henchmen lead me to the basement. The heavy metal door pushes open with a creak of metal on metal, and I poke my head inside. There are two girls in each cell now.

"Amelia!" Carrie yells. "Did you come to take us out of here?" I run to her cell door.

"No, honey, I'm sorry. I made a deal with him to let me come to make sure you're all okay."

"What kind of deal?" Jen asks as she comes to the bars.

"Don't worry about it. I'm here now. I don't have much

time. How is everyone?" I reach my arms through the bars and get a half hug from Carrie, then Sandy and so on.

"When are we leaving?" Monika asks.

"In a few days. Are you all eating?" They nod their heads. I see empty water bottles lying in the corners of the cells, so they've been giving them water to drink.

"Why did he take you away from us?" Sandy asks.

"He has other plans for me."

"Other plans?"

"I'm in love with his son. He's using me to get to him."

"Oh my God, look at your hair," Beth chimes. "What happened?"

"He cut it and sent it to my boyfriend as a warning."

"Has he hurt you?" she asks.

"Just a few hits, but I'm fine. He says he won't hurt any of you, as long as you do what they say. He can't sell damaged goods, so do as you're told, and don't argue with them." My glare shoots to Beth.

"Are they going to rape us?" Carrie asks softly.

"That's not the plan." I try to be positive and let them know I'm still here for them. "I know Freddy is looking for me. He'll find us all and get us out of here." I look around to the new girls cowering in the corners of the cells.

"Talk to them." I move my head in the direction of the other girls. "Help them. You know how scared you were when we came here." They all nod in understanding.

"Time's up. Let's go," my guard shouts.

"No! Not yet!" the group grumbles.

"It's going to be okay. Don't give up hope." I blow them kisses and leave.

When I enter the foyer of the house, I try to pass the living room without being seen, but he stops me with one snap of his fingers.

"Get back here." Anxiety surges through my body. My feet feel like they weigh a ton as I will them to move into the living room.

"On your knees, bitch. Time to pay your debt." He points at the floor in front of him. My eyes fill with tears, and I shake my head.

"Please don't do this."

"We had a deal, Amelia. Now get on your knees," he says, grinding his teeth. I square my shoulders and take a deep breath. *The girls are fine, and that's the most important thing,* I tell myself.

I can do what must be done.

Chapter 27
Freddy

Lori knocks on my door.

"Yeah," I yell, and she lets herself into my office.

"This came for you." She hands me a large white envelope.

"Where did this come from?"

"Courier brought it." She lingers in the room, as if she has something else to say.

"You good?"

"Yeah. Sorry. I just..."

"You just what, Lori?" My tone is impatient and bothered.

"I'm sorry about Amelia. I hope you find her soon."

"Thank you."

"I'm headed home."

"Night."

I use my blade to slice open the top of the envelope. I slowly slide out a photo, and my whole body clenches with the need to kill. It's a photo of Amelia taken from a distance. She's on her knees in front of a man, and he's not me. I can't see his face, but he has his hands fisted in her hair, while her wrists are cuffed behind her back. Her eyes are squeezed tightly closed, as if she's in pain. The clothes she wears are too big for her, and they're tattered and dingy. Her mouth is open, and her tongue is out. I pick up a book from my desk and heave it across the room.

"Goddamn motherfucking son of a bitch! I'm going to find you and rip your cold, dead heart from your chest!"

I flip the photo over, and written in black ink are the words…

I AM GOING TO MAKE YOU WATCH WHILE
I TAKE HER SWEET CUNT.

Blackness fills my soul, and I push everything off my desk with a roar. My chest heaves, and I choke out a breath.

"Holy fucking shit, Amelia! This is all my fault!" I beat my fists on my desk. Ethan bursts into the room.

"I can hear you all the way down the hall…" His words are halted when he sees me. "What the hell happened?"

"This!" Reaching out the photograph to him, I slam my fist into the wall.

"I'm gonna find this son of a bitch and kill him in the slowest, most painful way possible."

"Fuck!" Ethan joins in my rage.

"We've got to find her, Ethan, before he kills her. Before he-he…FUCK!"

"From the words on the back, it looks like he needs her alive to punish you."

"But what the hell is he going to do to her before I find her?"

My phone rings, and it's Daniel. I put him on the speaker.

"Tell me you know where that fucking plane went, Daniel." I say through clenched teeth.

"It looks like it flew into Texas, but I can't pinpoint where it landed because it was flying so low and close to the Mexican border.

"It could've landed in Mexico?" Ethan's eyebrows lift in speculation.

"I can't be certain. I'm sending Vito and Marco to the area

with the drone. Maybe they can spot something."

"We're running out of time. It's been almost three weeks since she was taken, Daniel."

"I'm doing my best, Boss."

"Well, do your best a little bit faster." I slam the phone down on my desk.

"Why don't you come home with me tonight? Lola's making lasagna, and maybe the kids will cheer you up."

"No, I can't be around anyone like this. I don't want to scare the kids. I need to rip something or someone apart."

"We should know something in a couple of hours. Go to the gym and work some of this shit off and get your anger under control. You won't be any good to Amelia if you're spiraling."

"I guess."

"You know you have full use of all of our resources. Anything you need. We'll find her." His palm slaps my shoulder as he heads out the door. I sit down at my desk, trying to take some deep breaths. I try to fill my mind with Amelia to calm me, but all I see is her on her knees with her mouth open. I decide to go to the gym and spar with Jerry.

Chapter 28
Freddy

"**G**oddammit! You hit just like the boss does when he's pissed," Jerry yells.

"I'm not pissed. I'm fucking furious." Jerry knows about Amelia being taken, and I told him about her hair and the picture. He likes Amelia, and he's worried for her safety too.

"Let's go hit the heavy bag, man. You're trying to kill me tonight." I huff out a breath and follow him to the bag. Jerry holds it steady from behind while he lets me pummel the shit out of it.

"Whose face are you seeing right now?" he asks while I punch the bag.

"What?"

"Answer me. Whose face are you seeing in your head right now?"

"Amelia's." I punch the bag, but Jerry holds on tight.

"What's she doing?"

"She's kneeling in front of that asshole with her tongue out, waiting to suck his cock."

Right. Left.

"Shit. What does he look like?"

"I don't know what he looks like. I couldn't see his face."

Left. Right.

"Who was the man in the picture?"

"I told you, I couldn't see his fucking face."

Right. Left.

"Think harder. What's he wearing?"

"Black boxer briefs down around his ankles."

Right. Left. Right.

"And a black T-shirt."

Left. Right. Left.

"Good. Tell me what else you see?"

"I can't, man."

"Yes, you can. Talk!" I close my eyes and try to concentrate on the photograph.

"There's a brown leather couch and a wooden coffee table."

"What else?"

"Her wrists are handcuffed behind her back."

Right. Left. Right. Left. Right.

"I don't want to do this anymore." I fall to my knees on the floor in front of the bag, exhausted. "What good did it do for me to tell you all that stuff?" I ask, looking up at him.

"The more times you say it, the more you deal with what you saw. Then you can start to think straight again. Are you still furious?"

"I guess not as much. I can breathe a little better now, and my heart stopped thumping."

"Good. Nothing anyone can say will help you right now, but you need to get control of your rage, so when you find this motherfucker, you can channel it all on him."

"I'm going to kill him with my bare hands."

"I wouldn't expect anything less from you, man."

I hang my head.

"Just sit there for a little while and try to come down off your adrenaline high."

"Thanks, Jerry." I sit on the mat for God knows how long.

My body is totally spent. Sleep wants to take over, but I push myself to my feet and get the hell out of there. I need to get the fuck home.

⌒

I pull my bike into the garage and head for the shower. I lean my head under the hot spray and try to burn this fucking day off my skin. I try to stay in control and not let the rage consume me again.

When Amelia is near me, the rest of the world falls away. She calms me with her touch. Maybe thinking about her can control my racing thoughts now.

We're lying on the blanket under the starry sky. Amelia fell asleep on my chest, exhaustion taking over just like I told her it would. I gave her what she asked for tonight, but I'm not sure I need my hard fucking ways anymore. Amelia makes me a better man. I respect her and want to treat her the way she deserves. I don't think I need all the down and dirty stuff anymore, but I'll always give my woman what she wants.

It's amazing how at peace I feel on this land. Our land. I can't take my eyes off her naked silhouette in the moonlight. Her breathing is shallow, and she's making the little cooing noise I love so much. I never dreamed of a life with a woman like Amelia. It breaks my heart that I can't say the words she needs to hear.

Our bodies are cooling down now, and I can feel the chill in the air. I need to move her inside the tent. Gently, I slide her body onto the blanket and stand. I dig through the pile of clothes at the edge of the blanket and find my boxer briefs. I unzip the tent and turn down the bed. I come back and lift her warm body from the ground and place her on the air mattress. I cover her with the fluffy pink blanket she loves so much. My girl likes things soft and cuddly. I'm not sure how this air mattress is going to take my weight, but I carefully cuddle in beside her.

This day was everything I hoped it would be and more.

Amelia agreed to live on the property with me. I'll spare no expense to make this house everything she wants it to be. I'll do whatever it takes to make her happy.

I fall into my first deep sleep on our own little slice of heaven.

We wake tangled in each other's bodies when the sunrise fills the tent. I find the little curl of her hair I love, wind it around my index finger, and give it a little tug.

"Mmm, morning," she says with a stretch and a smile.

"Morning, sweetness." She cuddles into my side, and I pull her in close and place a kiss on the top of her head.

"You were right about being able to sleep out here. I didn't wake up all night. Did you get some sleep?" she asks.

"I slept like a log. This place is perfect." I run the backs of my fingers up and down her arm. "Amelia. I..."

"Yes?"

"I...I..." What the fuck is wrong with me?

She leans up to look at me, and her palm comes to my cheek. The pad of her thumb slides back and forth.

"You didn't hurt me, Big Guy."

I'm trying to tell her that I love her. But she thinks I feel bad about last night.

"You gave me exactly what I wanted. Thank you." I nod my head and pull her into me tighter.

"I miss you so much, Amelia. I miss the way you softly breathe beside me at night. The way you giggle and make me smile. The way your touch calms my racing heart. I need you. Come back."

Chapter 29
Freddy

While I was lying in bed last night, my body too exhausted to sleep, I decided I need to find a way to feel closer to Amelia. The best place to do that is at our house in the country. I haven't been out here since before she was taken, and by the looks of it, all progress ceased the minute she disappeared.

I want the house ready for Amelia's return, so I begin making lists of things that need to be completed. She *will* come home. I call John, the foreman.

"John. It's Freddy."

"Have you found Miss Amelia?" His voice sounds hopeful.

"Not yet. But we will. Why isn't the crew working on the house?"

"I thought…"

"I don't care what you thought. I want the crew out here. I need the house to be ready by the time Amelia comes home."

"Are you sure you want to worry about the details right now?"

"I need to do this for Amelia. Do you understand?"

"I understand. I'll get the guys, and we'll be there in thirty."

"Good. I have a list of things to be completed, and I need your thoughts on a few things I would like to add."

"Be right there."

Why the fuck wouldn't I want to finish the house? What was he thinking? I'm going to have this house ready to carry Amelia over the threshold when she comes back to me. I'm going to make this place so amazing she'll never want to leave again.

"Freddy," a woman's voice calls from behind me. For a moment, I hold my breath and pray it's Amelia coming home. But when I turn my head, I see it's not.

"What are you doing here, Lola?" I don't want to see her. It's her fault Amelia's gone. I focus on my notepad, wishing she would turn around and leave, so I don't have to have this conversation right now.

"I thought I might find you out here." Her voice is calm and controlled.

"I don't have a lot of time, Lola. What do you want?" I turn away from her and continue making notes.

"I wanted to come and see how you're doing. I'm going crazy. What can I do to help?" Her hand touches my forearm. I look down at where her hand is, like her touch is burning my skin.

"Don't you think you've done enough?" I snap.

"This isn't my fault, Freddy. She begged me to help her get away from *you*."

"You sent her to a place where there was no protection. You gave her a step-by-step guide to get away from me."

"She asked me for help, and I gave it to her the only way I knew how."

I toss my notepad across the room, and she flinches.

"You helped her leave without any security. You know how fuckin' dangerous that was. You helped her leave me!"

"She begged me to help her find a safe place to go. She had her gun, and Jerry trained her well. She needed to think."

"Think? What did she have to fuckin' think about?" I toss my pen across the room in frustration next.

"You! She was trying to decide what to do about you!"

"We had a little disagreement. People have those all the time." I try to walk away from her, but she grabs my arm again.

"What was your disagreement about, Freddy?" She raises her voice to me.

"None of your business."

"I know what it was about. You! You keeping all your feelings bottled up inside and never telling her how you feel."

"She knows how I feel."

"But you never said what she needed to hear."

"Lola, I can't..." I walk over and stare out the window at the field of green grass.

"This is all *your* fault. My friend is God knows where, with some fucking maniac, and it's all your fault because you couldn't man up and tell her you love her."

"She wouldn't be with some fucking maniac if you hadn't helped her get away. Whoever took her was just waiting for the perfect moment to snatch her from me, and you handed her to them on a silver platter."

"I thought she would be safe at the cabin."

"Well, she wasn't. You're at fault here too."

"That's enough!" Ethan's voice booms through the space. "You two aren't doing Amelia any good by arguing over whose fault it is. That bastard would've found one way or another to get to her. To get to us!" We hang our heads like scolded children at his words. "We all want Amelia back. It doesn't matter anymore why she left or how she got away. We need to find a way to get her home."

Lola and I stare at one another. Neither ready to concede.

"What are you doing here, Ethan?" Lola asks.

"Jackson told me where you were going, and I thought you might need me. I didn't think it would be to break up a fight." Lola glares up at me. "What are you doing out here anyway, Freddy?" Ethan asks.

"This is my fucking house, Ethan."

I try to relax my shoulders and inhale a cleansing breath.

He is my Don Supreme, after all. I know I need to show him respect, but he's also my best friend in this whole fucked-up world, and sometimes I need to treat him like it.

I steady my breathing and try to calm down before I say, "I thought if I came out to the house, I would feel closer to Amelia. I thought if I were in *our* space, I could feel her somehow." I spin around and try to leave the room. "I don't know what to do anymore."

"We're going to find her, Freddy," Ethan says.

"We're no closer to finding her today than we were two weeks ago. How can you keep saying that?"

"Because when Lola was missing, you tried to help me keep it together by telling me the same thing. You kept me sane, even when I wanted to burn down the whole fucking world. You have to believe me now, Freddy. We *will* find her."

"I want to get the house ready for her."

"I can help, if you'll let me," Lola says.

"You don't have time. You have two little kids at home."

"Please. I can't go out and look for her like you can. I'm not a computer genius. But I know what she likes and how she wants things. Let me help you get the house ready. Give me your list. I'll keep everything moving, so you can concentrate on finding Amelia."

"I don't know."

"Let her help you, man. She'll stay out of your face if you give her a job to do," Ethan says. I clench my fists at my side and walk over and pick up the notepad. I hold it out to her.

"These are the notes I made this morning. I can get you the notes we took while daydreaming about the house before we started building. John is on his way with the crew. We can all get on the same page, and you can manage it."

"I won't let you or her down, Freddy."

"I'm sure you won't."

"I'm sorry. You know I never meant for this to happen."

"I know you didn't, Lola. I'm sorry too."

Chapter 30
Amelia

"Get up!" Lenny yells, busting into my room.

"What?" My eyes are still filled with sleep. What is it with these people and waking me up out of a dead sleep? He stands beside the bed and throws back my covers. I scream and pull my body into a ball.

"I said get! Up!" He pulls me to stand in one quick tug.

"Where are we going?" Fear takes over as he drags me into the bathroom.

"The boss can't have you looking like this on his arm at the auction. Go take a shower."

"I'm not going to the auction." He slaps me across the face.

"Would you like to try that again? I can strip you and put you under the water myself, or you can do it in private. It's your choice. Makes no difference to me." I take two steps back.

"I'll do it." My body trembles as I back farther into the bathroom.

"That's more like it," he snarls.

I take my shower and put on the robe he left on the counter

for me. When I enter the bedroom, two women are waiting for me, and Lenny stands by the door with his arms crossed over his chest. The women motion for me to sit in a chair, and they begin working on my hair. The first woman is on the shorter side. Her brown hair is piled high on the top of her head. She doesn't say a word as she goes right to fixing the chop job Mario inflicted on my hair.

When she's done styling it, the second woman steps forward and begins to apply makeup to my face. She's taller with her black hair in a Dutch braid. Neither woman would dare carry on a conversation with Lenny in the room.

Outside the window is a commotion. Lenny crosses the room and looks out over the compound. There's gunfire, and the three of us hit the floor, but Lenny doesn't move.

"Get up. What the fuck are you doing?"

I look at the others. The shorter woman nods her head, and we stand.

"It was just a drone, and the guys shot it down. Now get finished."

Was it Freddy? Is he looking for me? That must mean he's close. The three of us resume our places, and they continue to get me ready for the auction.

$$\backsim$$

Freddy

"I think we found them!" Daniel yells into the phone.

"Calm down. Tell me."

"Vito and Marco are in Texas with the drone. There's a small airport not too far from where we lost the signal. They got the drone up and searched the immediate area, but they didn't find anything. So I had them broaden the search, and they found a cleared, flat piece of land. It could've been used as a makeshift runway."

"That would explain why there's no record of the plane landing."

"They followed the runway to a dirt road, which led to an enormous warehouse."

"Warehouse?"

"Yeah. It sits in a valley between two hills. The terrain is mostly sagebrush and stone until you get closer to Mexico. Then it becomes mountains, cliffs, and rock. The warehouse is situated at the base of two mountains. Its location probably shelters it from any radar signals.

"What else did the drone find?"

"There's a two-story house, a building that looked like a bunkhouse, and a couple of smaller outbuildings. They're armed to defend, Boss. They have perimeter guards and sentries atop the buildings. There were a couple of motorcycles, a bunch of SUVs, two tractors, and two flatbed trailers.

"Did you see any planes like the skydiving one?"

"No, Boss."

"Women. Did you see any women?"

"No, Boss."

"You said they shot down the drone."

"Yeah, we got a little too close, and they saw it. But the guys have another one. They're waiting until dusk to launch it."

"It has to be her, Daniel."

"There's a really good chance she's there, Boss. There's nothing else around for miles except a national park and the Mexican border. It would be easy to smuggle them over the border and not be seen."

"You did good, Daniel. Now you and Holden rally the troops. We're going to Texas."

Chapter 31
Amelia

My hair is pulled up in a tight bun, and strands hang down around my face. The woman did a good job covering up the slap mark Lenny gave me earlier. I'm wearing a white dress with a flowing skirt and white pumps.

"How do you expect me to walk in these shoes?" I asked Lenny. He rears back his hand to smack me again, but the lady who did my makeup steps forward and grabs his hand.

"I don't think the boss would like you messing up my make-up job, now do you?" Lenny shakes his head and glares at me. I blow out a thankful breath and glance at the woman.

"Get moving," he barks and tilts his head to the door.

When he pulls me into the cell area where the girls are, I take a quick count, and all ten girls are here. They're all dressed in white gauze dresses that look more like sacks. Their hair is in wild and tangled messes, and they have no makeup on. They still have their yellow flip-flops on, and I doubt they're wearing any undergarments.

"Amelia!" they cry out as I enter the room. Some are in tears, others in a daze. I rush to the bars.

"Are you all okay?"

"They made us take a shower and put these clothes on," Monika says.

"Where are they taking us?" Sandy asks.

"The auction is today."

"No!" she yells.

"They can't!" Beth screams.

"We need to stay calm. Remember what I told you about watching your surroundings?" The original five nod. In the short time we were together, I tried to teach them some of the things Freddy taught me about surviving. Survey your surroundings. Keep your eyes and ears open and your mouth shut. Always look for an out. I only hope it helps tonight. If the drone was Freddy looking for me, I need to stall for time. I have to help the only way I know how. It's time to fight back.

"Why the hell do they look like this?" I yell at Lenny. His eyes grow wide.

"You better watch your tone with me, bitch!"

"They haven't even brushed their hair."

"They'll sell just fine whether their hair is brushed or not. We let them take a shower. At least their bodies will be clean when they're delivered."

"I want to see Mario!" Lenny backhands me, and I fall to the floor.

"We're loading up in five minutes. He's busy."

"I want to see Mario!" I grit my teeth, stand, and head for the door. He grabs me by my bun and yanks me back to him. The girls yell for him to stop.

Lenny draws me in close. Our faces are just inches apart, and I can smell the cigarettes on his breath. "You little bitch, I knew you were going to be trouble."

I spit in his face. He punches me in the face this time, and I fall in a heap on the floor. The heavy metal door swings open, and Mario steps inside.

"Lenny! What the hell do you think you're doing?"

"Keeping her in line, Boss."

In three strides, Mario is across the room and takes hold of

Lenny's throat. He pushes him up against the bars to Monika's cage, and his head makes a thunk sound when it hits the bars. The girls gasp and back away.

"Ahh! I was just doing what you told me to do," Lenny pleads.

"And I told you, I won't get as much money for them if they're beaten and bruised, you dumb son of a bitch!" He throws him to the concrete floor beside me. My vision is blurry in one eye, and I'm a haggard mess now. My dress is dirty, and my hair is pulled from its bun. I have blood running down my face, and I wipe it on my white dress.

"Fuck, Lenny, look what you did to her! I wanted to walk in there with a beauty on my arm, and now I have this." His hand points at me in disgust. "Randy, get in here," Mario bellows.

"Yes, Boss."

"Take her inside and let her clean up. We need to get on the road." Randy comes over and helps me to stand. The room is spinning, and I almost fall off my shoes.

Mario looks around the room at the ten girls behind the bars. He nods his head in approval.

"Yes, yes, they'll do just fine." He walks closer to them. "Ladies, we've had a slight delay in plans. We'll be leaving shortly." He speaks to them like he's their host and not their captor.

"You," he says, pointing at me. "Hurry the fuck up and fix yourself." I turn and head for the door.

Chapter 32
Amelia

Randy returns me to my room, and the two ladies follow us in. Their eyes are wide, but they immediately start trying to fix my hair and makeup. They help me change into a different white dress.

The shorter woman whispers, "What were you trying to do?"

"I was trying to stall for time, but it didn't quite work out the way I thought it would."

"Are you trying to get yourself killed?" the other lady asks.

"No. I just wanted to delay the auction."

"You need to steer clear of Lenny. He'd kill you as soon as look at you, if he had his way."

"Thanks. I'll try to remember that." *I think I've already figured that out.*

They load the girls and me into the Navigators, and we head down the dirt road. Thankfully, the windows are closed, so we aren't smothered by dust again. We only travel a few miles when they pull off on the side of the road and make us get out.

They line us up and lead us to the riverbank. This has to be the Rio Grande. They're taking us across the border into Mexico.

"What do you want us to do, swim?" I ask.

"Just wait," Mario says. Darkness has fallen over the canyon. In the distance, I see one lone light coming toward us. A tattered old flat-bottomed boat pulls up, and they usher us across a thin plank of wood to board. The rickety old boat travels a short way up the river and docks on the other side. More cars wait to take us to God knows where. These vehicles are beaten up and covered in dried mud. Not the luxury Navigators we just left on the Texas side.

There's no road, and it's so dark. I don't know how they can see where they're going. We bounce around like balls as we cross the desert and come to a stop at the base of the mountain. The driver honks three times, and a big door slides open. This place looks like it's straight out of an action movie. The tunnel is dark and only lit by our headlights, as we slowly make our way deeper into the mountain. The hard stone opens up into a large space, and we park.

The sounds of a crowd yelling fill the air as we exit the vehicles. The girls huddle around me as I walk closer to the edge and look down into what can only be described as a pit below. Rows are carved into the rock to stand or sit on, and at the very bottom is a flat surface. I'm sure it's meant to be a makeshift stage of some sort. Right now, two men are fistfighting. I look at Mario for an explanation, but my mouth can't seem to make words.

"A lot of activities are planned for tonight. My auction is just one of them." I nod and try to snap myself out of my haze. Now is my chance to find a way out of here. I can't waste it.

Lenny leads the way, and we follow him down the stairs to the base of the pit. Sliding into a row, we all sit and watch the carnage taking place in front of us. Blood covers the two men, but they continue to pound each other to a pulp.

I try to casually look around the pit. Guards are standing around the surface, looking down at the crowd. Guns are held in front of each of them, watching every move. I raise my eyes and see cameras in each corner, and I don't see any doors leading out of the space, unless they are magical like the big door leading us in here.

"What are we going to do?" Beth asks me quietly.

"Keep your eyes open. There has to be a way out of here."

I'm not really paying attention to the fight taking place in front of us when the girls all gasp and shield their eyes.

"What's wrong? What's happening?" I turn my head to see one of the men just broke the neck of the other and is standing above him in triumph. His hands are lifted above his head.

"He killed him," Carrie cries. Her huge eyes have tears streaming down her face. I try to comfort her, but Lenny gives me a growly look.

"Close your eyes. Don't look," I say.

Two muscular men come down the stairs, pick up the dead body, and carry it back up and out of the arena. From the way everyone is using the stairs, I would say there's no other way out.

Mario isn't running the show. A short, dark-skinned man points at Mario, then at the stage. Mario nods, and he motions to Lenny, who, without hesitation, climbs up the stairs.

When Lenny returns, he's flanked by men carrying black crates like I saw in the warehouse. The parade of ten crates is a menacing sight to see. They set them on the stage, remove the lids, and step out of the way. Mario takes his place at center stage.

"Good evening, my friends." His loud voice is commanding. "Tonight, I have several items up for auction." He reaches into a crate and pulls out an AK-47. He raises it above his head and shows it to the crowd. It draws the audience's attention, and a low hum fills the room.

"Each crate holds twenty of these beauties. Who would like to start the bidding at forty thousand dollars?"

The bidding starts, and before I know it, Mario yells, "SOLD for eighty-five thousand dollars. How many crates do you want, sir?" A husky man with black hair steps forward.

"I'll take two," he says in a deep voice.

"That leaves eight. Who else would like a crate of these magnificent weapons for eighty-five thousand?"

From up above, someone yells, "I'll take two!" People crane their necks to look. A short man with gray hair stands tall and proud as he nods to Mario.

"That's two to the man in the back. I have six more crates available, gentlemen. Who would like to claim them for their own?"

"I'll take two," a female voice calls from the middle of the crowd. A very attractive woman in a black leather dress stands. Her breasts are shoved up and spilling out of the top of her dress. Mumbling fills the vast space as she throws out her hip and stares Mario down. Her sultry voice says, "Or is a woman's money not allowed at this auction, Mario?" She's begging him to say the wrong thing.

"Your money is just as good as any of theirs, Delilah." A satisfied grin crosses her face, and she returns to her seat.

"Now, gentlemen, I have just four crates left. Who will be taking them home tonight?"

"I will!" A large Russian man stands.

"Vlad, my friend, I knew I could count on you."

"Sold to Vlad Vilkolov."

The team of men returns to the stage and removes the crates. The purchasers follow along behind as they make their way up the stairs.

Next comes a larger single box to the stage.

"Quiet down. Quiet down. Our next item up for bid is this Snipex Alligator. This Ukrainian Sniper Rifle is a 14.5mm caliber weapon. It weighs fifty-five pounds and is six-and-a-half-feet long. It has a range of 4 miles or 7,000 meters. Who would like to start the bidding at four hundred thousand dollars?

"Four hundred thousand dollars," a tall, thin woman standing near the front of the stage shouts in a brogue accent. She has short flaming-red hair in a bob and is wearing a pair of black sunglasses perched on top of her head. Her black leather jacket has a diagonal zipper and goes beautifully with her thigh-high black boots and a red leather miniskirt. The gun is bigger than she is.

"Four hundred and fifty thousand dollars," the same Russian man, Vlad, calls out.

"Five hundred thousand," Red yells.

"Five hundred and fifty thousand," Vlad returns.

"Six hundred thousand dollars," Red says slowly and sternly, as she stares down Vlad. He shakes his head.

"SOLD! To the lovely lady down front." She places the sunglasses over her eyes, squares her shoulders, and proceeds to follow the crate up the stairs. For a moment, I swear she looked at me, but her steps never falter as she leaves the arena.

One final crate comes into view. It takes four men to clumsily maneuver it down the steep stairs. The crate is the same size as the one Mario showed me in the warehouse. They pry off the wooden lid and lean the crate forward so the crowd can see. Everyone makes a collective gasp, and I search the crowd to see what all the fuss is about. This isn't a gun. This is a rocket.

"All of you know what you're looking at. I have two more just like it waiting to go home with you tonight. They were taken from the Turks. Let's start the bidding at thirty thousand dollars."

"Thirty-five thousand."

"Forty."

"Forty-five."

"Fifty thousand American dollars!" Vlad, the Russian, yells. The room stills, and Mario's eyes shine with excitement. "And I will give you another fifty thousand American dollars for that pretty little girl over there." The room vibrates.

"That's the next auction, Vlad." Mario dismisses.

"I don't care. I paid my hundred-thousand-dollar entrance fee to bid on them, and I want that one." His arm shoots out and points at Beth.

"No!" I yell and stand in front of her. Beth buries her face in my back and clings to me tightly.

Mario steps off the stage and snatches Beth's wrists and tugs her away from me. She tries to drop her weight to the ground, but he keeps dragging her across the rock floor.

"No! I won't go!" she screams and thrashes in his grip.

"Oh yes, you will!" he growls, pushing her toward the large Russian man.

"NO!" She twists and turns, but she can't break his hold.

"Come get your winnings, Vlad. She's a feisty one," Mario yells. The crowd laughs, and Vlad steps forward with two soldiers. They each pick her up under an arm and lift her seemingly weightless body from the ground and carry her out of the arena. Beth screams the entire way.

The girls huddle into one another, trying to protect themselves from what's about to happen. What good am I? I couldn't protect Beth. These huge men are no match for me.

Lenny and the soldiers begin to wrangle the girls and move them to the stage.

"Shut up!" he barks at them. I try to move with them, but he pushes me down on the hard rock bench. "Not you, bitch!"

Mario returns to the stage with the girls and instructs them to make a line and spread out.

"Tonight, I have these nine young ladies for your bidding pleasure. Who's going to start us out at…"

His words are cut off by a body rolling down the stairs. The girls scream and gather back into a huddle. The body lands on his back at the base of the stage. It's one of the guards from the top level. His throat is cut, and there's a note attached to his shirt. It reads: *RUN.*

Confusion spreads across Mario's face as shots ring out. Bullets ricochet off the rock walls and hit the guards at the top. Chaos ensues as people push for the stairs, trying to escape.

"Get down, girls. Get down!" I call out. The crowd scatters, and the thunderous sound of vehicles starting up makes the arena shudder like an earthquake. The gunfire ceases as fast as it began, and Lenny motions for us to move up the stairs. We quickly load into the vehicles and head for the river.

"What the fuck was that?" Mario bellows as his fists fly into the dash.

"What about Beth?" I ask. Mario turns in his seat, and his eyes connect with mine.

"She's gone. Forget about her."

Chapter 33
Freddy

Roscoe lands the jet on the makeshift airstrip in the middle of the desert. Marco pulls a truck close to the plane, and we load our weapons and gear. Roscoe wastes no time taking off and heading for El Paso to await further instructions.

We drive to the outskirts of the national park and set up camp.

In a short time, we're all gathered in the big tent. Maps are spread across a table as we plan our attack.

"We already know perimeter guards and men are stationed on top of the buildings," I say. "How many do you think there are, Marco?"

"At least twenty." My phone begins to ring.

"Go."

"Freddy."

"Sasha?"

"Yeah."

"What do you need? I'm busy."

"You know how I told you I was going to an auction to buy the Spinex?"

"Yeah, some secret location. Did you get it?"

"Yeah, I did. Six hundred thousand."

"Holy shit! That's a lot for one gun."

"I can take someone out from four miles away. Let's just say it's for my safety."

"Yeah, all right. What do you need?"

"I think I saw Amelia."

"Where?" I jump to my feet and pace around the tent.

All eyes are on me as Sasha explains, "She was at the auction. Her hair is different, and she looked kind of disheveled, but I'm pretty sure it was her. I think she's headed your way."

"Did you talk to her?"

"No. She was sitting with a group of young girls all dressed in white. When the auctioneer stood them on the stage to begin selling them, I created a diversion so everyone would vacate the premises." *That's a strange way to say it.*

"Vacate the premises?"

"Yeah, ya know, run for their lives." She laughs maniacally. Sasha can be so screwed up sometimes. "I stopped the auction, but not before one of the girls was sold to the Russians."

"Russians? Which Russian?"

"Vlad Vilkolov. She's just a kid, Freddy. We need to get her back."

"What does she look like?"

"Brown hair, about fifteen or sixteen. On the shorter side."

"I'll work on it. Where's Amelia?"

"They were headed toward the river."

"Thanks for the intel. And, Sasha?"

"Yeah, Boss?"

"Thanks for finding Amelia."

"She just fell into my lap, Boss. I didn't have anything to do with it."

"You did more than you know."

"I need to get this gun out of here. Be safe."

"Vito. Marco. Get that drone up. Sasha thinks she saw Amelia at the gun auction on the Mexican border. They're headed for the river."

Scrambling to their feet, they enable the drone. About ten minutes later, Marco speaks up. "Boss, there's a convoy of black vehicles speeding in the direction of the compound."

"Keep the drone out of sight this time. We're gonna need it."

We watch the live video feed on the computer monitor as four Lincoln Navigators fly down the dirt road, leaving a cloud of dust in their wake. The vehicles stop in front of the warehouse, and a group of white dresses exits.

"Boss. I have Lenny," Marco chimes. I move over to look at his screen. He points. "See? That's him, right there."

"I see the fucker."

"And there's Amelia." He points again.

"Oh my God. It is her!" A moment of relief floods my senses before everything moves to rescue mode. "Now we gotta get her the fuck out of there."

I watch on the camera as Amelia is fucking manhandled by Lenny when he pulls her toward the house. She's dragging her feet and fighting the whole way. *That's my little spitfire.* Another man follows, but I can't make out his face. We watch as the lights turn on inside the house. We can see bars on the windows. I guess we'll be going in through the front door.

"There are nine girls dressed in white," Marco confirms. We watch as the guards lead them to the warehouse, and they disappear inside.

"Boss, we need to recharge the drone. I need to bring it back."

"Wait. Can you zoom in on the second story? The last window on the left." He brings the camera closer. There, standing in the small window, is my Poppy.

"I'm coming for you, baby."

She looks up at the stars. I wonder what she's thinking right now. I wonder if she can feel me coming for her. She steps back into the room and shuts off the light.

"You can pull it back now."

Chapter 34
Freddy

I check in with Ethan.

"How's it going down there?"

"We found her. Well, Sasha found her."

"Sasha? How the fuck did Sasha find her? I thought she was off buying a sniper rifle in some secret location?"

"She was. Amelia was at the auction. Sasha spotted her with a group of girls who were about to be auctioned."

"Oh shit. These guys are into sex trafficking too?"

"Looks that way. Anyway, one of the girls was auctioned off before Sasha could create a diversion. I think she could be McAnally's daughter, Beth."

"How do you know that?"

"He came to me a week or so ago. Said his daughter was taken from some mall in Jersey the same day Amelia was taken. We believe they were transported on the same plane from St. Louis. I need you to work a deal."

"What kind of deal?"

"See if Ivan can convince his brother, Vlad, to give the girl back to McAnally. I'm sure he'll reimburse the money he paid for her, no questions asked. He just wants his daughter back."

"I'll get on it when we hang up."

"Ethan."

"Yeah?"

"You need to hurry before he hurts her."

"Yeah, if he rapes her, McAnally will lose his fucking shit, and we don't need a war on our hands."

"Thanks, man."

"You go get your girl back. Don't worry. I got this. Where are they keeping her?"

"At a compound outside of Redford, Texas. It's in a canyon out of view. There's a huge warehouse and a few other buildings on the property. It's being protected by a small force. Maybe twenty or thirty soldiers."

"What's your plan?"

"We take them at dawn."

"Send me the coordinates, and I'll send Ruck and some men to assist."

"I don't think they'll make it in time."

"You leave that part to me. You might need medical."

"Okay. Yeah. You're right."

"I'll let you go. Go get your girl, brother."

"I will, and then I'm never letting her go."

I hang up with Ethan and call Nico.

"What the hell is going on? Where are you?" Nico rages through the phone.

"We found her. She's in a compound outside of Redford, Texas."

"I'm on my way!"

"No! Wait. I need you to stay there and hold down the fort for me."

"Like hell I will, Freddy. You need backup."

"I can't worry about you *and* her."

"I'm a grown-ass man, Freddy. I'm not your little brother anymore. I'm a major in this fuckin' army."

"But you're my brother, and I can't lose you."

"Freddy. You need to stop this shit, man."

"Please, just stay away for now, okay?"

Nico lets out an irritated breath. "Fine. But when you get back here, I'm kicking your goddamn ass for this shit."

We work throughout the night formulating our plan to take down the compound.

Chapter 35
Amelia

Mario bursts into my room at dawn and scares the shit out of me.

"What the hell did you do last night?" His voice blares through the room as he rips back the covers and drags me from the bed. I don't think my feet ever touch the floor before he backhands me across the face and drops my body to the carpet. Pain shoots through my head, and I think he's reopened the wound Lenny gave me yesterday.

"I don't know what you're talking about," I cry, trying to shield myself from his blows. My brain is fuzzy, and I can't think straight.

"The gunfire must've had something to do with you or one of those girls." He hits me anywhere he can.

"We didn't know any of those people!" I try to shake the ringing from my ears and scoot across the floor to get away from him.

"Everything was fine until those girls took the stage," he growls. Towering above me, he grips my hair in his fist and hauls me to my feet.

"Ow! Please stop!" Pulling his arm back, he strikes me again. "Please don't! It wasn't us!" I plead.

"You cost me millions last night!"
"No, no, no. Please. It wasn't us."
Punch.
"It had to be you. You little bitch!"
Punch.
Darkness.

I'm lying on the floor when I open my eyes. My head pounds, and the left side of my face is raging. I use my fingers to assess my injuries. My lip is bleeding, and my left eye is swollen. My vision in the other eye is blurry, and my breathing is labored. My back hurts where he dragged me across the floor, and I wince as I try to ease myself up to lean against the side of the bed.

I don't know why he would think the girls or I had anything to do with last night. The more I'm around this man, the more I think he's lost his mind.

I make my way to my feet and stumble to the bathroom. I rinse my face with cold water, and it stings. *Freddy, where are you? I think he's trying to kill me.* I dab my face dry and make my way back into the bedroom.

I only make it a few feet before Mario fills the doorway once again. He has his hands on his hips, his body vibrating with anger. He walks toward me, and I cower into the wall.

"No, please. No more," I panic.

"You're coming with me. Let's go." Grabbing my upper arm, he pushes me out into the hall.

"Where are you taking me?"

"Go to the living room and sit your ass on the couch."

Still wearing the baggy T-shirt and shorts from last night, I do as he instructs. I can hear Mario talking on the phone. He's pacing between the dining room and living room, nursing amber liquid in a highball glass while he yells at the person on the other end of the phone.

"The faster you get everyone back together, the faster they get their little piece of ass." His words make me cringe.

"I'm not giving back their entrance fee. Tell them it's non-refundable."

"That's a million dollars, you fucking idiot!

"That's not my problem.

"Do your job and get everyone back there. The sooner the better."

He hangs up the phone and hurls the glass into the fireplace. It shatters everywhere, and I scream. In a flash, he's standing at the back of the couch behind me. The fist in my hair pulls my head back to look at him. Pain surges through my scalp and neck as his sweaty body hovers above mine, while he tries to force his slimy tongue into my mouth. I clench my lips closed as hard as I can, but he grabs my jaw with his other hand and forces my mouth open. Oh God, not this, not now.

"N… No!" I try to wrestle out of his hold, but I'm too weak from the last beating. I bring my hands up to his face, and I scratch him as hard as I can.

"You bitch!" He slaps me, and my body falls onto the couch cushion. He circles the couch and climbs on top of me. His face is an inch from mine. I close my eyes and pray he changes his mind as his liquor breath floods my nostrils.

"Please don't do this," I beg.

"I will use you however I fucking please, Amelia!" His hand moves down my body and stops at the top of my shorts.

"No!" I scream. His expression is different. He looks al-most…possessed. His pupils are blown, his breathing labored, his skin clammy with sweat.

"I don't think Freddy is coming for you, Amelia. I think he's forgotten all about you. So I guess I get to keep you, after all." His voice is evil.

"No. He's coming. I know he is," I whimper pathetically. His hands clench around my throat, and he starts to squeeze. His body is heavy on top of mine. I try to buck him off, but he doesn't budge. He's going to kill me. He's out of control. This is where I'm going to die.

I gasp for air, but nothing comes. Spots form behind my

vision, and I try to focus all my thoughts on Freddy. My Big Guy. The love of my life. I want my last visions to be of him, not looking into the eyes of my killer, so I close my eyes and picture Freddy.

"Would you care to dance?"

"Yes, that would be nice." His tall, muscular body fits nicely into that tight tuxedo. His chiseled jaw and those stunning eyes...

"Ya know, if you keep calling me Big Guy, I'm going to start calling you Poppy."

"Why Poppy?"

"Because poppies are used to make drugs like opium and morphine. And you make me feel high."

"What's your safe word?"

"How about...marshmallow?"

"Remembering you eating those damn marshmallows just makes me hard. It has to be something to make me stop whatever I'm doing."

"Hmm. Starlight."

"Thank you for sharing this with me."

"I want to share everything with you, Poppy."

Just a few more seconds without oxygen, and I'll be dead.

Pop!

Pop!

Pop!

The sound of gunfire comes from the distance, followed by

chaos and yelling. Mario lets go of my throat and drops me to the couch. I try to drag in a breath. My lungs burn with the small intake of air.

Too many people are spewing orders outside to make any sense of what they're saying. My head is spinning. There's a loud clunk on the roof and more gunfire.

"Well, maybe I was wrong after all, Amelia." An insane grin spreads across his lips. "Maybe Freddy is going to come take his punishment after all and watch me destroy you."

"Freddy, help me!" I try to scream, but my voice is hoarse and weak. Mario opens a tall cabinet, and when he turns back around, he has a gun trained on me.

"Get up!" He waves the gun at me. I do as he demands. I open my mouth to scream again, but before I can, Mario pulls me into him and points the gun at my head.

"Tsk, tsk, tsk. I wouldn't do that if I were you, Amelia." His fat hand comes up to cover my mouth. He backs us up until we're standing along the far wall of the living room in the shadows. Gunshots continue to explode around the perimeter of the house, and then all at once, everything goes silent.

I hear heavy footfalls on the wooden front porch. Something hard hits the front door, and it bursts open with such force that it slams into the interior wall. I squeal and struggle, but Mario's grip becomes tighter. I bite the inside of his hand and call out.

"Freddy!" His head snaps in our direction, and his eyes meet mine in the shadows.

"Amelia, baby, are you all right?"

"Watch out!"

Mario forces us into the light, and Freddy's brows scrunch in confusion.

"What the hell?"

A guttural laugh comes from Mario. "Is that all you can say to me after all these years?"

"Dad? How? You were dead," he sputters.

"You *thought* I was dead. You idiot."

"I checked your breathing and your pulse. There wasn't any. This can't be happening," Freddy says, shaking his head.

"Oh, this is definitely happening." He tugs me forward and into the light of the room. "You and I are going to have a little chat…alone. Tell your soldiers to stand down. We need some father-son time."

Just as he finishes speaking, Billy and Joey fall in behind Freddy. Mario takes aim and shoots Joey in the shoulder, and he falls to the ground, unconscious.

"NO!" I scream.

Mario shakes me violently. "Shut the fuck up!"

"Don't—"

Mario's cold voice cuts off Freddy. "Tell him to drop his gun and get out, or I'll shoot him too. And while you're at it, drop your weapon, Freddy."

Freddy's jaw stiffens, and he slowly lowers his gun to the floor and kicks it away.

"Billy, get out," Freddy growls, never taking his eyes off Mario and me.

"But, Boss?"

"I said get out! This is between my *father* and me." Billy's brows furrow as he drops the gun and begins to back out of the room.

"Wait! Take Joey with you." He points at Joey's body. He raises his chin to Mario in defiance.

"Fine, get him the hell out of here. He's bleeding all over my rug anyway." Billy takes Joey out of the house using a fireman's carry.

"There. You got what you wanted. Now let her go. Like you said, this is between you and me."

"Oh, fuck no. It's not gonna be that easy. I told you. I'm going to make you watch while I destroy her."

"Like hell you will!"

"Watch me."

Chapter 36
Freddy

"Don't you fuckin' move, bitch," Mario bellows as he pushes Amelia down on the same brown leather couch from the photograph. This confirms he was the man in the picture. He forced Amelia to her knees for him.

"It was you. You sent me the hair and the picture."

"I did," he says with a proud smile. "How did you like seeing your sweet Amelia on her knees for your dear ole Dad?"

"I'm going to cut your dick off and shove it down your throat, old man. That's how I feel about it."

Mario walks toward me with his gun aimed at my chest. He has no idea the comms in my ear are still live, and the whole team can hear everything he's saying.

"How are you still alive? You were dead."

"I was alive, but barely. Antonio saved me."

"Antonio saved you? No, that can't be. He helped *us*."

"He wanted you to think he was helping you. He wanted your loyalty and your trust."

"But why? We were just kids."

"Hell if I know. He made lots of deals over the years. He deceived everyone."

"Why did he help you?"

"I'd been working for Antonio for years. All those times I would leave for days or weeks, I was doing jobs for him."

"Jobs?"

"Don't act stupid, Freddy, you know exactly what I was doing for him. The same things you did for him and The Organization."

"Why didn't you just tell us?"

"Oh, don't cry like a little bitch. You both did just fine. When I 'died,' Antonio helped me create a new identity. I called myself Oiram Atsoca."

"You're Oiram Atsoca?"

"In the flesh."

"So you own Catch Me If You Can?"

"Sure do."

"Why did you choose that name, Oiram Atsoca?"

"It's my name spelled backward, stupid." *What the fuck? We were so busy trying to find Oiram Atsoca, we didn't stop to consider anything else.* It was right there in front of us the whole time.

In my peripheral vision, I can tell Amelia is still sitting on the couch, but she's using her foot to try to reach something. It has to be my gun. When she leans a little too far forward, Mario spots her movement and fires the gun over her head. She screams and curls into a tight ball.

"I told you not to fuckin' move, bitch!"

"Hey!" I yell, trying to bring his attention back to me. He turns and hits me with the butt of the gun, and everything goes black.

⤿

When I wake up, my earpiece is gone, my head is throbbing, and I'm duct-taped to a chair. Amelia is flat on her back in the middle of the floor with her arms and legs spread wide.

"It's about time you woke the hell up," Mario spits. The room is spinning, and I can feel blood dripping down the side of my face. "I wanted to be sure you had a clear view while I fucked your girl," he says, pointing down at Amelia.

"You motherfucker. Are you so afraid I'll kill you with my bare hands that you had to tape me to a fucking chair?" The room spins, but I keep my voice strong.

"Shut the fuck up. I told you that you're going to watch while I destroy her."

"Don't you fucking touch her!" I rage and pull at my restraints, but I can't get leverage to break the tape. He walks over to me and punches me in the face. My head whips to the side, but I shake it off.

"You're hurting an innocent woman because you're too scared to take me on. Coward."

Punch.

I groan and try to get my eyes to focus.

"You picked a nice one, Freddy. She's a fine piece of ass," he spits.

"Shut the fuck up!"

Punch.

"You should've seen how well she took my cock down that hot throat of hers. You would've been so proud."

"Son of a bitch!" I'm pulling and tugging on the restraints. I'll never give up.

"You chose well, *son.*"

"Don't call me that!" I zero my stare in on him.

"Where's my other son?"

"Out of the country on his honeymoon. Safe away from you."

"Oh, I'll find him, and I'll destroy him and his new bride next."

"You leave them alone!"

Punch

"Motherfuck!" I spit blood onto the rug beside me.

"I'll have his whore in front of him before he dies, just like I'll have yours."

"You sick fuck."

A sadistic grin fills his fat face as he steps away from me and begins to circle Amelia. Surveying her like she's a prized calf at auction.

"You stay away from her! Amelia. Amelia, baby, look at me." My words come out panicked and broken. My lip is split, and I can't see out of my right eye, but I don't care. I won't stop fighting for her. I pull on the tape trying to stretch it, but I can't get it to budge.

Her head turns toward me. Her glazed eyes stare in my direction, but her face is void of all expression. I'm not sure if she can really see me. Her face is swollen, and I can see blood and fresh cuts. Mario circles her like a shark waiting for the perfect time to take down his next meal.

When he reaches her left arm, instead of stepping over it, he stomps on it this time. She cries out in agony, and you may as well rip my heart out of my chest. Her pain is because of me, and I can't break my way out of this fucking chair to save her.

"I'm going to kill you," I growl.

Amelia's whimpering sounds fill the room as Mario laughs. "You don't look like you're going to do shit to me."

He focuses back on my girl. "See, Amelia, I told you he would come for you, didn't I? I told you he would come for you out of obligation, not because he loves you. He doesn't know *how* to love you. Isn't that right, boy?" I hate it when he calls me boy.

"It's no wonder I'm broken. You did everything you could to destroy me, to control me. I thought when I killed you, I would be free. But your words haunted my every thought for years. How I wasn't good enough. How I didn't deserve to be loved. How no one could ever love me. How I would never be able to love someone back, even if they did love me. My whole life was a lie. All of it. From you not being dead, to signing our lives away to Antonio. All the killings. All the damage he forced us to inflict on others, all of his fuckin' rules, constantly having to prove our loyalty to him. All the while, he had you tucked away down here running his business."

"His business, ha! I built this into what it is today. I did it! Not Antonio. I stole the weapons, I set up the transfers, and I created that stockpile out there. Me. I did it all. Not fucking Antonio Martinelli!" he seethes.

"You're just a fucked-up old man now, *Dad,*" I taunt.

"Shut your mouth, boy!"

"Why get into trafficking women if the weapons were moving so well?"

"I wanted to expand my empire with the girls, but he refused. This location was perfect. He couldn't see how much money there was to be made here."

"He didn't believe in hurting women and children. He may have been a prick, but at least he got that part right."

"When he died, everything became mine, and Rocco was never the wiser. The sex trade is on track to be just as lucrative as the weapons." He straddles Amelia. "Don't worry, little girl. I didn't forget about you." He rests some of his weight on her stomach.

"Uh." She gasps for air. He's hurting her.

"She can't breathe. Get off her!"

"I should've gagged you," he spits on the floor at my feet. He leans forward, holds her head between his hands, and licks her cheek with his filthy tongue. Amelia's eyes squint as if she knows what's coming before he slaps her across the face.

"No!" I scream. He slaps her again.

"Stop!" Again, he slaps her.

"You son of a bitch. Stop!" He slaps again.

Each time I yell, he hits her sweet face. He used to play this game when Nico and I were kids. I pinch my lips closed and hold my breath. His arm hangs in midair, just waiting for me to speak, but I don't. I hold it in. He stands and kicks her in the side and walks over to the window.

When he peeks around the curtains, his body tenses, and I know he can see all of his soldiers lying in the courtyard, dead. It only took the five of us to take them all out. We used the drone to seek and destroy as we advanced on the house.

"They're all dead. We killed all twenty-eight of them."

"Ha! There are twenty-nine. Sorry, you missed one."

"Nope, we kept Lenny alive on purpose." He turns to look at me. "Someone else wants to deal with him personally."

"Who?"

"Enzo Troponi. It seems he skipped town after an arms deal went bad. Mr. Troponi wants to have a little chat with him in private."

Troponi is a ruthless killer, like all Mafia kings, but he's known for destroying his enemies one piece at a time.

If the men are following my instructions, they've called Roscoe back to the airfield with the plane, rescued the girls from the warehouse, transported them to the plane, alerted Ethan of what's happening, and are tending to Joey's wound. That just leaves me to get us out of here. And I'm taped to this fucking chair.

Mario is growing antsy. He knows he's lost, and it's just a matter of time before my guys come back for us. He's stalking around the room in a frenzy. Pacing back and forth. Amelia is quiet. Too quiet. Her face is turned away from me, and I can only hope she's fallen into unconsciousness so she feels no pain from what this psycho has done to her.

"There's no way out of this, Mario." His eyes glare at me. "You have no men. You have no support. You may have a shit ton of weapons, but they're out there, and you're in here."

"Shut up."

"What's the matter, *Dad*? You seem nervous."

"Shut. Up!" He stalks to Amelia's body on the floor. He takes her shirt in both of his hands and rips it down the middle.

"Get your hands off her!"

"Oh, does it bother you when someone else touches your woman, Freddy? Tough shit!" he sneers. "She's mine now, and you're going to sit there and watch."

"You motherfucker! Don't touch her!"

He runs his filthy hands over her bare breasts, and my body fills with fire. He's touching Amelia, and she's mine! He's ruined everything in my life. I won't let him have her too. His mouth hovers over her breast, and he sticks out his tongue. When he sucks her nipple into his disgusting mouth, I snap. I break through the tape on my wrists with a roar.

"I'm going to kill you!"

Mario stands, and his eyes connect with mine once again. Like it's happening in slow motion, his brains blow out the side of his head, and he falls to the floor. Dead.

My mind doesn't comprehend what just happened. Where did that shot come from? Everyone's dead or gone to the airfield. It's just the three of us on the compound.

His dead body lies in a heap across Amelia's legs, and there's brain matter scattered everywhere. Thank God she's out cold.

I force my chair to crash to the ground, hoping it would break from the force, but it doesn't. Still connected by my ankles, I drag my body and the chair across the floor to Amelia. I push Mario's limp body off her legs and pull myself up to her as close as I can get. I tug the sides of her shirt together to cover her and pray someone comes for us soon.

Chapter 37
Freddy

I'm not sure how much time passes before I hear footsteps on the porch, and Sasha enters the room.

"Damn, that Spinex is amazing. It wasn't four miles away, but it worked great just the same." I lift my head, and through my one blurry eye, I see her, dressed in all black leather and standing in the middle of the room. She has her hands on her hips like she's goddamn Superwoman or some shit.

"I thought you took the gun and left?" I choke out.

"There's no fucking way I was going to leave you."

"Thank you. Thank you for taking him out. Call for help. Amelia needs a doctor."

"The troops are coming, Freddy. They'll be here in three, two, one…" Ethan bursts into the room with a team of our men on his heels.

"Get the fuck in here, Ruck! Amelia and Freddy need your help." The room fills with soldiers. My legs are freed, and the chair is pulled away. I crawl closer to Amelia.

"Amelia. Amelia, baby. It's me, Freddy." Her eyes remain closed, and she doesn't move. "Amelia! Speak to me, baby, please!"

I feel a hand trying to pull me away, but I throw it off. The hand reaches for me again, and I see Ruck's face in my blurry vision.

"Freddy. Man, it's Ruck. You gotta let go of her, buddy. Let me help her." His hand grasps me under my arm again, and this time, he yanks me away from my girl.

"Her arm! He stepped on her left arm, and he kicked her in the side."

"Thanks, man. I'll take real good care of your girl. Now, go with Ethan, and let the team check you out." Ethan drags me out of the way.

"Are you okay?" He forces me to look at him. His nose is wrinkled like he can't bear to look at me. I must look like hell.

"I'm fine. Amelia's hurt bad. Help her."

"Ruck's got her, buddy. I need to know where *you're* hurt, other than your face," he sneers.

"I can't leave her. I won't leave her."

"Okay, okay, we won't leave her. Let's move back a little farther. Give them room to work." He pulls me out of the way as the medical team surrounds her. Out of the corner of my good eye, I see someone striding toward us.

"Oh my God, Freddy, you look like shit, dude."

"Nico? What the fuck are you doing here? I told you to stay back and take care of things."

"I had to come."

Sasha enters my view. "I called Ethan after I called you."

"We brought Ruck, his medical team, and a few more soldiers on McAnally's jet," Ethan says as he holds out his hands to show me the room filled with people.

"Irish let you use his plane?" I ask.

"Well, his pilot flew the thing, but yeah. Our plane was already down here, and his daughter, Beth, was still in the area. I was brokering the deal to get her back, and he volunteered his plane."

"Did you save her?"

"We did, with a little payout on McAnally's part."

"I'm sure he thought it was worth every penny. Amelia will be glad she's safe." I turn to Sasha. "Thanks for taking care of Mario."

"I wasn't the one who shot him."

"I thought you used your fancy new sniper rifle?"

"We did. But I didn't fire the kill shot."

"Who did, then?"

"Nico." My head snaps to him.

"*You* did? I don't understand?" Not that I don't think Nico could make a distance shot like that, but why did he do it instead of Sasha? She's the master sniper around here.

"I waited for him to get in my line of sight and took the shot. That gun is fucking fantastic," Nico says with a big smile on his face.

"You killed Dad?" I still can't wrap my head around it all.

"We were all on the comms, Freddy. We heard everything until he smashed it. When I heard you say it was Dad, I knew I couldn't sit by and do nothing. It was bad enough to hear that Antonio had lied to us all those years and conned us into being his own personal murder crew, but to hear that Dad was alive the whole time was too much. I had to do this for you. I had to be the one to kill him."

"Thanks, man." I pull Nico in for a hug.

"I'll always have your back, brother. I'm just sorry it took us so long to get here," he says, pointing up at my face.

"Do I really look that bad?"

"Yeah, you do." He slaps me on the back.

Amelia is strapped to a backboard and carried out by six soldiers. They load her into the back of the pickup truck, and with a little help, I climb in beside her. She looks so helpless lying there.

Marco drives us slowly to the airfield to avoid kicking up too much dust, and we all board the McAnally jet. They leave Amelia on the backboard and place her in the center of the bed in the back of the plane. Ruck tends to her injuries on the two-hour flight home, and I stay by her side.

"Why isn't she waking up?" I ask, holding her hand.

"She's been through hell for weeks, Freddy. She's exhausted and hurt. It's probably best that she's unconscious. If she has broken ribs, at least this way she stays still, and her pain level is under control. It'll minimize any further damage she could give herself before we can get back home."

"What if she has a head injury?"

"Nothing I can see points to a head injury."

"I watched her take a lot of hits to the face, Ruck."

"We won't know for sure until we can get her to the hospital and run some tests. Until she wakes up, no diagnosis is conclusive. I really do think it's for the best if we don't try to wake her up on the plane."

"Okay."

Mid-flight, Ruck decides her injuries are too extensive for our small clinic, so he arranges for her to be taken directly to our wing at the Johnsonville Hospital.

The planes land, and we're met with ambulances to transport Joey, Amelia, and me. We're all taken, sirens blaring, to the hospital.

Doctors check me over and take some X-rays. I'm released to the waiting room. Joey had surgery and is now in a room upstairs. The doctor says he will have a full recovery. The waiting room is filled with members of The Organization, Lola, Ethan, and me. Ruck finally comes to speak to us.

"We've run a panel of tests, CT scans, and an MRI."

"And?" I ask impatiently.

"She has a broken left arm that will need surgery."

"Surgery?" Lola asks.

"Yes, she's going to need a pin to hold it in place due to the nature of the break. She has a pneumothorax…"

"What the hell is that?" Ethan chimes.

Ruck takes a deep breath. I'm sure he knew this conversation was going to be difficult. "It's also called a collapsed lung, and it means there's air between the lung and the chest wall. Hers is small. We don't want to use a needle to remove the air unless we have to. The team will monitor her condition to see if her body absorbs the air and her lung expands properly on its own."

"How do you monitor a lung?" I ask.

"We'll take X-rays, maybe another CT scan if we deem it necessary. She also has extensive bruising, swelling, and cuts to her eyes, lips, and face. We did an MRI, and there are no signs of a brain injury, but we'll know more when she wakes up."

"Thanks, Ruck," I say and shake his hand.

"She's on her way to surgery. I really need to go. I want to be there to assist the orthopedic surgeon. I'll come back when the surgery is complete."

Lola pulls Ruck in for a brief hug. "Thank you, Ruck. For all you do for us."

"That's what I'm here for."

⌣

Amelia is gone from my side for four more hours before Ruck finally returns to give us an update.

"How did it go?" I ask, standing as he comes into the room. Lola grabs my arm and hangs on to me.

"Everything went fine. He ended up needing to place a few extra pins to keep the break in place though. She'll get a cast in a few days once the swelling goes down and it's safe."

"Can we see her?" Lola asks.

"They're taking her to a room now. Only one person at a time."

"You'll let Freddy stay with her, won't you?" she asks.

"Yes, he can stay as long as he likes."

⌣

In a short while, the nurse ushers us to Amelia's room. I let Lola go in first because I think it'll kill her if she doesn't get to see her, and I'm not leaving Amelia's side once I get in there. When Lola comes out, she's crying. Her hand comes to my forearm, and she steadies herself. She opens her mouth, but no words come out. She buries herself in Ethan's side.

"We'll be back tomorrow. I need to take Lola home."

"Sure."

I take tentative steps toward Amelia's room. When I breach the doorway, I see why Lola was so upset. My eyes take in Amelia. Her skin is pale and emaciated. She's hooked up to all kinds of machines, and beeping fills the room. More tubes than I've ever seen come out of her soft skin. Her left arm is wrapped and is lying on a pillow beside her. Her beautiful face is bruised and swollen. My giggling ball of energy lies here motionless.

"Oh my God, Amelia."

I walk slowly to the side of the bed where a chair waits for me. She has to be cold because this room is freezing. The nurse watches me as I pull the blanket as high as I can around her waist and then scoot the chair closer to the bed and sit. My hands rest in my lap, and I wait for guidance from the nurse.

"Can I touch her?"

"Yes, sir, you can hold her right hand. Don't touch her left arm or lean on her torso in any way. If you need anything, push this button right here, and one of us will come in. I'll leave you two alone."

"Thank you."

I take her hand in mine and kiss her knuckles.

"I'm so sorry, Poppy. This is all my fault." Her hand is limp in mine. I open her palm and place it on my cheek, like she would if she were awake. It's cool on my face. "I was afraid someone was going to take you from me. I can't believe it was my own father." My eyes begin to fill, but I shake it off. I won't allow myself to become weak. I need to stay strong for Amelia.

Chapter 38
Freddy

Present Day

"No. No. No. No. No. This can't be happening."

I jump from the chair, ready to bust my way into her room. As I reach for the door, it swings open, and Ruck stands in front of me. He places his hands on my chest and pushes me back out into the hall.

"What the hell happened?"

"She had a cardiac event."

"What does that mean?"

"Her heart stopped."

"What? Why?" Panic fills my body. This can't be happening. I feel an unfamiliar wetness in the corners of my eyes. "Get back in there and do something!"

"We did all we could do, Freddy."

"No. This can't be happening." My hands find my hair again and pull until the pain matches the feeling in my chest. "He got exactly what he wanted. He took Amelia from me."

I try to move away from Ruck, but he grabs me hard by the shoulders and forces me to look at him.

"Freddy…"

I shake my head. "No. She can't be…"

"She's not dead, Freddy… She's awake." A smile creeps across his lips. I stare at him in disbelief. *No, she's dead. He killed her.*

"What did you say?" I can't wrap my brain around his words.

He gives my shoulders a hard squeeze. "She's awake."

"Awake? But the monitors went off, and you needed the paddles, and…"

"Freddy. She's. Awake!"

"She's awake? She's awake! SHE'S AWAKE!" I yell, and Ruck laughs. "I need to see her." I try to push past him, but he holds firm.

"Give the nurses a minute to clean her up, and then you can see her."

"She's awake. Oh my God." I scrub my hands over my face.

I feel giddy with excitement. I pull him in for an awkward hug before sitting back down in the hard-as-fuck chair in the hall. I lean my elbows on my legs and rest my head in my hands, trying to come to grips with the fact she's awake. Amelia's awake.

The door opens, and an older nurse steps out.

"Mr. Acosta."

"Yes!" I jump to my feet.

"You can come in now."

"Thank you."

I move past them both and stop in the doorway. My eyes connect with Amelia's. She's pale, but a small smile curls the edge of her lips when she sees me. I don't feel like I'm in my body anymore as I float to her bedside. I pull up that stupid chair my ass knows too well and lower myself into it.

I take her hand in mine and press it to the side of my face. This time, it opens on its own and finds its way to that familiar place. I feel the wetness return to my eyes, but this time I don't push it back in. I let the tears finally flow freely. I haven't shed a tear since the day we buried Momma and Laura. I had to be strong for Nico, I had to be strong in front of Antonio, I had to be strong for Amelia. I have my girl back. I won't keep my feelings in any longer.

My head falls to the bed beside her, and my body convulses as I cry. They are tears of happiness. Tears of relief. Thankful tears that the devil didn't take her from me. Amelia came back to me, and I'm never going to let her go.

Her hand moves from my face and runs through my hair. She gently brushes the wet strands from my face.

"Freddy." Her words are weak and quiet as a whisper. "Freddy… look at me. Please…Freddy." I tilt my head to the side.

"I can't believe it. I can't believe you're awake and talking to me." My voice quivers.

She uses her thumb to wipe away my tears and softly asks, "What happened?"

I take her hand in mine and move closer to the head of the bed so she can lie her head back on the pillow.

"Mario. He taped me to that damn chair and made me watch while he beat you."

"Oh, Freddy."

"I'm sorry. I tried to get free. I tried to save you. I'm sorry I-I couldn't."

She runs a finger across the multicolored bruises on my face.

"Did he do this to you?" I nod. I'm so ashamed he got the upper hand and beat me.

"How did we get away?"

"Nico killed him with a sniper rifle."

"Nico?"

"Amelia, I'll tell you everything, I promise, but I need to tell you something important first."

I stand and lean over her, cupping her face in my hands. Being careful not to hurt her. I've watched these bruises change colors with the passing days. The swelling around her eyes has gone down, and her split lip has healed. I'm so thankful those beautiful pools of blue are staring back at me once more.

"Amelia." My words catch in my throat like they always do.

"What is it, Freddy? What's happened?"

"This has been the longest eighteen days of my life."

"Freddy, what is it? You're scaring me."

"I…I…I love you." The words burst from my lips.

"Freddy."

"I. Love. You. Amelia. I think I've loved you since the night we met. The way you make me feel. The way your giggles fill my soul. I've always known you were the one for me. I'm sorry I couldn't tell you before. I'm sorry I kept so much inside. I promise you. I won't let a day go by from now on without telling you how much I love you." I kiss her softly.

"I love you so much, Freddy."

I kiss each bruise on her face, willing them to heal from my kisses.

"I love you." *Kiss.*

"I love you." *Kiss.*

"I love you." *Kiss.*

"I'll never stop saying it, Amelia. I promise."

Tears fill her eyes. "Oh, Freddy." Her words come out meek and soft. "Can you get in bed with me and hold me?" I turn and look at Ruck and the nurse, who are still standing in the doorway, witnessing our professions of love.

He motions for me to go ahead. "Be careful of her chest though. She's been through a lot today."

I climb in on her right side and carefully pull her body into me.

"Everything is better when I'm in your arms," she says.

"Try to rest, Poppy. We have our whole lives to talk." I feel her body relax into mine, and I let myself drift off, holding my girl in my arms.

I hear the door squeak when Ethan and Lola enter the room.

"I love her," I say quietly and point at Amelia, as if they don't know who I'm talking about. Lola's face lights up.

"I love Amelia," I whisper-shout again.

"We heard you the first time," Lola whisper-shouts back with a grin.

"You'd better get used to it because I'm never going to stop saying it."

"It's about fucking time," Ethan growls.

Chapter 39
Amelia

One Week Later

There's a knock on my hospital room door, and Ethan ducks his head in.

"Can you handle a few visitors?"

"Yes, of course. I'm so bored," I whine.

My arm is still in a cast, and they won't let me get out of bed alone yet. My lung has healed, but my chest is still sore from where they used the defibrillator.

He holds the door open, and in walk the girls from the cells.

"Oh my God! You're all right!" I open my arms wide, begging them to come closer and hug me. Nine girls surround my bed. I didn't get a chance to get to know the new five, but I don't care. They're all alive and well, and they look healthy and happy.

"We're so glad you're okay, Amelia," Carrie says.

"We were so worried about you." Monika hugs me.

"I was worried about all of you. How are you? Did you contact your parents?"

"Our parents came for us," Sandy says.

"Mr. Martinelli is flying us all home today *first class*. But we wanted to come and see you first," Carrie replies.

"I'm so glad you did. You all look amazing. Are you eating?" They all nod and chuckle.

"Yes, and Mr. Martinelli bought us new clothes," Jen adds.

"Thank you, Ethan," I say sincerely.

"Anything for the girls."

I look at all the faces around my bed, but I realize one is still missing. Beth. "You didn't find Beth, did you?"

"Here I am!" Beth chimes as she enters the room.

"Beth!" We all yell in surprise.

"You can't get rid of me that easy. I told you my dad is a powerful man." A tall man with light-brown hair walks in behind her. He shakes hands with Ethan. Beth comes to my side and hugs me.

"Thank you," she whispers. "Dad, this is Amelia. She saved us."

Tears fill my eyes. "No, I didn't…"

"Yes, you did," Carrie argues. "You helped us to be strong and told us to never give up hope."

Freddy enters the room.

"Are you having a party in here without me, Poppy?" All the girls turn to look up at my man.

"These are the girls. They came to see me before they left to go home."

"Hello, ladies. It's an honor to meet you." They all swoon over Freddy, like he's a Greek god or something. Which he is. My Greek god. He walks through the crowd to the side of my bed and gives me a quick kiss on the cheek.

"Aw." All of the girls gush.

"Come on, ladies. I promised your parents I wouldn't keep you too long," Ethan chimes. They all give me hugs and kisses and say goodbye.

"If you ever need anything, please let me know. I'll always be here for you," I say to all of them.

"Thank you, Ethan," I say as he crosses the room and takes my hand.

"When are they going to break you out of this place?" he asks.

"Soon, I hope. I need some baby love from the kids. How are Dominick and Alessia?"

"Keeping their mommy busy as usual. You come and see them anytime you want."

"Thank you. There's nothing like that sweet baby smell."

"I gotta get going." He claps Freddy on the back. "Take care of our girl."

"I will."

Ethan leaves the room, and I pull Freddy close to me.

"Did you talk to Ruck? Is he going to let me out of here today?"

"I'm sorry, sweetheart. He wants you to stay one more night."

I cross my arms over my chest and let out a huff. "But I'm ready to go home now. I want to sleep in my own bed."

"I know you do, but it's only one more night. Come on, you need to get out of this bed and take your walk."

"Whatever."

"I love you," he says so sweetly that it makes me smile. I still can't believe those words are coming out of his mouth.

The nurses told me how devoted he was to me while I was unconscious. How he never left my side. How they would come in to check my vitals and catch him talking to me and telling me stories. One nurse even told me she swore she heard him singing to me.

He walks beside me as we head out the automatic door to sit on a bench in the flower garden. I can't believe how tired I get, but each day I can walk farther than the day before.

"How do you feel? Can you breathe all right? Does your chest hurt?" Freddy pummels me with questions.

"Freddy, I feel fine. Stop worrying about me."

"Never."

"I was listening to some of the nurses talking about you today."

"Talking about me. What were they saying?"

"They are all very taken by my handsome boyfriend," I say cheekily.

"Oh really?" I swear I see a blush on his cheeks.

"Yes. They were talking about how you never left my side. How they would come into the room while you were talking to me. Telling me stories. *Singing to me*." Freddy gulps hard, and his Adam's apple bobs.

"Singing to you." He chuckles uncomfortably. "You know I don't sing, Amelia." He tries to brush me off.

"I'm just telling you what they were saying. Why would she say that if it wasn't true?"

"Um, uh. Okay, fine."

"What?"

"I was getting desperate, okay? Ruck told me to talk to you. I had talked until I was blue in the face."

"What did you talk about?""At first, I told you about life after my momma died. High school. My dad. Nico. Working for The Organization. Nothing was working. I remembered Ruck told me to sing to you."

"You really sang to me?"

"I was so desperate for you to wake up, Amelia. You don't know what it was like watching you lie there hour after hour. Never moving. Just the sound of those damn machines beeping. I would've done anything for you to wake up."

"So what did you sing to me?"

""You Are My Sunshine."" His voice is quiet and almost…shy.

"Why did you choose that song?"

"Laura used to sing it all the time."

"Aw, Freddy. That's so sweet. No wonder they were gushing about you. Sing for me, please," I beg.

"Nope."

"Aw, come on."

"Nope. It was a one-night only performance. Besides, it didn't work anyway. You didn't wake up until I started talking about us."

"Us?"

"Yeah. The night we met. Our night under the stars. Stuff like that."

Freddy is so sweet. I wish I had heard him singing to me. I wish it had woken me up. That would have been an amazing moment for him.

We hold hands and just be. I enjoy these moments of peace and calm we spend together. The lady pops in my head again. I wish I could remember who the heck she is.

"Whatcha thinkin' about so hard?"

"It's really weird."

"What is?"

"I can't get this lady out of my head."

"What lady?"

"I don't know if she was one of my nurses or if she came to visit me or what."

"Amelia, you were unconscious for eighteen days. Do you even know any of your nurses?"

"Not really."

"Maybe you met her somewhere else."

"I know it's crazy, but I feel like I met her *here*."

"I saw every person who entered your room. Let's try to figure this out."

"Okay."

"What did she look like?"

"She had shorter brown hair and perfect skin. I wish I had her skin."

"Was she dressed in scrubs like a nurse or a white coat like a doctor?"

"No."

"What was she wearing, then?"

"She had on a pink dress."

"What did she say to you?"

"It's not what she said to me, so much as…I knew what she was trying to tell me."

"What was she trying to tell you?"

"To go back. Go back."

"Go back?" Freddy's eyes grow wide.

"What is it? Do you know who came to visit me?"

"Maybe."

Freddy reaches into his pocket and takes out his wallet. He pulls out an old picture and holds it out in front of me. "Is this her?"

"Yes! That's her!"

"Oh my God."

"Who is she? Why do you have her picture in your wallet? Freddy..."

"That's my momma."

Chapter 40
Freddy

Today couldn't have gotten here soon enough for me. Thanks to Lola, the new house is finished and ready for Amelia's arrival. I swung by for one final walk-through this morning and deposited her favorite fluffy things throughout the house. When I finally show up at the hospital to discharge my girl in the late afternoon, she's sitting on the side of the bed with her arms crossed over her chest and a big pout on those pink lips of hers.

"Freddy Acosta, where have you been?"

"Getting everything ready to take my girl home. Where do you think I would be?"

"I don't know, but I've been waiting all day."

"Has Ruck signed your discharge papers yet?"

"Did I hear my name?" Ruck asks, strolling into the room.

"Can I please go home now?" Amelia whines. Ruck looks from her to me, and I give him a wink.

"Of course, that's what I came here to do, check on your arm and sign your discharge papers. How does it feel?" He takes her casted arm into his hands and turns it this way and that.

"It feels okay. A little itchy in spots where I can't reach under the cast, but okay, I guess." She goes right back to badgering him. "You took long enough to get here."

"Sorry, Amelia, I had an emergency I had to tend to."

"What happened?" I ask.

"Vito sprained his wrist wrestling with Roscoe."

"Oh no," she says.

"He'll be fine."

"Those dumbasses know better than to get themselves injured. They're our only pilots," I bark.

"It was a minor sprain, no big deal," he says, waving me off. I think maybe that was supposed to be part of the diversion. "Now, Amelia, I need you to sign by the X, and you'll be free to go. Oh, and remember to come by the clinic next week so I can take the cast off."

"Finally," she huffs as she signs the paper and gives me a big grin. "Can you please take me home now?"

"Yes, Poppy, I'll take you home now." I kiss the top of her head. "Thanks, Ruck."

"Anytime, man. See you tonight." I shoot him a glare. "I mean, see you around." He grimaces as he closes the door. I'm going to kick his ass if he ruins Amelia's surprise. Her mouth flies open, I'm sure to ask what he meant, but I cut her off.

"Lola packed you some clothes to choose from to wear home." I pull things out of the duffel and lay them on the bed beside her. "Pick what you want to wear, and I'll help you get dressed."

"I think I can dress myself, Freddy. You don't have to help me."

"Oh, I'm going to help you get dressed, and I'm going to wait on you hand and foot when we get home."

"You don't have to do that." A blush spreads across her face.

"That's what a good boyfriend does for the woman he loves."

"Are you my boyfriend, Freddy Acosta?"

"God, I hope so."

"I'm not sure what to do with this version of you," she coos, taking my hand.

"What do you mean, version of me?"

"You're supposed to be this mean ole Mafia boss. Everyone cowers in your presence." She holds up spooky hands. "It feels strange having you do things *for* me. And you've been smiling a lot lately."

"I've never been this happy before, sweetheart."

"I told you life would get better when you let yourself love."

"And you were right as usual. My whole world changed when I saw you lying in that hospital bed. I was so afraid I was going to lose you, and I couldn't bear the thought of my life without you." I take in a deep breath and try to let those negative thoughts go. I have my Poppy back, and that's all that matters. "Let me help you until you get your cast off, and then we can renegotiate."

"Okay, if you insist."

"I insist."

I help her stand from the bed and take her in my arms. I kiss those pouty lips of hers, hoping she likes the surprises I have waiting for her tonight. "Now. Let's get you dressed so we can get the hell out of here."

"Fine by me. I've seen enough of the inside of this hospital to last me a lifetime."

I help her change her clothes and repack the bag with all the cards and gifts she received. Transport brings in a wheelchair, and she doesn't argue. She just sits down to enjoy the ride. Marco pulls the Escalade up to the automatic doors, and I help Amelia inside. I thank the guy for his help and step around to the other side and get in. I scoot close to her. Her arm wraps around my bicep, and she leans her head on my shoulder.

"It's great to have you back, Miss Amelia."

"Thank you, Marco. It's nice to be back."

"Home, Boss?"

"Yes, Marco. Take us *home*." His eyes connect with mine in the rearview mirror, and he winks.

As we leave the city, Amelia is finally starting to catch on.

"Freddy."

"Yes, Poppy."

"Where are we going?"

"Home."

"But he missed our exit."

"We don't live there anymore."

"What did you do?"

"I finished the house and moved us in."

"You finished the house?"

"Don't worry, I didn't make the final decisions on the decor. I took the lists you made to Lola. She added the finishing touches."

"She has two little ones to worry about. Why would she do that?"

"Because you're her best friend. And we wouldn't let her help with the rescue."

"I bet that pissed her off."

"Sure did. It was too dangerous to involve her in the rescue operation. We knew she would've gone in guns blazing if we left it up to her. She needed something to keep her busy, so I agreed to let her help with the house."

"That was so sweet of her."

"She was a big help. If you don't like something, tell me, and we'll fix it."

"I can't wait to see it. Did you get the Alaskan king bed we talked about?"

"Yes."

"And the giant soaker tub we can both fit in?"

"Yes."

"And the…"

"Amelia, just wait until you see it. I don't want to ruin all my surprises before we get there."

"I'm sorry. This is just so exciting." She giggles those little giggles I've waited weeks to hear. They're music to my ears. I kiss the top of her head, and we melt into each other as we ride the rest of the way home.

She runs her hand over the heavy, hand-carved mahogany door as we enter the foyer. Amelia's eyes spring to life, and her mouth flies open as we make the left into her kitchen.

"Oh, Freddy. It's amazing." Her eyes dart around the room. I know she's ticking off all the little things on her list in that detailed brain of hers: the cabinets, the island, the pendant lights…

"If you don't like the stools, we can change them."

"No, they're perfect. I love them." Her hand slides over the top of the island. "Freddy."

"Yes."

"Is this…quartz?"

"It is."

"I thought you said you wanted marble?"

"You thought quartz would clean up easier, and since this is your kitchen, I thought it best to get my girl what she wanted."

"Thank you."

"I respect your opinion, Poppy. I would give you the moon on a platter if you just asked."

"Oh, Freddy." She takes my hand, and we walk into the pantry. "Wow!"

Inside, the shelves are organized and labeled, just like I knew she would want them. All her crazy appliances are lined up on the shelves. The opposite wall is stacked with canned goods, condiments, and everything else she needs to bake desserts and cook the dishes she loves.

"Do you like it?"

"Like? I love it. I love all of it. It's perfect!" She motions for me to come down to her level, and she kisses me hard and deep. I want to bury my cock deep inside her right here in the pantry, but we have to take it slow for a while. I don't want to hurt her, and I don't want to ruin all the surprises yet to come.

"You're the most considerate man I've ever met."

"Well, wait until you see the rest of the house before you come to conclusions."

I lead her to the living room, and it's filled with oohs and aahs at the furniture, the pillows, and the rugs. She stands in front of the fireplace, pointing up at the photographs lining the mantel. There are some of our families, Ethan, Lola, the kids, and more.

"You thought of everything."

"I'm glad you like it."

"It's incredible."

Moving upstairs to the primary suite, she opens the door but doesn't utter a single word. *Oh my God, she hates it.* I ordered the bedding I thought she would like. Maybe I should've waited and let her pick it out.

"Amelia. If I ordered the wrong bedding, I can take it back." She shakes her head. "What is it, baby? I'm sorry." She shakes her head again, tears streaming down her face now. I pull her into my chest and hug her. "Poppy, what's wrong? Are you hurting somewhere? Maybe I brought you home from the hospital too soon. Tell me what the hell is happening."

She walks over to the huge bed and sits down. Running her hand over the comforter, she pats for me to sit beside her. The comforter is covered in some kind of flowers, and it's a soft pink. It's exactly what I thought she would like, but I guess I was wrong.

"I can't believe you." My stomach churns. What have I done to upset her so much?

"I thought you liked flowers," I say gently, taking her hand.

"I do."

"They reminded me of your bedroom in the tiny apartment. Remember your bed? It was so small my feet hung off the end." We both laugh.

"I remember," she says, wiping her eyes.

"I took your virginity on that bed."

"You made it so special for me."

"I don't understand. What did I do wrong?"

"You didn't do anything wrong. You did everything perfect."

"If everything is so perfect, why are you crying?"

"Because my big Mafia boyfriend, who loves black and gray, decorated our bedroom with flowers. *Pink* flowers."

"I would do anything for you, Amelia."

"You made our house a home. Thank you."

"Why are you crying, then?"

"Not all tears are sad tears, Big Guy. You make me so happy." I breathe out a sigh of relief. I still don't understand how she can be so happy she cries, but I'll take it just the same.

"I missed you so fucking much, Amelia. My heart was breaking without you."

"I don't want to think about the time I was gone. The time I was with *him*." She squeezes her eyes closed and takes a deep breath. She's the strongest woman I've ever known. "I want to enjoy this time together. This is all I've ever wanted. Just you and me…together."

"I have something else to show you."

"Oh my gosh, what else is there?" I stand and take her hand.

"C'mon, let's go back downstairs."

As we approach the living room, I move Amelia in front of me. There, filling the space, are our friends and coworkers from The Organization and the shelter, to welcome my girl home. Everyone yells, "Welcome home, Amelia."

"Oh my gosh," she squeals, and her hands cover her mouth. She moves into the room and sees Lola first.

"Thank you, Lola. The house is perfect."

"I just followed *your* notes."

Dominick is running between Ethan and Lola with Jerry's grandkids hot on his heels.

"Boys!" Ethan yells, and I feel the sound rumble through my chest. "Take it outside!" The boys run out the patio door and into the backyard, laughing the whole way.

Chapter 41
Amelia

This evening has been amazing. Everyone came to welcome us to our new home. I tried to spend a few moments with everyone. My security team brought me the biggest bunch of flowers I've ever seen. They were all very sweet.

It was nice to see Jerry with his wife and grandkids. They really bring out the softer side of him. Marissa filled me in on some of the new residents who have come to the shelter, and Gilly told me all about her honeymoon with Nico. I pulled Nico aside to talk to him in private.

"You saved me," I say, hugging him.

"I'm glad I was there to help."

"Thank you, Nico."

"He loves you so much." We both look across the room at Freddy, who is laughing with Ethan.

"I always could feel it, even when he couldn't say it."

"I'm not sure what all happened down there, but I'm glad he figured his shit out."

"Me too."

"I'm sorry it took our father's wrath to make him see what he had with you."

"In a strange way, I think it finally gave him some peace." I shake the thoughts from my head. "It's over now. I only want to think about our future." Freddy comes in behind Nico and gives him a bear hug.

"What are you filling my girl's head with now, Nico?" He laughs.

"Embarrassing childhood stories about you, of course."

"No, he's not." I wave him off.

∽

I sit on the couch and hold baby Alessia while she sleeps. Her baby smell consumes me and all is right with the world. Freddy is never far from my side, watching over me and making me drink water.

∽

By nine o'clock, the crowd has left, and I'm exhausted. Dominick is thrown over Ethan's shoulder, fast asleep, and Alessia is tucked in Lola's arms as we walk them to the door. I lean in and hug Lola.

"Thank you for all you've done. It means so much to me."

"You're family, Amelia. Don't you ever forget it. I'm so glad you're home safe."

"Thank you." I swipe my index finger down Alessia's little face, and she coos.

"Thanks, man," Freddy says, doing that bro hug thing with Ethan.

"Take a week off to be with Amelia, but then I'll need you to get your ass back to work."

"Ethan," Lola reprimands and swats his arm.

"It's okay, Lola. I've been MIA long enough."

"Thank you, again," I say as we close the door to our new home.

Chapter 42
Freddy

One Week Later

"Amelia. Amelia, baby, wake up." Her body is curled into the fetal position, and her face is wet with tears. She's been screaming for help in her sleep. I couldn't bear to let her suffer any longer.

"Wh-wh-what's wrong?" Her voice is groggy and hoarse when her wet eyes flick open.

"You were having another nightmare, sweetheart." I sit down on the bed beside her.

She looks up at me and down at herself. Whimpering, she crawls into my lap. Her tears become sobs as she curls up against my chest.

"Shh, I've got you. You're safe. You're home. I'll never let anything bad happen to you again." Her hands grip my arm for dear life, and I gently rub circles on her back .

"Why is this happening to me?"

"I don't know, baby. Maybe you're holding too much in. Do you want to tell me about your dream?"

"I don't remember it." *That's what she always says.*

"Do you want to talk about what happened in Texas?"

"I don't ever want to talk about that again."

"Maybe your subconscious mind does. Maybe if you could talk about it, you would feel better."

"I don't think I can," she says, shaking her head.

"I could make you an appointment with a professional, if you would be more comfortable."

"I don't know."

"What about Lola? You could tell her what happened. She knows what you're going through." I feel her shrug her shoulders against me.

"I just want it all to go away. I want to forget." I tuck a strand of her hair behind her ear.

"I'm here for you. Whatever you decide to do."

"Thank you."

I lay her back on the bed and climb in behind her. I pull her shaking body in tight to mine, massaging her temples until she falls back to sleep. She's had a nightmare every night since I brought her home. How can I go back to work in the city tomorrow when I'm not sure if I should even leave her alone? The only time she's left the house was to go to the clinic and have the cast removed. What if she takes a nap and has a bad dream? No one will be here to soothe her. I never want to think of my Amelia scared and alone ever again.

The following morning, I make her a cup of coffee and place it on the stand beside the bed. I lean down and whisper in her ear, "Time to get up, Sleeping Beauty."

She whines and pulls the covers over her head like she always does.

"Is that coffee I smell?" Her words come out muffled from under the covers.

"Your favorite…Americano," I singsong. She pulls the covers down and breathes in the rich blend.

"It smells amazing." She sits up in bed, and I hand it to her.

She warms her hands on the sides of the cup and gently blows on the dark liquid.

"What are you going to do today?"

"I don't know. Hang around the house, I guess," she says, taking a drink of the dark roast blend.

"Do you want to come into the city with me?"

"No, I'm good, thanks. I'll just stay here."

"You could take a drive and stop by the shelter." She places the cup on the stand, throws back the covers, and sits on the edge of the bed.

"Nah, I'm good, really."

"Amelia, you can't stay in this house forever."

"I know!" she yells.

Well, this is a new side of Amelia I've never seen before. She never raises her voice like that. She takes in a deep breath and pushes up to stand. Her body wavers a little before heading for the bathroom.

"I've only been home for a week, Freddy."

"I know, Poppy, but I thought you would be anxious to get back to your life. You were always so active."

"Well, I'm tired!" she snaps again. *Oh fuck. Be understanding. Be understanding.*

"Okay, you know best." *But does she really know what's best for her right now?* I kiss her on the head. "Get some rest. Maybe take a nap on the back porch. The fresh air will do you some good."

"Mm-hmm. Have a good first day back to work."

Chapter 43
Freddy

At the end of my second week back to work, I don't know what I was expecting, but this definitely wasn't it. Amelia used to be so busy. She had a full schedule every day. Now all she does is lie around the house in her pajamas.

I climb into the truck and head for the city. While I drive, I call Ruck.

"Hey, man. How's our girl doing?" His voice booms through the truck.

"I'm not sure."

"What's wrong?" His voice is filled with concern.

"She's acting strange."

"Strange how? Is she still having nightmares?"

"Yes, and she won't talk about them. She won't talk about anything. She just lies around the house. She won't go to the shelter. Won't go for a walk. She just naps all day and hardly says a word to me anymore." I sound like a whiny little bitch when I say it all out loud.

"Amelia went through something very traumatic in that desert. She was physically and mentally abused. Who knows what else Mario did to her down there."

"I know that, Ruck. I'm worried about her, and I feel so selfish."

"It's not selfish to want Amelia to feel like her old self, but she needs time. More time than maybe you were expecting. You need to be patient." I let out a deep exhale and run my hand through my hair.

"How much time before I'm allowed to freak out, Ruck?"

"There's no right answer to your question. It could be days, weeks, or months before she deals with her trauma. Call me if she has any major changes for the worse."

"Like?"

"If she sinks further into depression and won't get out of bed, won't take a shower, or eat. Don't push her, but keep an eye on her."

"Okay, I will."

The following week goes by the same way as the others. She won't leave the house. She has at least moved to the back porch, where she's getting fresh air. When she's not napping, she's staring out at the land in a daze. I feel like she's slipping further and further away from me. I keep an eye on her like Ruck instructed. She combs her hair, takes a shower every day, and puts on clean clothes. I usually cook or bring in dinner on my way home, or I'm afraid she would starve. She's stopped sobbing all the time, but she's so damn quiet. I want my energy-filled, bouncy Amelia back.

It's late in the afternoon on Saturday. She's in her usual spot on the back porch, sitting on the small couch. The light blue throw is draped across her legs, and she holds a cup of coffee.

"Hey," I say.

"Hey."

"Wanna go for a walk?"

"I don't know." She crinkles up her nose.

I sit on the couch beside her and motion for her to give me her legs. I lay them across my lap and massage her calves and feet while we look out over the lush green field. A warm breeze blows her hair gently around her face.

"It might do us both some good." She shrugs. "I can make us a snack, and we can go down by the waterfall. You love it down there." I stand. "Aw, come on." I smile and pull on her hand like a child wanting to go to the playground.

"Okay. Let me go change."

Finally, a little progress. I go to the kitchen and make a couple of sandwiches. I throw them in a backpack along with a couple of apples, water bottles, and a lightweight blanket.

Amelia walks into the kitchen twenty minutes later. Her hair is braided into two ponytails, and she's wearing blue jean shorts, a pink tank top, and her gym shoes.

"Ready to go?" I ask. She nods and takes my hand. We head out through the screen door, letting it close behind us with a bang.

Our hands swing between us as we walk through the tall grass.

"How do you feel today?"

"Fine." She doesn't elaborate. Just the same short, clipped answers she's given me the past few weeks.

"Amelia…"

"Yes?"

"I'm worried about you."

She looks up at me with a confused expression. Like she doesn't realize the way she's been acting.

"You don't seem happy. Don't you like the house?"

"I love our house."

"Don't you love…me, anymore?" I look down at the ground in front of me as she pulls us to a stop.

"Freddy Acosta, why would you say that?"

I haven't been this insecure since I was ten years old.

"I don't think I'm giving you what you need."

"What do you mean?"

"I think you need to talk to someone, but you don't want

to talk to me. We haven't been *together* since you got home. You're still having nightmares. You won't go to work. You won't go to visit Lola and the kids. You won't go see Ruck or a therapist. I-I-I'm afraid."

"Afraid of what?" she murmurs.

"I'm afraid I'm losing you all over again, but in a different way this time." She wrings her hands.

"I can't tell you what happened in the desert."

"Why not? Because you don't think I can handle it?"

"Because it was your *father*, Freddy."

Both of us have been living in denial these past few weeks. It's not just her. I'm just as guilty as she is. I haven't told her about the notes or the hair. How exactly do you start a conversation like that? *Oh, by the way, Amelia, my dad sent me an envelope of your hair and told me he was going to fuck you and make me watch.*

"I don't want to upset you," she whispers.

"Amelia…"

"Can't we just agree to never talk about it again?"

"No. I don't think that's good for either of us. We both need answers."

"What kind of answers?" I'm getting tired of her answering my questions with a question. I drop the backpack and rake my fingers through my hair in frustration.

"I need to know if… if… Fuck!" I throw down my hands and turn my back on her. I can't bear to look into those beautiful blue eyes when I ask her this question.

"I need to know if he fucked you." The words spew from my lips.

"Does it matter?" she snaps. I was just hoping for a yes-or-no answer, not really wanting to discuss it.

"Yes, I mean no. I mean. I need to know if he…hurt you like that."

"Why do I have to say it?" When I turn around to face her, she's turned her back on me now. I encircle her body from behind. The feeling of her body against mine calms me.

"Because maybe I need to hear the truth."

"You can't kill him all over again, Freddy."

"I didn't kill him the first time, Amelia." I didn't think about what I was saying. It just flew out of my mouth.

She turns in my arms and looks up at me. "Is that what's bothering you? You're upset because you didn't pull the trigger?"

"It should've been me who killed him. I spent hours while you were gone, planning how I was going to kill the fucker who took you. How I would torture and mame him before I ripped him apart limb by motherfucking limb. But I was taped to a *fucking* chair…helpless."

"He hit you in the head and knocked you out."

"It doesn't matter what he did to me. I didn't protect you. That was my only job, to keep you safe, and I fucked it up."

"You brought an army to save those girls and me."

"But all I could do was watch while he slapped you, kicked you, punched you…" I clench my fists by my sides. I can't have my hands on her when I'm angry.

"Freddy, I don't love you any less because you weren't the one to pull the trigger." Her hand slides to my chest.

"I failed you."

"Oh, Big Guy. You didn't fail me. I ran away from you. I should've stayed and talked to you that night. Instead, I ran and hid like a child. I talked Lola into lying to everyone for me, and I got her in trouble with Ethan." Her fingers play with the hem of my shirt. "You didn't know they were tracking me. You can't do this to yourself. The monster is dead. That's all that matters."

Her sweet body pulls me in for a hug. I need her so much. I need to touch her soft skin and hear her call my name. I need her to be all right.

I take her braid in my hand and roll it between my fingers. Then I realize she got me to talk, but she still hasn't answered my question.

"Poppy." I hold her firmly to my chest.

"Yes, Big Guy."

"Did he rape you?"

"No. Freddy. He didn't rape me." I hold her, and tears roll down my cheeks and land in her hair. I'm so relieved we were able to get to her before he went there.

Neither one of us releases our hold on the other. I feel like I'm drowning, and she's my lifeline. I continue confessing.

"He sent me your hair." She releases a breath. "Can you tell me what happened?"

"I went to sleep, and sometime during the night, he dragged me from the bed. He didn't give me any time to think or argue before he grabbed my hair and started cutting it. He pulled it so hard," she says, running her hand over her head as if she can still feel it.

"Someone got into the house while I was gone and left the envelope on the kitchen counter," I say.

"He told me he put a note inside," she softly says.

"Yes, there was a note."

"He said he told you I didn't love you anymore. I was going to live there with him forever or until he got tired of my… cunt."

"That's not what the note said."

"What?"

"It said 'I'm going to make you watch while I destroy her.'"

"That's all?"

"Yes."

"Why would he tell me one thing and you another?"

"To control you. To make you feel like I didn't want you anymore." I pull the elastic bands off her ponytails and unravel the braids. Her hair is wavy as I run my fingers through it.

"He also sent me a picture," I say cautiously.

"A picture of what?" She looks up at me with worried eyes. I swipe my thumb over her cheek to remove the wetness. I move her head back to my chest so I don't have to look at her while I tell her.

"It was a picture of you." I feel her body tremble. "You were on your knees in front of him, with… your mouth open." Her body sags against mine, and I take all of her weight. I gently stroke her hair while her tears soak my T-shirt.

"I never wanted you to see me like that."

"Amelia, it's okay."

She shakes her head. "No. No. No."

"Hey. Look at me. I told you during your training—you do whatever you have to do to survive."

"I didn't want to do it," she cries.

"Oh, baby, I know you didn't."

"But he made me a deal."

All these fuckers and their deals. "What kind of a deal?" I say through gritted teeth.

"I'd been begging him to let me see the girls since he made me move to the house. I needed to be sure they were all right."

"Of course."

"He kept putting me off, telling me to wait till tomorrow. Wait till tomorrow. But tomorrow was never coming, and we were running out of time."

"Why were you running out of time?"

"Because when they took us, the guards told us we would be auctioned off in three weeks. And there were only a few days left."

"Oh."

"One night while we were eating dinner, there was a loud scream. I was terrified they were hurting one of the girls. When I begged him to let me go check on them, he told me there had been a new shipment of girls that day. It was probably one of them getting used to their new surroundings. I pleaded with him to let me go to them, but he just laughed at me."

"Bastard."

"Then he got this evil look on his face and said he would let me go see them if I would give him a blow job." She buries her face in my chest.

"Shh, it's okay." I rub circles on her back.

"I told him no. But when the screaming started again…"

Her hands cover her ears as if she can still hear their screams. "I had to help her." Her words became frantic.

"Of course you did." Her sobs are breaking my heart. "You were so brave."

"If I was so brave, then why couldn't I get us out of there?"

"Amelia, hey, look at me. There were twenty-nine guards, a shit ton of weapons, and six of you. Not to mention, they were young girls. You were locked in a basement. I don't know how you would've ever escaped them."

"But I should've—"

"No. You shouldn't have. Stop blaming yourself."

"What if Sasha hadn't seen me at the auction? What if she didn't fire those shots and break up the auction? What if…"

"Baby, please, stop doing this to yourself." Her cries are harder and louder now. I hold her tightly and let her purge the demons from her soul.

"You did everything you could with what you had. I'm so proud of you."

"You aren't disgusted by me?" She pulls back from me and lowers her head.

I raise her chin to look at me. "Disgusted? What the fuck are you talking about?"

"Because I. You know. What I had to do to him."

I drop to my knees in front of her and clutch her around the middle. My head rests on her chest as my tears begin to fall. I've never felt so vulnerable in my entire life.

"I love you with every piece of me. With every piece of my heart. I'm so glad you're back in my arms, Amelia. Nothing else matters. Nothing that he said or did matters. I have you back. Can't you see? You could never do anything to make me love you less. Never."

She runs her fingers through my hair.

"Freddy. I love you so much. You're all I've ever wanted." She holds my face between her palms and swipes my tears away with her thumbs. "Please come up here." She motions for me to stand, and I do. "I've never seen you like this before."

"I've never allowed myself to feel like this before. Maybe this is what we both needed to heal from this horrible nightmare. No more secrets."

"No more secrets," she agrees.

"From now on, we tell each other everything."

"Everything."

"No matter how painful it could be for the other person or ourselves."

"Yes. I promise."

"Me too."

We stand in the middle of the field for a long while, holding on for dear life to one another.

Chapter 44
Amelia

We never make it to the waterfall. We were both emotionally exhausted and couldn't hike the rest of the way. The sun is starting to set, so Freddy spreads out the blanket on the grass, and we sit down to watch.

"I made sandwiches," he singsongs, trying to lighten the mood. He pulls two half-smashed ham sandwiches from a plastic baggie, and I can't help but giggle.

"I love that sound."

"What sound?" I take my squished sandwich.

"Your giggle."

"You're silly." I playfully bump my arm with his.

"I would've given anything to hear you giggle, just once while you were gone."

"Freddy," I sigh.

"I love you, Amelia."

"I love you, Freddy. Don't you ever doubt my love for you again."

"I won't."

I climb between his legs and lean my head back on his chest. He wraps his arms around me, and we sit in silence as we watch the orange sun slide behind the tree line. Darkness falls around us, while we eat our squished sandwiches.

"I need you, Amelia. All of you. I need your body pressed against mine. I want to please you and hear you say my name when you come."

"Freddy, I need that too," I purr. "I thought you didn't want me anymore."

"I'll never stop wanting you, Poppy. My thoughts of you were the only thing that calmed me while you were away."

I stand, look down at him, and then straddle his lap. My pussy is nestled over his hard cock. I rock over his hard length while he grips my ass and squeezes.

"Freddy, make love to me under the stars like you did the first night on our land."

"I'll do anything for you, Amelia."

Our lips, teeth, and tongues collide in a heated kiss we've waited too long to reignite. In one quick flip, I'm on my back. We're grabbing at each other's clothing as the darkness surrounds us, making it feel like we're in our own little cocoon. Freddy's hand slides down my body, finding its way to my wet heat.

"You're drenched."

"Make love to me." I take his hard dick in my hand and squeeze. "I want to feel you inside me, Freddy. Now."

I know exactly what he's thinking. He needs to get me ready for his huge cock, but I need him inside me. He nods in acknowledgment and kisses me sweetly.

"Whatever my girl wants."

Freddy

The full moon illuminates Amelia's soft features while I watch her for signs of discomfort as I press my throbbing cock in a little deeper. Her lips part on a moan, and her hooded eyes open to see me staring at her.

"Amelia, I don't want to hurt you."

"Don't stop, Freddy. Please, keep going."

I do as I'm told and press into her completely. Kissing her tenderly, I begin to rock slow and steady. Making love to the only woman I've ever loved…

Chapter 45
Freddy

Covered in my T-shirt, she sprawls across my chest as we lie beneath the night sky. Her hair is shorter than it was, but I can still find a soft curl to wind around my finger to calm me.

"This is what I thought about," she says softly.

"What did you think about, sweetheart?"

"Us being together."

"Be specific." I tug on her curl.

"I thought about how peaceful it was lying in your arms the night you brought me here."

"You mean the night you demanded sex from me?" I smirk.

"And it was fucking amazing, wasn't it?"

"Yes, it was. Now go on."

"I thought about what our life together would look like."

"What did you want it to look like?"Sitting on the back porch watching the sunset like you promised. Swimming in the pond…naked."

"Oh. Naked, huh?"

"You told me no one would see us out here.""You're right. I did say that."

Her small hand strokes back and forth across my chest. "Staring at the stars made me feel closer to you somehow. So each night before I went to bed, I would go to the window and look up at the stars and beg you to come for me." She brushes her finger over my nipple, and it pebbles beneath her touch. "I guess I was hoping you were looking at them too and could hear my plea."

"I was always trying to find a way to feel closer to you too."

"Did you?"

"When I walked through our house, it helped. The night before we raided the compound, we *were* looking up at the sky together.

"How do you know that?"

"We were staking out the house with the drone. I saw you come to your window and stare up at the stars."

"At that moment, we were both looking at the stars," she coos.

"Yes."

There's a long silence before I say, "I'm so sorry I hurt you by not telling you I loved you. I was being selfish. I was just afraid..." My words get caught in my throat.

"I understand now. You were holding on to so much pain. You never made peace with your father. I never could've imagined how mentally cruel he was to you. I was wrong to try to force you to put those feelings into words before you were ready. And how your poor mother and sister died. I wish you could've shared it all with me, but I understand."

"I couldn't deal with it myself, let alone put it into words."

"I know that now."

"The way you said, 'your poor mother and sister,' what did you mean by that?" I ask.

"It was something Mario told me."

"Can you tell me?" Her body tenses. "It's okay, Amelia. He can't hurt me anymore."

"But I don't want to be the one to hurt you." I pull her tighter to me.

"I can take it. Whatever it is. As long as you're by my side."
I feel her take in a deep cleansing breath and begin to speak.

"He said the accident that killed them wasn't an accident."

"What?"

"He said he worked at a car lot. He made a good living, but he wanted more for his family. So he borrowed some money from the Albanians. When he couldn't pay it back, they murdered your mother and sister to send him a message."

"Oh my God."

"He said he made a deal with Antonio to keep you and Nico safe."

"What kind of deal?""Antonio would get the Albanians to back off if Mario went to work for him."

"That must've been when he started leaving."

"He said Antonio would send him overseas to do jobs because no one knew who he was, so they never saw him coming."

"Holy shit."

"I'm so sorry, Freddy."

"No. I'm glad you told me. It's just another piece of the puzzle that is my father."

"So it's true then?"

"What's true?"

"He wasn't a bad person until he got in with the wrong people."

"I guess. He wasn't a bad dad when we were little," I admit.

"So..."

"Tell me what you're thinking."

"Antonio Martinelli seems to be in the center of everything. He made deals with everyone and lied about everything. Mario went to him to protect his sons. And you went to him to protect your brother," she explains.

"Antonio was the master of the deal, all right. Maybe he liked being everyone's savior."

"Or maybe he liked controlling everyone like his own little puppets."

"He really fooled us, didn't he? I feel like such an idiot. We thought he was helping us."

"You can't do that to yourself. You didn't know what else to do. You were kids."

"But I dragged Nico into this life. He could've gone to college. He could've made something with his life."

"You can't think like that."

"Did you hear my conversation with Mario?"

"I heard some of the awful things he said about you and Nico. He had no remorse for the way he treated you."

"There were so many unanswered questions, and I couldn't come to grips with a lot of the things he put us through. But you got those answers for me, Amelia. I'm sorry for all the horrible things he did to you. I'll never hold anything back from you again, I swear. No matter how it makes me feel, I won't ever leave you out again."

"Thank you. That means the world to me."

"Please, promise me something."

"Anything, Big Guy."

"No matter how angry I make you…you won't run away from me again."

"Never again, I promise. Can I ask *you* something?"

"Anything."

"What's Ethan going to do with the warehouse in Texas?"

"I'm not sure, why?"

"I think I need to go there."

"Why in the hell would you want to go back down there, Amelia?"

"Maybe it will help me let it all go somehow. I guess in my mind, he's still out there somewhere, waiting to come back and get me, like he promised."

"Sweetheart, I guarantee he can never hurt you again. Nico made sure of that when he put a bullet through his brain."

"I know, but I was unconscious for that part."

"I'm glad you were."

"But…"

I press my finger to her lips to stop her from continuing. "If you need to go back to Texas for some kind of closure, we'll go. I'll work it out with Ethan. Whatever you need to move on with your life, I'll make it happen."

"Thank you."

"Let's pack up and get back to the house. I don't want my girl getting chilled out here in the night air."

Chapter 46
Freddy

Two weeks later, we're on the private jet, headed for Texas. Ethan has had a team at the compound inventorying everything for weeks. The dead bodies are long gone, and the blood stains scrubbed away. There shouldn't be anything left to trigger Amelia but her own memories.

Vito lands on the makeshift runway, and Tommy meets us with a car. As we ride to the compound, Amelia's face is glued to the window, and her hand has a death grip on mine in her lap. The car comes to a stop in the courtyard, and Amelia's face grows stark white.

"Amelia, baby, you don't have to do this. We can turn the car around right now and go back to the plane."

"No. I need to do this." She opens her door and is out of the car before I can protest any further.

"Why don't you start at the beginning?" I suggest, catching up with her and taking her hand in mine. I'm not going to let her go one step without me by her side.

Chapter 47
Amelia

Freddy takes my hand, and I lead him to the warehouse. I show him the showers and tell him how the girls and I had to shower in front of everyone. In front of Lenny. He takes a lot of deep breaths, but he keeps his cool as I guide him to the cells.

"This cell was mine," I say, pointing at the one on the left. "Carrie was there, Sandy was there, Monika was in that one, Jen was over there, and Beth was here. We would come to the edge of our cells and talk. Well, everyone but Beth."

"Why not Beth?"

"She was very defiant at first. It got her a few slaps in the face by Lenny too. I tried to tell her to keep her mouth shut, but she wouldn't listen to me. I guess now that I know who her father is, I understand her need to stand up for herself."

"McAnally's a bad man to cross."

"She didn't act like she knew he was the head of the Irish Mafia though. She kept saying he was some important businessman in New York City."

"Oh, he's important all right." Freddy chuckles. "I'm glad we're on the same side."

"I'm glad Ethan was able to broker the deal to get her back home."

"Yeah, Vlad wasn't very happy, but Ivan is the head of his family and the Pakhan, so he has to do what he says."

"What does that word mean? Pakhan." I butcher the pronunciation, but he knows what I mean.

"The families in the Bratva each have a head. Like our Don Supreme is Ethan. But when all the families come to the table, the one in charge is called the Pakhan. That's Ivan."

"Oh, wow."

"Yeah, so I wouldn't mess with him either."

As we walk across the compound to the house, I ask, "What is Ronan's title?"

"He's the Leader of the Irish Mafia."

"Your father really was messing with the best of the best of all the families, wasn't he?"

"Yes, and he stole from them all and then sold their weapons to the highest bidder."

"He told me no one knew who he was because Mario Acosta was dead."

"They didn't know he was Mario Acosta because he called himself Oiram Atsoca."

"Why did he choose that name?" I ask.

"That's what I asked. He said we were idiots because we couldn't figure out it was actually his name spelled backward." I try to imagine all the letters shifted around in my head.

"I never would've figured that out."

"Yeah, neither did we. We were so focused on finding that name that we never considered it could be different. We searched all over the world for the company he owned, Catch Me If You Can Enterprises."

"He really was snubbing his nose at everyone, wasn't he?"

"He sure was."

Chapter 48
Freddy

We enter the house and stand silently in the middle of the living room. I don't want to be here anymore than she does, but if this is what she needs, I'm all in.

"Baby, are you okay?" I ask, squeezing her hand.

"Yeah." The word comes out so soft it barely registers. She pulls me through the living room and up the stairs. We walk down the hall and into the last bedroom on the left. She heads straight for the window and looks out.

"This was my room." She sounds like she's a million miles away. I listen and watch as she stares out at the desert. "I wasn't allowed to have a mirror. This window was the only way I could see what he did to my hair." Her hand reaches up and touches the window. "When it was dark outside, I could see my reflection in the glass." The other hand plays with the ends of her hair. "It's grown back a little, don't you think?"

"It sure has. But you know you could be bald, and I wouldn't give a shit, right?" She gives me a soft smile and nods her head in agreement.

When she's done looking around the small room, she leads me back downstairs. We walk through the kitchen and into the dining room. Her hand glides over the dining room table and over the back of one of the chairs. I can only assume it was hers. She stops as we enter the living room again.

The room has been cleaned. The blood stain from Joey's gunshot wound has been removed from the carpet, and the glass has been replaced in the window where Nico's kill shot broke through. A tear rolls down her cheek. I engulf her body from behind to protect her as we look over the floor where she was bound, the chair I was restrained in, and the ugly brown couch.

She clears her throat and stands up straighter. "I'm done in here. Can we go outside?"

"Of course. Whatever you need, Poppy." I follow her out the door and onto the front porch. "Where do you want to go now?" I follow her gaze to a little enclosed area across the way.

"Over there." She points at the fenced-in space.

When we reach the gate, it's unlocked. She gives the door a shove and walks inside. She sits down on a bench, leans her head against the fence, and closes her eyes. Her strength entrances me. These places she's showing me are laced with trauma, and she moves through each one with ease.

"This is where I used to sit and daydream about us." She taps on the seat for me to sit beside her. Sitting, I lean my head back against the fence and close my eyes like she does.

"My thoughts of you brought me peace and solace."

The sun is hot on my face, and it doesn't take long for me to begin to sweat in the desert heat. Amelia suddenly shifts and sits straight up as if she just remembered something. She scrambles and drops to her knees on the dirt.

"Amelia, what's wrong. What are you looking for?"

"A rock."

"A rock?"

"Yeah, there was a rock I used to hold in my hand. It's shaped like a heart." Her searching becomes frantic.

"We'll find it." I fall to my knees beside her, running my hands through the dirt and rocks.

"It has to be here."

I don't understand why in the hell we're down on our hands and knees in the dirt searching for a rock, but I'll find the one she needs if I have to look at every rock in Texas.

"I found it!" she calls out. Relief floods my gut. "See, look, it's shaped like a heart." She holds it out flat in her palm for me to see.

"Can I hold it?" I ask tentatively. She looks at me with hesitation but lays the rock in my hand. I run my finger over the smooth surface, and I imagine my girl clinging to this little rock. I imagine her begging it to give her whatever strength she needed to get her through the day, and it makes my heart clench.

"It's beautiful," I say, as I place it back into her hand and cover it with mine. "I think you should take it home with you."

"Really?" Her face lights up.

"Yes. It brought you hope and comfort. We can put it on the mantel, and you'll always have it close by if you need it." She hugs me around the neck.

"Oh thank you, Freddy."

"Where to next?" I ask.

"I think I'm done." Her voice sounds almost…content. This is not what I was expecting. I was prepared for tears and breakdowns, but there have been none. My phone chimes with a text from Ethan.

"Do you mind if we go back to the warehouse? Ethan's here, and he wants us to touch base with him before we leave."

"Sure."

I take her hand in mine, and we walk back around to the front of the warehouse and find Ethan standing with a group of men.

"Oh, good. Here they are now," he says, pointing at Amelia and me. "Come on in, you two." He waves us into the warehouse. We hesitantly follow them. I scan the faces of the men waiting for us. I had no idea this was going to be a meeting of some of the most powerful men in the world, but here we are.

"Gentlemen, this is Freddy Acosta. Some of you already

know him, but for those of you who don't, he's my second. He's also in charge of all illegal operations for The Martinelli Organization."

"Gentlemen," I say with a nod, not letting go of Amelia's hand for one second.

"And this brave woman is Amelia Peters," Ethan says. Amelia blushes as she turns to him. He nods his head, and her businesswoman mask falls into place.

"Gentlemen. It's a pleasure to meet you." I give her hand a quick squeeze to reassure her she's doing great and continue to hold on tight. Her face is soft and relaxed. If she is intimidated by these men, she isn't showing it.

"Freddy, Amelia, I would like to introduce you to Ronan McAnally, Leader of the Irish Mafia, New York City; Enzo Troponi, capo de capi, Cosa Nostra, Italy; Ivan Vilkolov, Pakhan, Bratva, Russia; Heimlich Klein, capo di tutti capi, Germany; Branimir Tola, Albanian Mafia; and Diego Montcheska, boss of the Mexican Cartel from across the river. We've come together today to discuss what to do about the weapons housed in this facility."

"You gentlemen don't need me…" Amelia tries to release my hand. If she thinks I'm letting her out of my sight in this place, she's sadly mistaken.

"Amelia. Stay, please," Ethan urges. She nods her head in understanding, but her face is etched with confusion. I pull her in closer to my side.

Ethan directs his attention to my girl. "Mr. Tola is looking for a particular weapon that was taken from his possession a few months back. It's a very *delicate* piece of machinery, and he would like to have it back," Ethan explains. "Amelia, I thought possibly while you were being held here by Oiram Atsoca, you might've seen said weapon?"

"I was only brought to this part of the warehouse once," she says.

"Did you see any large weapons?" She focuses on Ethan, and her grip on my hand tightens.

"The one time he brought me here, he told me he stole a weapon from the Albanians." Her eyes flicker between Tola and Ivan and back to Ethan. "He told me he was going to sell it to the Russians." My blood pressure rises as I remember the fact that the Albanians are who killed Momma and Laura all those years ago. The only thing keeping me in control is the fact they were under different leadership back then.

"Do you know what it was?"

"No, but it kind of looked more like a rocket than a gun." The men grumble, and the room seems to prickle with anticipation.

"Do you know where the *rocket* is now?" Ethan continues the questioning.

"He told his men to close it up and get it ready for delivery."

"Delivery where?"

"I don't know."

Ivan adds to the conversation. "My brother was supposed to purchase the weapon after the auction. But the auction was interrupted, and everyone fled before they could make the transfer."

"That was the night your brother *bought* my daughter," Ronan snarls.

"Gentlemen, please. We've already dealt with that situation, and your daughter is home safe and sound."

"For a price," Ronan says snidely under his breath.

"Amelia." Ethan turns back to her. "If the weapon wasn't delivered the night of the auction, do you know where he might've put it, you know, for safekeeping?"

"I never saw the crate again. Maybe it's still in the mountain."

"The mountain?" Mr. Troponi asks.

"Yes, the auction was held inside a mountain, not too far from here in Mexico. Everyone tore out of there so fast when the shots were fired. Maybe the truck is still there somewhere," she says.

"I assure you, there is no truck inside my mountain," Diego quips.

"Then you wouldn't mind if we see for ourselves then, would you, Diego, old friend?" Branimir asks.

"Go look for yourselves, but you won't find it."

"Amelia, do you have any idea where it could be?" Ethan asks. Amelia looks around the massive space.

"Did you look in the basement?"

"Basement?"

"When they would move us in and out of the basement, we would pass a room that was always padlocked. Maybe it's in there?"

"Marco, Tommy. Take some tools and go check the basement." His tone is sharp and quick with them. But when he speaks to my girl, his voice is calm and respectful. "Amelia, would you mind showing them where to go, please?"

"Yes, of course." Gesturing for Amelia to lead the way, I follow her down the stairs with Marco and Tommy bringing up the rear. She leads us to a thick metal door, and sure enough, there's a heavy padlock on it.

Tommy comes in behind us with a box of tools and bolt cutters. They work for a few minutes, and the lock finally breaks free. Opening the creaking door, we see a large wooden crate sitting alone in the center of the room.

"That looks like the box he showed me," Amelia confirms.

We step inside the room. Marco and Tommy pry the top off the crate. Wrapped in straw is the largest rocket I've ever seen. The only rocket I've ever seen.

"This is it. Marco, radio Ethan and tell him we found it."

"On it, Boss."

All the men file into the basement. Once Branimir confirms it is his rocket, the tension in the room lessens. "Thank you, Amelia," he says. "You're a very brave young woman to live through what you did here and still come back to help us."

"Oh, I…" Amelia speaks, but I cut her off.

"Yes, she is very brave. Now, gentlemen, if you don't need anything further from Ms. Peters, I would like to take her home."

Nods and expressions of agreement and thanks come from the men as she sweetly thanks the group, and we exit the building. When we're safely in the car waiting for Tommy to drive us back to the jet, Amelia asks, "Why did you let them think I came back here just to help them?"

"Because, sweetheart, you just won the hearts of some of the world's most powerful men. Why disappoint them? Besides, you never know when they might come in handy." She takes the rock out of her pocket and holds it in her hand. I watch as her thumb slides over the smooth surface. Who am I to say what should bring her comfort? *Maybe I need a rock.*

Vito is waiting to take off when we arrive at the jet. When we're high above the clouds, I can't take my eyes off my girl as she stares out the window, lost in her thoughts. I stroke the top of her thigh with my thumb.

"How are you feeling? Did you find what you needed back there?"

She gives me a smile, and her expression seems different. Her eyes are soft, and her skin is glowing. In that moment, I have my Poppy back.

"I feel really good. I feel like a weight has been lifted off my shoulders."

"I'm glad to hear that. You should try to get some rest." She nods her head and cuddles into my chest. I pull her close and take a deep breath. I think she's going to be okay.

Chapter 49
Amelia

It's been a month since we took our trip to Texas, and I feel more like my old self. Lola invited me to a girls' night out at Scarlett's, so I accepted.

Freddy is driving us in the Chevelle. I forgot how the rumble of the engine makes me feel inside. He pulls into Scarlett's and parks.

"Take it easy tonight, okay," he says.

"You're such a worrywart," I tease.

"This is your first night out with the girls in a long time. I just want you to be careful."

"I'll be careful. Don't act like you guys won't be in the control room stalking us." I giggle.

As we enter the club, the girls raise their glasses to me. I see Lola, standing with Ethan's sisters, Lil, Gilly, MeMe, and the assassin for The Organization, Sasha.

"Oh, stop it," I say, waving them off.

"You need to catch up. Here, drink this." Lola hands me a shot, and I pound it back just as Freddy walks by on his way to the security office. I smile a big grin in defiance at him, and he shakes his head.

"Before we all get drunk, I need to talk to you ladies about something. Personal."

"Ooo personal, I like that," Gilly says. "What is it?"

"Is everything all right, honey?" Lil asks, putting her hand on my arm.

"I feel a lot better since we went to Texas, but I still feel… I feel…"

"What is it, Amelia? You can say anything to us. You should know that by now," MeMe says.

"I feel like a part of me is still missing."

"Missing?" Gilly asks.

"I don't feel like I'm in full control of my life yet."

"More details, please," Lola says.

"I used to be more confident. I used to feel powerful, like I could take on the world."

"Powerful, huh?" Sasha asks.

"What can I do to get that feeling back in my life again?"

"I think you should take control in the bedroom," Sasha says.

"In the bedroom. What do you mean?"

"You need a night of being in control of your man to get your confidence back."

"Oh, I don't know if Freddy would go for that. He's usually the one who leads in the bedroom. I was a virgin, remember?"

"So what? That was years ago. You need to get past that shit."

"I know, but I don't know how to control him in the bedroom. Have you looked at him? He's six foot five, Sasha. How do I control a man who towers over me by almost a foot?"

"I can teach you." She's so confident, sometimes it scares me.

"Teach me?"

"Yeah. It turns Gary on when I'm the boss."

"Oh God. Do we have to hear this?" MeMe says, covering her ears.

"I know when Nico took me to The Black Room Den, I felt powerful when we left there," Gilly says.

"Gilly! The Black Room Den, really?" MeMe cringes.

"It was something from a book he read." She waves off her nervous Nellie sister.

"I'll teach you," Sasha offers.

"Teach me?"

"Sure. I'll take you to pick out an outfit, teach you how to walk, how to stand, what to say, and what to do to drive your man wild."

"Hey! Can you teach me too?" Lil pipes up.

"Lil! You too?" MeMe chimes.

"Yes, MeMe. Come on, don't you need a little spice in the bedroom too?"

MeMe lets out a huff but agrees. "Fine, I'm in."

The group pulls in close as Sasha speaks. "All of you, really?"

"I'll take some lessons if you're giving them," Lola chirps.

"It might be nice to learn something new," MeMe says sweetly.

"It looks like we're all in, Sasha," I say.

"Okay, everybody, meet me at the sex shop on Elm tomorrow at six." Everyone's eyes bug out of their heads at her words. She puts her hands on her hips. "If you want to learn, we're starting at the beginning. Now, can we please drink? I have some things planned for Gary tonight." She waves up at the camera, knowing he's watching. We all shoot back our screaming orgasms and head for the dance floor.

The next evening, we basically take over the Black Whip Sex Shop. Sasha helps each of us pick out an outfit and some items to use on our men. She tells us how to bring them to an explosive climax, all the while taking control of the scene and feeling more confident and assertive in the bedroom.

"You know, you could do this for a living," I tell her.

"Nah, too much work. I'll just be the personal sexual liaison for women of The Organization." Laughter fills the store as we proceed to buy the place out.

Chapter 50
Amelia

It's Friday afternoon, and I've decided tonight is the night. I'm going to take control of Freddy Acosta and become the powerful, confident woman I was before all this shit happened to me. I call him at work.

"Poppy, what's wrong? You don't call me at work very often."

"When do you think you'll be home tonight?"

"Umm, about two hours. Why? What's wrong?"

"Nothing's wrong. I have a surprise for you," I singsong.

"A surprise, huh?"

"Mm-hmm."

"I could finish up here and be home sooner if you want," he croons.

"No. Two hours will be perfect."

"Okay, see you in two hours."

⌒

I spent the time setting up the bedroom, taking a shower, putting on sultry makeup, and making dinner. Spaghetti carbonara. Sasha says carbs are good for energy.

Freddy comes in the door right on time.

"Honey, I'm home," he sings.

"You're so silly." I greet him at the door, wrapping my arms around his neck.

"I like it when you meet me at the door like this." He smothers me in kisses.

"Come on, dinner's ready." I take his hand and try to pull him toward the kitchen, but he stops me.

"Let me wash up first."

"Okay, but do it in the powder room down here. Don't go upstairs."

"Why can't I go up to our bedroom, Poppy?"

"Because I have a surprise for you up there, and I don't want you to see it yet."

"Oh, a surprise. Is it a sexy surprise?" He waggles his eyebrows at me.

"I think you'll like it. Now, hurry up. We need to eat before it gets cold."

Freddy

Amelia is almost giddy. I haven't seen her like this in a long time. I wonder what her big surprise is.

"How was your day?" I bellow as I wash my hands in the half bath.

"Good. How was yours?"

I meet her at the kitchen island.

"Fine. Did you do something different with your makeup?"

"Yeah. Do you like it?"

"It makes you look…mysterious."

"Good, that's the look I was going for." She snickers.

I help her carry the food to the dining room table, and we proceed to eat our pasta and talk about our day.

I set my fork on my plate. "I'm done. Can I have my surprise now?"

"Someone's anxious."

"The anticipation is killing me." I scoot my chair back and stand. I pull on the back of her chair, and she stands.

"I need to clean up the table."

"Fuck the table. I need my surprise." She breaks out into laughter.

"Okay, but you go first, and I'll follow."

I take her by the hand and lead us up the stairs to our bedroom door. When I push it open, I can't believe my eyes. The whole room has been transformed.

"Do you like it?" she chirps.

The pink is gone, replaced by black curtains and black satin sheets. A black comforter rests folded across the foot of the bed, and candlelight warms the space. In the center of the bed lies a pair of leather handcuffs. *She's going to let me cuff her tonight. My cock twitches with excitement. I love to control my girl.*

"Amelia. You want me to—" I point at the cuffs.

"No," she coos and shakes her head. "You're not going to cuff me tonight. I'm going to cuff you."

"Me?" *What the fuck?*

"I'm going to be in control tonight." Her voice is different. It's firm and determined.

"Amelia…" She cuts me off with a finger to my lips.

"I know what I've been missing."

"What are you talking about, missing?"

"I miss my old self." Her shyness temporarily returns, and she looks at the floor. Then she takes in a deep breath, squares her shoulders, and speaks.

"I was always in control at the office and in my life until… Mario. He took something from me in that desert, and I need to take it back."

"And you think if you control me in the bedroom, it will help you in your everyday life?"

"That's the premise, yes. Are you up for the challenge, Mr.

Acosta?” *I don't want to sound like a bumbling idiot, but fuck yeah, I'm up for it.*

“I'm up for anything you need, Poppy. And if you think chaining me to the bed is going to help you, by all means, I'm in.” *I'm an understanding guy who can take one for the team.* With a flip of a switch, her demeanor changes.

“Good. Now, take off your clothes and sit with your back against the headboard,” she demands.

“Fuck, woman, you're getting right to it. No foreplay?”

“Oh, there will be foreplay, just not the kind you're thinking of. Now scoot,” she says, slapping my ass. *Who is this woman?*

I do as I'm told and remove my clothes and sit with my back against the headboard. My dick is ready for the party, but I wait patiently for whatever comes next.

“I see someone is happy to see me.” She approaches the bed and looks over my hard cock standing at attention.

“Do you blame me? You're blowing my fucking mind right now.”

“Give me your hands.” Long gone is her smiling, happy demeanor. Enter a strong and powerful Amelia.

I hold out my hands in front of me, and she attaches a leather cuff to each wrist and clips them together with a D-ring. I pull on them to show her I'm under her control.

“Now, I'm going to go change. Sit there and think about your punishment.”

“Punishment? What did I do wrong?”

She doesn't answer me but lets out a sly giggle as she walks into the bathroom. I look around the room while I wait for her. Something is lying under a cloth on the dresser, but I can't make out what it is, and the room smells of jasmine and citrus.

“It's chilly in here.” There's no reply. “I'm naked, ya know. You know what the cold does to a man, don't you…Amelia?”

Finally, the door swings open, and Amelia takes over the space. She's not my sweet Amelia anymore. She looks more like Dominatrix Amelia. She's dressed in a black latex corset pushing her tits to the sky, with a matching micro-mini skirt and thigh-high black boots that make her at least six inches taller. All the air rushes from my lungs at the sight of her big hair and bloodred lips. She looks like she might beat the shit out of me if I step out of line. My cock joins the party, and a little worry runs through me, wondering what the hell I signed up for tonight.

"Amelia…"

"Quiet." She holds her hand up, and my mouth snaps shut. "Tonight, you will call me Mistress. Do you understand?" Her voice is low and sultry. She speaks slowly, and her words are deliberate.

"Yes, Mistress."

"Good boy." *Oh fuck. Did those words just turn me on?*

"What's your safe word?" *Safe word? Why the hell do I need a safe word for this?*

"Uhh. Red."

"Good. And if you don't want to stop, but you need a break, what do you say?"

"Yellow."

"Good boy." *Fuck. Do I have a praise kink I never knew about?* Her eyes are dark as she stalks to the side of the bed.

"I need to know your limits." The low hum of her voice sends chills through me.

"My limits?"

"You know. Is there anything you don't want me to do to you tonight?"

"What?" *I'm going to make her work for this one.*

"Do you have any no gos?"

"No gos?" She lets out an exasperated breath, like I should know what she's trying to ask me.

"You know… things that are a hard no for me to do to you."

"Oh! I guess… hmm…no butt stuff."

"Anything else?"

"I think I can handle anything else you want to do to me, Mistress."

"Fine. No ass play…tonight." *Tonight? Shit, my girl's going to do this again?*

She turns and slinks away from the bed, swinging her ass from side to side. She stands by the dresser, and my cock is begging to know what's under the cloth.

"On your knees in front of me."

"Yes, Mistress." I scoot my way to the side of the bed and drop to my knees before my queen. I can smell her arousal. Her fingers glide through my hair, and I groan. She places one foot up on the bed and cinches up her skirt. Her bare pussy is directly in front of my face, and I breathe in her scent. "Oh fuck."

"Do you want a taste?" she teases.

"Yes, Mistress. I would love a taste of your hot pussy."

"Yes, Mistress, is fine," she corrects. "You may lick my pussy."

Her confidence is exhilarating. I run my nose over her mound and inhale deeply before I flatten my tongue the way I know she likes and lick her wet slit from back to front. Her pussy is intoxicating, and I need more. I lean in for another taste, and her hands grip my hair and pull me away. My tongue is still jutting out as I look up at her.

"Greedy boy."

"Please, Mistress. May I have another taste?"

"That's my Good Boy. Yes, you may." I lean my head forward and lick her again. This time, my tongue moves slowly and deliberately, lapping up her juices.

"Very nice." Her eyes are dark with desire. "Suck my clit."

"Yes, Mistress." I lick her engorged clit and suck it into my mouth.

"Yes, just like that." Her words come out as a breathy moan, and I know I'm pleasing my Mistress the way she needs. I breathe through my nose and don't release the pressure as I flick her clit with the tip of my tongue. Her hips begin to rock. She moans, and my cock weeps.

"Right there. Good Boy."

I raise my cuffed hands toward her pussy, and she yanks my head away from her center sharply. She definitely got my attention with that move.

"No hands. Just your mouth."

"Yes, Mistress."

"You may continue." I return to my position with my head between her legs, and I suck her clit back into my mouth. I know my girl's body well, and she's close. I double down on the pressure and flicks.

"Yes. Don't stop. Right there." Her hips grind on my face until her whole body convulses, and her cries of satisfaction fill the room. I know I've made my mistress proud. I continue to lap up her sweetness until her hands grip my hair and pull me free.

"Very good, now get on the bed," she says sternly. "Head down, ass up."

"But…"

"Do you doubt your Mistress?"

"No, Mistress."

"Then do as I say. Head down. Ass up."

I scurry to the bed like the good little boy I am. My cock is so hard I want to wrap my fist around it and give it a tug for some relief, but I don't think my Mistress will allow it. I rest my head on my forearms with my ass in the air.

"I like it when you obey me, brat." *My brain is about to implode from her words*. She stands at the side of the bed and runs her palms over my ass and down my back. Being in this position makes me feel vulnerable. Now I know how she feels when I have her body on display for me. She smacks my ass before she leaves my side and goes over to the dresser. I see the cloth drop to the floor, and when she leans over to pick it up, her juicy ass peeks from below her skirt. I groan with more discomfort as my dick begs for release.

She climbs on the bed behind me, and she runs something soft over my skin. I try to turn to see it, but I can't.

"Do you like the way that feels?"

"Yes, Mistress. May I see?" She runs it over my back and holds it out in front of my face. It's a small red flogger with black tails, and I know what's coming.

"You did a beautiful job making me come, so I want to reward you."

"Thank you, Mistress." I hear the whirling sound of the flogger as it spins. It touches my ass cheeks lightly, and the strange feeling causes my body to jerk. No one has ever tried to control me. I'm always the one on the other end of the flogger or the paddle.

"What's your color?"

"Green, Mistress."

"Good," she purrs. She continues to spin the flogger up my spine and across my shoulders. It moves back down to my ass and across the back of my thighs. All at once, there's a crack as the tails connect to the skin on the back of my thighs.

"What's your color?"

"Green, Mistress."

Again, she snaps the flogger, but this time, it's a little bit harder. I flinch and shut my eyes, sinking into the feeling. Again, it snaps and again.

"Your color?"

The word green comes out on a moan, and my mind anticipates the next sting and where it will land. It cracks again, and again. Over and over until I'm lost in the sensations she's giving me. I feel like I'm floating from the pleasure. When she stops, she rubs her hands over my hot flesh to soothe it.

"What a good boy you are."

"Thank you, Mistress."

"Turn over onto your back."

I do as I'm told. The skin on my ass and upper thighs twinges, and my cock is so hard I could pound nails with it. Should I tell her she has me so close to the edge? She's doing so well controlling the scene, I don't want to throw her off her game, so I try to hold out a little longer.

"Your cock looks like it's about to explode. The head is so big and red. Do you need to come, Freddy?" she coos.

"Yes, please, Mistress."

"Maybe I should edge you like you do me, hmm?"

"No. Please, Mistress. I need to come."

"Do you think you've been a good enough boy to come?"

"Yes, Mistress. I made you come. I can make you come again."

"Oh really?"

"Yes, Mistress. I'll do whatever you want. Please, I need to come."

"Don't come until I tell you to, Freddy. I wouldn't want you to be a bad boy."

"Yes, ma'am."

"What did you call me?" she says sharply.

"Mistress. I'm sorry. Yes, Mistress."

"That's better."

"Mistress, can you take the cuffs off, please, so I can touch you?" She looks confused. Like she wasn't expecting my question.

"I-uh. Yes, but only if you continue to do what I say."

"Yes, Mistress." She removes the cuffs, and I rub my wrists. She looks concerned but stays in character.

"Thank you, Mistress."

She climbs on the bed and straddles my thigh, not my cock. She slides her wet pussy up and down my thigh, covering it in her arousal. She grinds her clit into my leg, and the action makes my cock ache.

"Please," I groan.

"Please, what? Use your words, Freddy."

"Please, may I come?" my voice pleads. *What the fuck is wrong with me? I sound like a needy little bitch. Normally, I could fuck her all night, but she's edged me so long I could embarrass myself at any minute like a schoolboy.*

"By mouth or pussy?"

"Pussy, please, Mistress."

"What's your color?"

"Green," I moan. *I refuse to go to yellow or red. But oh my God, she's trying to kill me!*

She lowers her mouth to my cock and licks the precum from the tip. I grab the sheets with both hands as she licks me from base to tip. She looks up at me under her sooty lashes and smiles a wicked grin.

She wastes no time climbing above my cock and notching my tip at her entrance. Slowly, she lowers her wet cunt down onto my length, surrounding me in her warmth, and a guttural moan escapes my throat. She says low and sultry, "I want you to cry my name when you come."

"Mistress, oh shit," I hiss.

I'm trying not to come until she allows me, but goddamn, she feels so fucking good on my cock. Her hands are on my chest as she gets the leverage she needs to slide her tight pussy up and down my shaft. The sensation is almost painful.

"Oh fuck. You're so deep," she moans.

Her pussy flutters around my cock.

"Come for me, Freddy. Fill my pussy with your release." Her words roll over me like thunder. My hands move to her hips, and I thrust up into her. I hold her hard against my cock as I explode into her center.

"Oh shit. A-A-Amelia."

"I can feel your cum pumping into me. Oh. Fuck."

Her body shudders over mine as we ride the wave together. Our combined release slides out of her and runs down my ass crack. She collapses on my chest, and I wrap my arms around her.

"That was so amazing, Freddy."

"You made me so feral for you, Amelia."

"You really liked it?" she chimes as her head pops up. Her face is beaming as she looks down at me. My silly, carefree girl is back. All of my Amelia is back.

"Fuck, yes, I liked it. You're such a badass. Where did all that come from?"

"The girls and I had a little instruction."

"Instruction? Who the fuck was the instructor?"

"Sasha."

"Gary says she does some nasty shit to him," I say, and we both break into laughter.

"I love you, Amelia."

"I love you, Freddy."

Chapter 51
Freddy

Ten Months Later

Now that everything has cooled off, I think it's time Ethan and I have a meeting.

Ethan is behind his desk when I enter his office. I take my usual spot in the leather chair in front of his desk.

"So what did you want to talk to me about?" he asks, pushing his seat back and crossing his right leg over his left knee, rubbing the tension away from his temple.

"I wondered if you knew when my debt to Antonio would be paid."

"Your what?"

"My debt. You and I have never really talked about it."

"Explain."

"Antonio made a deal with Nico and me."

"Yeah, I know about that. You both came to work for The Organization the day after graduation."

"Right. But he never told us for how long. He just used the word *indefinitely*."

"Knowing Antonio, he would've found a way to keep you

forever," he snarks. He scoots closer to his desk and rests on his elbows. "Do you want to leave The Organization?" That's a loaded question in the mob. You don't just quit or leave. You're in for life. Even I know that, but Nico and I never took an oath or had a ceremony. We're not related to Ethan by blood, and we are Greek, not Italian. Technically, I shouldn't even hold the position I do. But Ethan doesn't follow the rules. He makes his own.

"I like what we've done since you took the reins. I just think there may be a time in the future when I might be ready for a change. I wanted to know your thoughts."

"I guess I just assumed you were happy here. You've never complained or said you didn't want to be my second." There's a defensiveness to his voice.

"I am happy, and it's not that I don't want to be your second. I like the shit we get into together." We both chuckle under our breath. "I just don't want to be one of those old fat bosses who gets taken out in a restaurant by a gun under the table."

Ethan strokes his chin. "Well, I don't really want to go out that way either. I was trying to avoid that whole scenario by going legit. I remember what it was like when Sasha came toward me in the restaurant, guns blazing. It was all fake, but the sickness in my stomach was very real."

"Making Johnsonville a safer place for all of us has been your top priority. And you've done an amazing job turning this city around."

"Look, if you want out, just say it. Don't blow smoke up my ass."

"Damn, man. I'm not blowing smoke up your ass. What you've done for this city and our soldiers has been a fucking miracle. You've made everyone's lives better. Be proud of yourself and accept a little praise once in a while."

"Fuck." Ethan gets up from his chair, walks over to the window, and looks out at the city. "You and Nico are family. He's my damn brother-in-law, and you're the best friend I've ever had. The only real friend I've ever had. I'll let you go peacefully. You know that."

"I haven't made any decisions yet. I guess I just wanted to know my options."

"Talk it over with Amelia. Hell, maybe I need to have the same conversation with Lola. We're all still relatively young. Maybe there's something she wants to do in life she hasn't told me about yet. I thought she was content running the shelter and the coffee shop, but I could be wrong on so many levels."

"Don't start doubting everything you've built. I've just been thinking about what I want my life with Amelia to look like in ten, twenty, thirty years, ya know?"

"Let's talk to the girls and come back together and talk again, soon. Okay?"

"Sounds like a plan." We both meet at the door and shake hands. "Thanks for listening."

"Anytime, Freddy. My door is always open to you. You know that."

Relief floods my veins as I walk down the hallway. Now I need to talk to Amelia.

Chapter 52
Amelia

Freddy and I have some new additions to the homestead. Yep, we're country folk now. We went to the local animal shelter and brought home two dogs. Henry is a chocolate Lab. They think he's about two years old, and Tallie is a yellow Lab, and she's a little over a year old.

An elderly woman brought them into the shelter after she fell. Her daughter is moving her into an assisted living facility, and she can't care for them anymore. We wanted two dogs, so they were a perfect fit for us. They're so sweet and well-mannered. They've been well-behaved with all the kids when they come to visit and have been wonderful protectors from the critters. They have already scared off a few who ventured out of the woods. Neither Freddy nor I have ever had pets before, so it's been a learning experience for both of us.

Freddy knows how much I love the pond with the waterfall, so he cleared some of the land around it and built a shelter. He had a gravel road constructed that leads straight from the house to the pond. The shelter is complete with electricity and running water. There is a giant built-in grill, a refrigerator, and a heavy-duty ice machine we added after hauling ice a few times.

We wanted a space where we could have everyone over for a barbecue. Even mobsters need some downtime. I've even brought some ladies from the shelter out to enjoy a day in the sun.

Today, we're having a relaxing day by the pond. Everyone in The Organization is invited to bring their wives and children for a day of good food, fellowship, and fun. Soon, the field will be filled with cars, trucks, and motorcycles.

Gilly and Nico are the first to arrive. Gilly is nine months pregnant and waddles like a duck. I take the salad bowl out of her hands and point at the lounge chairs.

"Go find a chair and sit your ass down," I order. She waves me off, but does as she's told. I hand her a cold bottle of water, and she fans herself with a paper plate.

"Are you okay?" I ask, sitting in the lounge chair beside her.

"Why does it have to be so damn hot?"

"It's July, Gilly. What do you expect?"

"I don't know, maybe just a cloud or two for today. Would that be too much to ask for?" she asks, looking up at the sky like she's having a conversation with God.

Nico comes over carrying a tray. He places it on the table and sidles up behind her and rubs her shoulders. "Can I get you anything, babe?"

"No, I'm okay. But I don't know how long I'll make it out in this heat, so you'd better go do your visiting now." He chuckles and kisses the top of her head.

"Okay, I'll be back. Holler if you need me. Here comes Lil, she'll keep your ass in line."

"Gilly! How are you feeling, Little Momma?" Lil comes in close and talks baby talk to her belly. "And how is my little niece or nephew?"

"Kicking the shit out of me." She looks up at her with tired eyes.

Lil comes over to me. "Where do you want me to put this, honey?"

"Over on that table," I say, pointing off to the left.

"Be right back."

Lil sets the bowl on the table and grabs a drink from the refrigerator. She heads back to us and sits down in the lounger on the other side of Gilly. "Now, really, how are you feeling?" Her voice is sympathetic and understanding.

"How do I look like I'm feeling, Lil? I'm fat and hot."

Lil laughs. "You're almost to the finish line. You're doing so well." She rubs her hand over her swollen belly. "Did you think of anything else you need before the baby comes?" she asks, taking a swig of her beer.

"No, I think we're all set. This baby can't get here soon enough for me though."

Freddy brings an industrial fan and points it straight at Gilly.

"Oh my God. Thank you, Freddy!" she exclaims.

People begin to arrive. Marco, Tommy, Vito, Roscoe, Billy, Max, Franco, Johnny, Chris, Phil, Joey, and all of their significant others file in with bowls and trays of food in hand. Children of all ages and sizes run toward the playground.

Freddy said we couldn't have a space out here for the adults without a place for the kids to play safely, so he built a large area for them. There's a slide, swings, a jungle gym, and a small zip line from one end to the other. All the kids love it. I've even caught some of the guys *testing* the zip line out for safety reasons. *Of course they were.* The area is fenced, and a canopy roof completes the structure and keeps the kids out of the sun. Tallie and Henry don't let the kids out of their sight.

There are even his-and-hers bathrooms. But they aren't close enough for Gilly because she's off to go pee and grumbles the whole way about "Why did he have to build them so far away?"

The noise level ramps up as more people arrive. MeMe and her husband, Giovanni, and their son, Ricky; Lil's husband, Alessandro, and their three kids, Mario, Damian, and Lucia; Jerry and his wife, Alice, and their three grandkids; and, of course, Lola, Ethan, Dominick, and Alessia. Lola just found out she is pregnant with their third child, but she doesn't seem bothered by the heat yet.

Lawn chairs and blankets litter the grass as Ethan fills the grill with hamburgers, hot dogs, chicken, and steak. Everyone pitches in, bringing the meat of their choice, and Chef Ethan cooks it up on the grill.

Freddy is at the pond with some of the kids, showing them how to walk behind the waterfall. There are squeals as he starts tossing kids through the falling water, and they splash down into the pond.

Gary and Sasha stroll in an hour late as usual.

"Hey there, glad you both made it this time," I tease.

"Hey, we're single. It's hard for us to leave the bedroom," Sasha says with a coy grin.

"I'll get us something to drink," Gary says as he holds the back of the lawn chair for Sasha to sit.

"Just water for me," she says. He gives her a goofy grin and a thumbs-up.

"Well, that wasn't creepy or anything," Gilly says.

"Yeah, he's acting weird," Lola adds. All at once, we all stare at Sasha with wide eyes.

"What did you do to him?" I ask.

"Me? Why do you think I did something to him?" She turns her head and grins widely when he hands her the water bottle.

Gary lifts an eyebrow when he notices all of us staring at him. "Yeah, I don't know what you women are talking about, but when you look at me like that, it's time to leave. I'm gonna go help Ethan." As he walks away, we all burst into laughter.

"I got a new toy for us to play with," she says slyly.

"Oh God, I can't listen to this," Gilly says, rubbing her belly. "Close your ears, baby."

"Seriously, when are you two just going to break down and get married?" Lil asks.

"Married? Shit. I'm not getting saddled to anyone. You all go live your happy homemaker lives. I want excitement and danger," she declares.

"You can have excitement and danger and be married."

"Yeah, right. We're good just the way we are, thank you.

How about you, Amelia?" All of their eyes turn to stare at me. *Thanks for throwing the attention on me, Sasha.*

"What do you mean? What about me?" I ask nervously.

"When are you and Freddy gittin' hitched?" Sasha and her fake country accent slay me.

"You'll have to ask Freddy that question. I'm happy just the way we are. He tells me at least twenty times a day he loves me, and that's good enough for me."

"Don't you want more?" MeMe asks.

"More? More is what got me into trouble in the first place. No, I don't need *more*. I have everything I want."

"But, girl, Freddy is getting old. What is he like, fifty by now?" Sasha says.

"No, he's not! He's only thirty-eight and a half," I balk.

"Well, that's old in baby-making years," Gilly says.

"That's for women, not men, Gilly. Who said anything about babies anyway?"

"You want kids, don't you?" she asks.

"Yeah, someday, maybe, I guess," I stammer before taking a drink of my beer. "We have plenty of time. I don't need to be a baby-making machine. I love sharing my life with Freddy and the puppies. I'm not going to rush it. Besides, I get my baby fixes from all of your kids, and then you take them back home. No yelling. No crying. No mess. It's a win-win."

Ethan, Gary, Freddy, and Nico come to join us after everyone has eaten.

"What are you ladies discussing so intently?" Gary asks, gesturing for Sasha to get up and sit on his lap.

"Oh, nothing you guys would be interested in," I say.

Ethan places a kiss on the top of Lola's head. When he drops down in the chair beside her, he looks melancholy.

"What is it?" she asks him.

"I was just thinking."

"About what?" Lil asks.

"Mother and how she would've loved the shit out of this."

"Yeah, my momma would've loved this place too. She loved a good picnic. Right, Nico?" Freddy says.

"Yeah. When we went on trips when we were little, she would pack a picnic lunch. We'd have to stop at a rest area along the way. She would spread out a picnic lunch on a blanket. I can still taste it. Cold fried chicken, potato salad, lemonade, and chocolate chip cookies."

"Why does cold fried chicken always taste so good from a picnic basket?" Freddy says.

"I know, right?" Nico agrees.

Freddy takes my hand and pulls me onto his lap. I cuddle into his chest, and the conversation continues.

"Dude, what the hell is wrong with you now?" Gary asks. Motioning to the stupid grin on Ethan's face.

"I was just thinking. You're all together because of me."

"No, we're not." Sasha laughs. "Lola and Amelia arranged the seats on the airplanes and the hotel reservations in the Grand Caymans.

"That's correct, but who do you think set the wheels in motion by forcing you to go on vacation?" Ethan has a stupid grin plastered across his face. "Me." He points his thumb to his chest.

"Well, you didn't set up Nico and me. We didn't even like each other. Remember, I begged you to take him off my security detail."

"Who made him head of your security detail in the first place?" Again, he points at his chest. "Me."

"You didn't set up Amelia and me," Freddy says.

"I left you there with her after I took Lola away for our masked one-night stand, and you two have been together ever since. I'll take that as a win. Thank you."

Everyone's mouths are agape at how proud our Don Supreme is to be our *matchmaker*.

"You're really proud of yourself, aren't you?" Lil scoffs.

"Yep. I'm the king of matchmaking around here."

"Whoever would've thought Rocco Ethan Martinelli, Don Supreme of The Martinelli Organization, is a matchmaker," Gary says with a belly laugh.

There are whistles and catcalls while Ethan stands and takes a bow.

The crowd starts to thin, and our little group is still sitting together when Gilly makes a whining sound. "Dammit."

"Are you okay? You look kinda flushed," Lil says.

"What's the matter, Gilly?" I ask.

"I. Uh. I think I just peed myself." She tries to get out of the lounge chair, but her belly keeps her from standing. Ethan stands and offers her a hand. She moves to the edge and places her bare feet on the grass.

"It's hot as shit out here," she says, wiping her hand over her face. "And this chair is starting to hurt my back." She lets out a low groan.

"Nico!" everyone yells at once.

Gilly frowns at us like we just tattled on her or something. Nico is playing ball with Damian, and his head snaps in our direction.

"What's wrong? Angel, is everything all right?" he asks as he jogs over.

"I think I just peed myself," Gilly says shyly.

"You what?" He gives a little chuckle, and we all glare at him. "Oh shit. Okay. What do you need me to do?"

"Can you go to the car and get my bag, then walk me to the bathroom?"

"Sure, Angel. Be right back." Nico takes off running for the car. By the time he comes back, Ethan and Gary have Gilly out of the lawn chair, and they're moving in the direction of the bathroom. Nico catches up to them and takes Gary's place by her side. They help her the rest of the way to the bathroom.

When Nico and Gilly come back a few minutes later, her eyes are huge, and Nico is acting nervous.

"What the hell took you so long?" Ethan asks.

"I think we need to leave," Nico says. Everyone's face drops.

"Why? What happened?"

"I don't think I peed myself. I think my water broke."

Gasps and cheers of "oh my God" and "get her to the car" fill the picnic area.

Chapter 53
Freddy

We caravan to the hospital. They deposit Gilly into a wheelchair and whisk her and Nico away to some forgotten land of pain and screaming. The rest of us find our way to the waiting area and set up camp. Excitement quickly turns to boredom as the hours click by. Amelia's head lies on my lap as we wait and wait and wait.

"How long does it take to push a baby out anyway?" I say in a long, agitated breath.

"It can take days, Freddy."

"For fuck's sake, let's hope it doesn't take this baby days." I tap Amelia's shoulder to let me up. "I gotta get up and stretch, baby."

"Okay." Amelia sits up and sets me free.

"I'll go find us some coffee."

I walk the halls until I find the cafeteria. I stand behind a lady in line for coffee. She has one kid in a stroller and another hanging off her hip while she tries to dig out money to pay. At first, I feel aggravated, but when I see the tears running down her cheeks, I have to step in.

"Here. Let me take care of your coffee." She looks up at me with sad, tired eyes.

"Oh, you don't have to do that." Her voice cracks.

"Really, it's no problem."

"Thank you."

The little boy in the stroller grabs my leg.

"Billy, don't touch the nice man." Nice man. If she only knew the things I've done.

"It's all right, isn't it, Billy?" I lean over and shake his outstretched hand. He smiles wide and bright, and I realize I'm smiling back at him too.

"I know it's not my place to ask, but is everything all right? You seem very upset." I don't know why I asked, but something about this lady makes me want to know more.

"It's my husband. He's upstairs in surgery."

"Surgery. Would it be rude to ask why?"

"Someone shot him in the alley behind Don's Pub on Main."

"Do you know who?"

"No. All I know is my husband owed money to some very bad men."

"He did. Why?" She looks at me with confusion on her face. "I'm sorry. I don't mean to pry." She shakes her head and blows her hair out of her face. She moves the baby to the other hip as she steps aside and waits for her coffee order. I place my order and step to the side with her.

"My husband isn't a bad man. He borrowed money from some men he shouldn't have so we could buy a car. Our old car gave out, and he works all the way across town. If he couldn't get to work, we couldn't pay our bills. I told him I would get a job, but the daycare cost alone would take everything I'd make, so it doesn't make any sense for me to work."

"What does he do for a living?"

"He works for Martinelli Construction. He loves his job, so he did the only thing he knew to do. He borrowed money from the Irish." *Oh shit. He borrowed money from McAnally.*

"How much does he owe?"

"What?"

"How much?"

"I don't know exactly. He paid a little bit back, but then we got behind on the payments."

"How much was the loan for?"

"Ten thousand dollars."

"They shot him for ten thousand dollars?" She nods. The barista calls out her name, Evelyn, just as the baby girl on her hip lets out a high-pitched wail. I take the drink for her and set it on the counter.

"Would you mind watching Billy for me for a minute?"

"Me?" My voice cracks.

"Please. I know we don't know each other, but I'm about at the end of my rope, and I can't juggle them both right now. Just long enough so I can change Maggie." Her eyes are swollen from crying, and her cheeks are flushed pink when she looks up at me with those big, pleading eyes.

"Um, yeah, but hurry, okay? Kids don't like me much."

"I'll just be one sec." She takes Maggie and the diaper bag and heads for the ladies' room. I pick up her drink and pull the stroller over to the nearest table. I sit down in front of Billy. He smiles a big grin up at me again, and I find myself unconsciously smiling back at him.

"Hey, buddy," I say awkwardly. He claps his hands and lets out a giggle.

"Up," Billy beams. "Up."

"No, I can't take you out, little guy." Billy's face scrunches up and starts to turn pink.

"No, no, no. Don't cry. Please don't cry." My heart beats wildly in my chest. Please don't let this kid cry. I search the stroller for a toy or something, but they must all be in her diaper bag.

"Hey. Hey. Look at this." I do the only thing I can think of. I put both hands in front of my face.

"Peek-a-boo."

Billy sniffs his nose, and his eyes light up. I try again. This time, I make a smiling face when I say it.

"Peek-a-boo!"

Billy cackles with glee. What the hell is it with this kid? Why is he so stinking cute?

"Peek-a-boo!" I chime again, and now we're both laughing.

His mom exits the bathroom and heads straight for us. She has a confused look on her face as she approaches.

"Look, there's Momma," I say, pointing at her. Billy's eyes are as wide as saucers as he tries to turn to see her. I move the stroller so he can, and his smile beams brightly.

"Thank you so much," she says with an exhausted sigh, sitting in the chair across from me.

"It was no problem. We had a few laughs, didn't we, buddy?" Just then, my name is called.

"What's your husband's name?"

"John."

"Last name?"

"Why?"

"So I can check on him later."

"Oh." Her brows scrunch together, but she tells me anyway. "John Jacobs. Room 304."

"Great. My friend is having a baby, so I might take another walk to stretch and see you later. I hope he comes out of surgery soon. I'm sure he'll be just fine."

"Thank you… What was your name?"

"Uh. Freddy."

"Thank you, Freddy."

The barista calls my name again, and I move forward to pick up the cup carriers.

"Bye-bye," Billy's tiny voice says. When I turn around, his little hand is waving back at himself, but he's looking at me. I nod my head in his direction and say bye. Walking back to the waiting room with an armload of coffees, I decide I'm going to help this woman.

Chapter 54
Freddy

It's been almost three more hours, and I'm not sure how much longer I can take sitting here when Nico appears in the doorway. He has a glazed look on his face. He's dressed in blue scrubs, and he has a weird cap on his head.

"Nico. Is everything all right?" Lola jumps from her seat to stand in front of him. Nico just nods. Amelia comes in beside Lola.

"Are Gilly and the baby okay?" Nico's mouth hangs open, and he nods again.

It's going to take the big brother to snap him out of this. I stand and come in behind the two girls and gently push them to the sides.

"Nico!" I snap, taking him by the shoulders and giving him a little shake. "What the hell's going on? Is the baby here yet?"

He nods. "It's a boy." His eyes light up, and his smile begins to grow until it can't grow any farther.

"It's a boy," I mimic.

"I'm a dad."

"You're a dad!" I pull him in for a hug. "Oh my God! You're a dad!" We all congratulate him, and the room grows loud.

"What's his name?" Amelia questions.

"When can we see them?" Lola asks.

"In a little while. They're getting them settled in a room. They want her to try to breastfeed first."

"Okay. You come out and get us when she's ready," Lil says.

"I will," Nico beams. "I have a son."

"You have a son," I repeat calmly.

Nico walks off in a haze, and the rest of us hug each other. Since we're going to have to wait a little longer, I decide it's time for me to step away and do a little business. I excuse myself from the group and call Ronan.

He picks up on the third ring.

"Freddy, my friend. How are you these days?" he says in his thick brogue.

"I'm good, and you?"

"Fine. Fine. What can I do for you?"

"I found out one of our employees owes you some money."

"Really? What's their name?"

"John Jacobs. Supposedly, he borrowed ten thousand dollars from you to buy a car and couldn't pay it back. Someone shot him last night behind Don's."

"Shot him for ten grand? That wasn't me. I only break bones for anything under twenty-five," he says with a sardonic chuckle.

"Good to know. Can you check whether what they say is true and let me know? If he owes you, I want to take care of it."

"Sure. Give me…fifteen minutes."

"Thanks, Ronan."

I make my way to the rooms on the third floor. I hear a child crying, and when I reach the nurses' station, I see a nurse bouncing Billy on her hip. His face is as red as a beet and flooded with tears. Another nurse is holding a sleeping Maggie on her lap while she types on an iPad. As soon as Billy sees me, he holds his arms out to me.

"Excuse me," I say. "Is everything all right with Mr. Jacobs?"

"Are you family?"

"No, but I'm a family friend."

"I'm sorry, sir. I can't give out any information unless you're family." Billy is hanging out of her arms as she tries to hold him. I reach out for Billy and take him from the nurse.

"Look. Obviously, something bad has happened for you to have the kids. Where's Evelyn?" Billy lays his head on my shoulder. I pat him on the back, and he immediately quiets down.

The nurse lifts her eyes down the hall, and I turn toward room 304. I rub circles on his little back, and I swear he's already asleep. I move down the hall and stop in the doorway. I hear a woman crying and know this isn't going to be good. Pushing the door open farther, I see Evelyn crying by her husband's bedside.

"Evelyn," I say quietly, and her head pops up.

"Freddy? Oh my God. Is Billy okay?" She moves away from the bed, and we meet in the middle of the room.

"He about jumped out of the nurse's arms to get to me, so I took him. I hope that's okay." She wipes her tears away and pushes Billy's hair back out of his face and rubs his cheeks.

"Yes. That's fine."

"What happened?"

Her tears begin to flow once more.

"They did everything they could, but the doctor said…he's never going to wake up."

"Never?"

"No. They explained that he must've had a stroke on the table because he's unresponsive now."

"I am so sorry, Evelyn."

"I have to... I have to…"

"What do you need to do. Can I help you?"

"I have to let him go." She bursts into tears. I try to pull her to my side to comfort her, but it's hard with my arms full of Billy.

"C'mon, let's sit down." We all land on the sofa by the window, and she cries her heart out. What the hell can I do to help this woman? My phone rings, and it's Ronan. I lay Billy on the couch beside me and take the call while she leans against me and sobs.

"Go."

"What is that awful sound?" Ronan asks.

"Never mind. What did you find out?"

"It was fifty grand, not ten."

"I see."

"And it wasn't me. It was the Russians."

"Thank you for the information. I'll take care of it." This is going to take a little more time to fix than I thought. I call Amelia.

"Freddy? Where are you?"

"I'm in room 304. Can you come up here, please?"

"Room 304? Are you okay? What happened?"

"I'm fine, baby. But I'm going to need your help."

"I'm on my way."

〜

Amelia

I make my way to room 304 and slowly open the door. I see Freddy sitting on the couch by the window. A distraught woman is leaning on his arm, and a little boy is sleeping beside him.

"Freddy?"

"Amelia." He looks relieved to see me.

"What's going on?" I say cautiously, walking closer to them.

"This is Evelyn. Evelyn, this is my girlfriend, Amelia." Evelyn sits up and wipes her eyes.

"Hi," the woman says softly.

"Amelia is here to help you."

"I am?"

"Amelia can get you somewhere safe." He stares me in the

eye. I know by the way he uttered those words that Evelyn really needs protection.

"Why do I need to go somewhere safe?"

Freddy turns to her and takes her hands.

"Evelyn, I did some checking. I wanted to make sure that if John worked for Martinelli Construction, I could help him."

"How would you help him?"

"I know them."

"Oh."

"You told me he borrowed ten thousand dollars from the Irish."

"Yes."

"He really borrowed fifty thousand dollars, and it was from… the Russians."

"No. That can't be."

"I'm sorry it is. And there's more."

"He did work for Martinelli Construction, but he was fired for not showing up at the jobsite a month ago."

"A month ago? I don't understand any of this."

"I can only assume when he couldn't pay, he started hiding from the Russians. They shot him last night when they caught up to him."

"Why would he lie to me? Why would he endanger our family? Our babies!"

"I think you need to take the kids and go with Amelia to the women's shelter. They can keep you safe until I can work out a deal with the Russians."

"How are *you* going to work it out with the Russians?" She raises her voice a little, and it causes Billy to stir.

"Shh," Freddy soothes as he rubs the child's back. *What the hell am I seeing here?* Freddy always says kids don't like him. He looks so comfortable with this little family.

"I really work for The Organization." Evelyn's eyes grow wide. "I can help you and your kids, if you'll let me."

She shakes her head. "This is too much. He wouldn't do this to us."

"Unfortunately, it happens all the time. You borrow just a little money to get by and then a little more. Before you know it, you're in so deep you can't pay. The shelter will be a safe place for you and your children, Evelyn."

"But I have to say goodbye to John first."

"Of course." I step in. "I'll go out in the hall and get everything set up. Would you like me to take Billy out in the hall with me?" I ask, and she nods.

I scoop the little one up and take him out in the hall. I call Marissa and have her get a room ready. I have her send Bennie here to pick them up and take them to the shelter.

Staff members enter the room. Soon, I no longer can hear the beeping of machines. Evelyn's cries seep from beneath the door as she mourns for her husband. I don't know how much time passes until Freddy exits the room with her under his arm, sobbing.

"The car is waiting," I say respectfully.

We stop at the nurses' station, and Evelyn takes a little girl from a nurse. She holds her close and strokes her back. Freddy picks up the diaper bag. We all ride the elevator in silence to the ground floor, where Bennie waits.

When we step back onto the elevator, Freddy pulls me into his arms, and I can feel his body shudder. He's crying. I squeeze him tightly and hold on. I don't know what all happened today, but I know that when he's ready, he'll tell me.

Chapter 55
Freddy

Nico leads us down the corridor and turns right into a room. The lighting is soft, and the linens are pink. Gilly is sitting up in bed holding a little bundle in her arms. Her smile is wide, and her cheeks are flushed. Lil, MeMe, and Amelia move to one side of the bed and gush all over her. They bombard her with questions. How do you feel, and how bad was the pain? Ethan and I stand on the other side by Nico.

Nico leans down and takes the bundle from Gilly, then turns to me.

"Do you want to meet your nephew?"

"Me? Uh, yeah, sure."

"Here, you can hold him."

"Oh, I don't think…" Before I can complete that sentence, Nico pushes him into my arms.

"Hold your arms like mine. It will be a smoother transition." *A smoother transition? Oh fuck.* I hold my arms like he instructs, and he awkwardly deposits the bundle in my arms.

"He's so tiny," Amelia coos.

"Look at the big Mafia boss now. He's turning into mush, right before our eyes," Gilly teases.

I look down at his little face. His eyes are closed, and his cheeks are chubby. Dark hair swirls on the top of his head, and when Amelia plays with it, it turns into curls.

"His blanket is awfully tight. Is he okay in there?" I ask.

"He's fine. Babies like to be swaddled tight. It makes them feel like they're still in the womb," Lil says.

"Oh." I get a whiff of the baby smell the girls are always talking about, and my thumping heart begins to calm.

"So… What did you call this little guy?" I ask Nico. He looks down at Gilly. She nods for him to go ahead.

"His name is Nikolai Frederick Acosta."

"What?"

"Nikolai Frederick Acosta."

"You named him after…me?"

"You're my big brother. You've always protected me. You made sure we stayed a family. I want Nicky to have a great role model to look up to, and I couldn't think of a better man than you."

The girls all coo a collective "aw."

"Thanks, man."

"Hi, Nicky. I'm your Uncle Freddy."

♋

We pass the baby around the room, and everyone gets a short turn before the nurse comes in to shoo us all away. Amelia deposits him into his mother's arms, and Nico follows us out into the hallway. He pulls me into a hug, and tears fill my eyes.

"I won't let him down, brother."

"I know you won't."

♋

In the car on the way home, Amelia can't stop beaming.

"That was so worth the wait. Don't you think, Freddy?"

"Yeah. That was pretty cool. I can't believe Nico named him after me."

"I can tell it touched your heart."

"More than you could ever know. You were right about the baby smell."

"I know, right?" she agrees loudly.

"Have you changed your mind about having a baby?" I ask. Amelia chokes. "Are you all right?"

"Yeah, my drink just went down the wrong pipe. Why would you ask me that?"

"Just the way you were looking at Nicky."

"Me? What about you?"

"What are you talking about?" I laugh.

"You turned into a big ole softy holding the baby."

"I did not."

"Oh really?"

"Well, he was pretty cute."

"Did you change *your* mind?" she asks.

"Maybe? I don't know. I never saw myself as a dad before. Shit, I never saw Nico as a dad before either. But he looked so happy."

"He did, didn't he? But we have lots of time, so let's not think about it now, okay?"

"Right. Time. Sure."

Why do I feel like holding baby Nicky just changed my whole life?

Chapter 56
Amelia

It's been a few weeks since baby Nicky was born, and we've all been spending more time together as a family. Uncle Freddy turns into a big softy whenever he's around, and I hardly get my turn to cuddle him because Freddy hogs him. He talks to him about playing ball in the field out back and riding the horse.

"Look what I bought you, Nicky." Freddy holds up a ball glove and shows it to the baby.

"I think that's too big for him right now, don't you?" I chuckle.

"He'll grow into it," he says, turning back to the baby. "Your daddy and I used to throw the ball around when we were kids. I'll teach you like I taught him."

"Aw. That's so sweet," I say. "See, I told you. You're just a big ole teddy bear under all those muscles."

"Shh. Don't let anyone hear you say that. I have an image to uphold," he says, walking away with the baby.

"Freddy. I wanna hold him. Come back," I whine.

Chapter 57
Freddy

Having baby Nicky around has made me think about having a family with Amelia. I never thought it was something I wanted, but Nico always looks so happy. Well, except when the baby cries, and he panics a little. *That's kind of funny.* Before we can have the baby conversation, I think we need to discuss a few other things.

"Amelia, can you come here, please!" I yell.

"What is it? What's wrong?" She comes out of the kitchen with concern etched on her brow.

"Nothing's wrong. I have a surprise for you."

"Ooo, a surprise. What is it? Where is it?" She circles me, checking my hands.

"It's not here."

"Where is it?"

"You'll see." I can't help but laugh at her excitement. I take her by the hand and lead her to the Gator in the barn and strap her in.

"Let me put this blindfold on you."

"Where are you taking me, Freddy Acosta?"

"Would you just play along, please? You'll find out soon enough."

"Okay." She concedes and lets me cover her eyes.

I drive us through the field behind the house. To the spot we spent our first night here together. To the place we made plans to build our dream home. To the place we came to heal after she was taken.

"Can I take the blindfold off now?" she asks when the Gator comes to a stop.

"Nope. Just a little longer."

"Ugh," she grumbles.

I help her exit the vehicle and lead her to the spot I've prepared for us.

"Okay, you can look now." Amelia lowers the blindfold, and as her vision comes into focus, I see her face change.

"Freddy. What did you do?"

Chapter 58
Amelia

"There's a bed in the middle of the field," I say in awe. I can't believe my eyes. It's covered with a white duvet and lots of pink throw pillows. The area is circled by tiki torches that cast a warm glow.

"Freddy. What is all this?"

"I wanted to surprise you. And I wanted it to be a little more comfortable than an air mattress this time."

I move into the space and look at all the details. There's a small table with candles, champagne, and hors d'oeuvres sitting on a silver tray.

"I thought you hated hors d'oeuvres?"

"I didn't hate them the night we met at the ball. They tasted good. It just took a hundred of them to fill me up."

"It's all so beautiful." I pull him in for a hug.

"I would do anything for you, Amelia. You know that, right?"

I nod as he picks up the tray and reaches it out to me and says in a fancy voice, "Hors d'oeuvre, madam?"

"Why, yes. Thank you, kind sir," I chime back. I pop one into my mouth.

"Oh my gosh. It's amazing." My mouth is filled with savory goodness.

"The chef from the masked ball made them. Champagne?"

"Thank you." I take a sip from the glass, and the bubbles tickle my nose. "I can't believe you did all of this. Are you a closet romantic, Freddy Acosta?"

"Maybe." He takes my glass from me and sets them both on the table. "Would you care to dance?"

"Why, yes, thank you."

"I wanted this evening to be special." He takes me in his arms like we're going to dance.

"You know there's no music." I giggle.

"I can fix that," he says, reaching into his pocket and pulling out his phone. He presses a few buttons, and soft music comes over a speaker system. He takes my hand and pulls me close to him.

"Mmm. This is like a dream," I whisper.

"We're going to have more nights like this on our land, Amelia." We sway to the music while the crickets chirp in the distance. I think I've died and gone to heaven.

Freddy

"Are we really going to sleep out here under the stars tonight?" Amelia asks as we dance.

"Sure, why not?"

I spin her out and back into my chest, and she giggles. I do it once more and lower her into a dip.

"Marry me."

"What?"

"Marry me, Amelia. Make me the happiest man on earth."

"Freddy…" Her eyes fill with tears.

"I love you, Amelia. I want a life with you, and I want everything that comes with it. The kids, the dog, the cat, and the white picket fence. I want it all."

I pull her to stand

"There's a problem with your plan."

"What?" I begin to think maybe she doesn't want this after all.

"We have *two* dogs, no cat, no white picket fence, and I thought you didn't want kids," she says.

"I'll build you a white picket fence, and I'll get you a cat."

"What about the kids?"

"I think I can do that…with you."

"Really?"

"Sure. Look how much Nicky loves me." I smile cheekily.

"He does love you a lot."

"Think of how much our kids would love *me*."

"And me too." I chuckle at her frustrated tone.

"Who wouldn't want a momma like you?" I kiss her on the forehead. "So. Will you marry me?"

"Yes, I'll marry you."

"Really?" She nods her head vigorously. "Woo-hoo!" I pick her up and spin her until I realize I've forgotten the most important detail of the night. "Wait. The ring. I forgot the ring." I set her down and dig into my pocket. I pull out a black velvet box and drop to one knee. "Amelia Peters, will you marry me?" Tears fill her eyes again.

"Yes." She nods, and I slide the ring on her finger.

"Now it's official."

"Oh, Freddy, this is the most beautiful ring I've ever seen."

"It's a six-carat cushion-cut diamond. I got it at Cartier in New York the last time I went to meet with McAnally."

"You've been planning this for two months?"

"Yes. I was trying to find the perfect time to ask you. Then baby Nicky came, and we've been helping Evelyn and her kids get settled. I decided I was done waiting. I couldn't wait for the perfect time any longer. I had to *make* the perfect time. So here we are."

"And it is perfect."

Chapter 59
Freddy

Amelia and I ate, drank, and danced. We blow out the torches, cuddle down in the bed, and look up at the stars.

"You're right, this is a lot more comfortable than lying on the ground or on the air mattress."

"See, I told ya."

I hold this beautiful woman in my arms. She has agreed to be my wife. Now, we have to talk about our future. Twirling a curl of her hair between my fingers, I say, "Poppy."

"Hmm?"

"I need to know what our future looks like to you."

"What do you mean?"

"I'm not getting any younger."

"That's what Gilly says." She chuckles and then stifles herself. "Sorry, go on."

"Well, I *am* older than you."

"Would you stop? Twelve years isn't that much in the grand scheme of things. What's this really about?"

"I need to decide whether I want to keep working for The Organization, or if I want to give it up."

"Give it up?" She leans up on her elbow and looks down at me. "Why would you give it up?"

"Because I don't want to die an old fat mobster." It sounds so stupid when I say it out loud, but it's true.

"Freddy, stop it." She slaps me on the chest.

"Ow! I'm serious. You know what happens to old mobsters, don't you?"

"No. What?"

"Some young guy comes along and thinks he can do better. So he invites you out to dinner and shoots you in a public place to make a statement." Her eyes grow wide.

"Have you talked to Ethan about this?"

"Yes."

"And what did he say?"

"He doesn't want to die that way either. The main reason he wanted to go legit was to keep his family safe."

"And they are safer. We're all safer with Ethan at the helm."

Should I say what I'm thinking? I know it's my insecurities filling my head, but I swore I wouldn't keep my feelings from her again.

"I can't lose you again, Amelia."

"Freddy."

"Losing you almost killed me. I don't think I could live through it again. And if we have kids—I could never live with myself if something happened to them."

"You don't want to have kids because you are afraid they'll be kidnapped?"

I turn my head away from her. "Maybe." She pulls my face back to hers.

"So you think if you quit The Organization, the world will leave us alone?"

"Yeah. Maybe."

"Wasn't it you who said that if they want something you have, they'll try to take it?"

"Yeah."

"What makes you think anyone is going to forget what you do for The Organization? What you did for Antonio?"

"Why would anyone still want to hurt my family if I don't work for them anymore?"

"Knowledge. You know every aspect of how The Organization works."

"I didn't think of it that way."

"Look at all the good you do."

"What good? I'm just the muscle. I handle all the deadbeats who can't pay. All the businesses that don't follow the rules."

"You know you are so much more than that. Don't put yourself down. Look how you took care of Evelyn. She started out as some lady you met in a hospital cafeteria."

"I held her kid for her, big deal."

"As soon as you found out her husband was a Martinelli employee, you knew you had to help her. You did so much more for her that day, and you don't even know it."

"He was one of us. At least for a time, he was."

"See."

"See what?"

"You're such a big ole softy under all this gruff exterior."

"I can't come off soft though, Poppy. I've told you this before. Weakness isn't allowed in our world."

"Well then, help people under a different name. Ooh, or wear a mask."

"I'm not fucking Batman."

"Okay then. Hmm. I know…start a foundation, and you be the secret benefactor. Let someone else run it for you."

"Like who?"

"Me."

"You would do that?"

"Sure. We can do it together."

"Now that just might work." I'm amazed by this woman. She has so much brilliance in that tiny body of hers. "I've done so many bad things in my life, Amelia. A few good deeds aren't going to make up for it."

"Maybe not. But it might help heal your soul and help you feel better about yourself."

"I'll talk to Ethan. But you didn't answer my question."

"I'm sorry. What was your question again?"

"What does our future look like to you?"

"Hmm…I like to travel and go on adventures. Can you take some time off to fly your future wife off to some faraway lands?"

I pull her back down to my chest and snuggle her in tight. "Yes, I think that could be arranged."

"And can we have a wedding? A wedding on *our* land. Ooh, we could have it in the barn!" she squeals with excitement.

"We can do it wherever you want. But I have one more question for you."

"Okay, shoot."

"We need to talk about kids. Do you want them?"

"If we're blessed with kids, yes, I would be thrilled. But if we're not, that will be okay too. I like the life we're building together. What about you?"

"I always thought the answer would be emphatically no. But…"

"But?" Her voice draws out.

"But since Dom, Alessia, and Nicky came into our lives…I really love them, ya know."

"Yeah, I know." Her smile is soft as she rubs my chest with her hand. "But I also like the part where they go back to their parents when they cry."

We both laugh.

"Yeah, the panic on Nico's face is hilarious." I belly laugh.

"But he'll get used to it. Ethan did. He's a great father, and Nico will learn to handle every situation that comes along too." Her words become softer. "Just like you would."

"What if we have kids and I drop one, or smoosh them in bed between us, or yell and make them cry. I-I-I don't know, Amelia." My insecurity is creeping back in.

"You're not your father, Freddy. Besides, we'll both make

mistakes. Parents don't know everything until the second or third kid anyway." She shrugs off the worry. "You make all your mistakes with the first kid. Then the rest are easy. Ask Lola."

"We don't have to worry about kids right now. I'd like to make love to my fiancée under the stars tonight."

"Yes, please."

Chapter 60
Freddy

Six Months Later

Over the past few months, our city has become even safer. Ethan supplied the other families with a shit ton of weapons from the Texas haul, for a hefty price of course. Don't get me wrong, he stocked up our arsenals first, but The Organization had no use for all the heavy hardware.

We set up a movie screen at the pond and had a party as we watched Marco and Vito blow the Texas compound to smithereens. Hopefully, all of our bad memories went up in smoke with it.

Ethan and I discussed our work situation with the girls, and we have decided to stay in our current positions for the foreseeable future. We like the progress we've made with The Organization and the collaboration. However, we've made a few changes.

I'm stepping down as Ethan's second-in-command, and Beckett will be stepping up. He has always been a loyal member of the team. Whether it was watching over Guilia when she was in Europe, being on Lola's security detail, or heading the team that took Buddy down. He has always proven himself to be the right man for the job.

Roscoe has been my second-in-command since I took over illegal operations. I'll be training him to seamlessly fill in for me when I need to whisk my woman off for a romantic getaway. Maybe someday, The Organization will be led by Beckett and Roscoe. Only time will tell.

Chapter 61
Freddy

"I think I'm gonna throw up," I declare, as Nico and I walk down the path to the altar. "Everybody's looking at me."

"In a minute, they'll all be looking at your beautiful bride, and no one will remember your name."

"Gee, thanks, man."

"Whatever you need, brother. I'm here for ya," he says, clapping me on the back.

Amelia wanted to have the ceremony in the grassy field where all the major events in our lives together have taken place. The grass is cut thick like a carpet, and crisp fall leaves cover the aisle. The hundred or so guests are seated on chocolate-brown folding chairs with white cushions. The first chair in each row is decorated with flowers of deep burgundy, rust, and harvest gold.

When we reach the arch, I made out of extra timbers from the barn, I stare out over the field, and I can see why Amelia chose this spot. The fall leaves on the trees behind us make an amazing backdrop.

Nico taps me on the shoulder as "A Thousand Years" by Christina Perri pipes through the speakers we rigged in the trees. The guests turn to look down the aisle. Dominick and Alessia are first.

Dominick is dressed in a cowboy hat, brown boots, blue jeans, a white shirt, and a brown leather vest, matching Nico and me. He's pulling a little red wagon carrying his sister. She's a bundle of frills in a cinnamon-colored dress. She claps her hands and laughs the whole way down the aisle. Lola lifts her from the wagon, and you get a glimpse of the tiny brown cowboy boots on her feet. She settles her on her hip as Dominick comes to stand by Nico.

Next down the aisle is Sasha. She was the only sister or friend who was not pregnant or had just given birth. I've never seen her look so stunning. Her short dress is a soft cinnamon color to match Alessia, and she wears a blue jean jacket over it. Brown cowboy boots complete her look as well. Her hair is up in an elaborate braid configuration circling her head with some little flowers tucked in the back. She's carrying a bouquet of fall flowers. She smiles sweetly at Gary as she approaches the end of the aisle.

My stomach is filled with buzzing bees as I see Amelia in the distance. She's a ball of white as she approaches. She's wearing the princess ball gown she's always dreamed of. The crystals sparkle in the sunlight. Her hair is in a soft, messy bun with little pieces floating around her face. Little white flowers are tucked around the bun, and a long veil is attached at the back of her head, stretching down the aisle. Her bouquet matches Sasha's, but it's three times as large.

Her hand is wrapped around Ethan's arm as he guides her down the path of leaves. He's dressed like Nico and me. It's strange to see him out of a crisp suit and in a white shirt, vest, and jeans. The cowboy boots are so out of character for him, but he would do anything for Amelia.

My heart skips a beat as she gets closer. Everything around me becomes a blur, and all I can see is Amelia. Her ocean-blue eyes stare into my soul, and her cheeks glow in the sunshine. I can't believe we're here, after everything we've been through.

Ethan brings her to a stop in front of me, and we wait for

the minister to speak. I mouth, "You look beautiful," and she blushes.

"Welcome, everyone. Today, we come together in this beautiful location to celebrate the union of this man and this woman. Who brings them to be married today?"

"I do," Ethan declares. He kisses Amelia on the cheek and shakes my hand before he links her hand in mine. He turns to stand by Lola, and Alessia shouts, "Da Da," and everyone chuckles.

Amelia and I walk forward to the arch and face the female minister. All of the jitters are gone. All I can see is my bride, and all I can hear is the minister.

"Dearly beloved, we are gathered today to witness the union of Frederick Alexander Acosta and Amelia Mae Peters. Please face one another and join hands."

Amelia's dress swooshes around her as she turns to face me. Her smile is as wide as can be.

"Amelia, do you take Frederick to be your lawfully wedded husband? Do you promise to love him, trust him, honor and keep him? In sickness and in health. In good times and in bad. Forsaking all others, as long as you both shall live?"

"I do."

"Frederick. Do you take Amelia to be your lawfully wedded wife? Do you promise to love her, trust her, honor and keep her? In sickness and in health. In good times and in bad. Forsaking all others, as long as you both shall live?"

"I do." My voice cracks as the words come out.

"Our bride and groom have written their own vows to share today. Amelia, if you would go first, please."

Amelia clears her throat. Her eyes are glued to mine as she begins to speak.

"Freddy, I love you with every beat of my heart. You loved me when I didn't love myself. You give me strength and let me be myself every day. You always know what I need, even when I don't. I will stand by your side and support you every day of our lives. I will protect your heart in this lifetime, and in every lifetime to come. I love you."

"Frederick." The minister motions for me to speak. My mouth is dry. I search my pockets for the paper I wrote my vows on. I take it out and unfold it. Taking in a deep breath, I begin to speak.

"Amelia, I never thought I would find someone to love. But when you breezed into my world with your bubbly personality, my life finally began. You are beautiful, smart, and funny. Your giggles brighten even my worst day. I promise to be by your side, supporting you, protecting you, and loving you from now until forever. I love you."

"May I have the rings, please?" the minister says. Nico nudges Dominick. He holds out a piece of wood cut from a tree on our land. Burned into the wood are our names and the date. The rings are attached with a piece of ribbon. Nico removes the rings and places them in the minister's hand.

"The circular shape of these rings represents eternity. A symbol of love and commitment with no beginning or end. Amelia, please repeat after me. Frederick, I give you this ring as a symbol of my love and devotion."

"Freddy, I give you this ring as a symbol of my love and devotion."

The minister turns to me and repeats the words for me to say.

"Amelia, I give you this ring as a symbol of my love and devotion," I repeat.

"Please bow your heads and pray with me. Lord, please bless Frederick and Amelia. We pray that they share an endless and selfless love for all the days to come. Please continue to strengthen their commitment to one another and hold them in the palm of your hand. What God has joined, let no man put asunder. In your name we pray. Amen."

The crowd replies, "Amen."

"Ladies and gentlemen, I present to you for the first time, Mr. and Mrs. Frederick Acosta!"

We clasp hands and turn to face the crowd. Everyone yells and applauds.

Chapter 62
Amelia

We greeted all of our guests, and they've moved in-side the barn for cocktail hour. Freddy and I stand patiently, waiting for Sasha to join us to take photo-graphs. She's standing under the big oak tree having an intense conversation with a man I've never seen before. I'm sure I would've remembered his jet-black hair, full eyebrows, per-fect skin, and pitch-black eyes. He looks dangerous in his ex-pensive, tailored black suit, like he's going to a funeral, and not a wedding.

We watch as Sasha stands before the intimidating man. Her head is tilted up so she can concentrate on his every word. She shakes her head and tries to step away, but the man grabs her by the shoulders and forces her to look at him. Her body stiffens, but she squares her shoulders and pushes his hands off her. With her long fingernail, she jabs him in the chest, getting her message across. His jaw tenses as he leans down and whispers something in her ear.

She points over her shoulder at us and shakes her head. The man sweeps his hand under his chin and glares at her.

"What the hell does that mean?" I ask.

"I've seen Ivan do it before. It means 'I don't care.' It's a Russian thing," Freddy explains.

"You think he's Russian?"

"I don't know, could be."

Sasha crosses her arms over her chest in defiance.

"I'm going over there. This is crazy." I move toward the couple before Freddy can say a word.

"Sasha." I smile with a song in my voice. "Are you ready to take pictures? The sun is setting."

Sasha's head whips in my direction, and she steps away from the man like he just burned her. "Yes. We're done here." She waves him off with a flick of her hand.

"I'm leaving. But we *will* talk again."

"If you say so," she snarks.

The man calmly strolls away, climbs into the back of an obsidian-black Mercedes G 580, and drives away. Freddy and I wait a beat for her to explain who the man was, but she doesn't acknowledge his presence. Instead, she pastes a smile on her face and says, "C'mon, we're burning daylight." Freddy and I exchange glances and follow along behind.

The pictures are all taken, and Sasha acts like her meeting with the mystery man never took place. Freddy and I stand at the barn doors ready to enter.

"Well, Mrs. Acosta, are you ready to party?"

"Yes, Mr. Acosta, I think I am. Are you?"

"I think I would rather leave and make love to my new bride."

"Freddy." I giggle. "You have to wait until after the reception, and then you can have your way with me."

"Oh, I intend to fuck my new wife long and hard, just how she likes it." He pulls me in for a kiss just as we hear the music cranking up. The doors swing open, and the DJ introduces us. As we step inside, everybody screams.

The barn is decorated exactly how I wanted. Each of the

twelve-foot wooden tables has a long, thin white table runner down the center. There are slices of the log we cut down, dotting the length of the runners. On top of each is a glass vase filled with what looks like water. Baby's breath floats inside, and a white votive candle floats on top. Tall tapered candles and Mason jars filled with dried fall flowers complete the decoration. A huge chandelier mounted on the ceiling brings the whole country-chic look together.

When everyone has been well-fed, Nico begins the toasts. With a ding on the side of his glass, the crowd settles, and silence fills the barn.

"Big Brother, I can't tell you how happy it makes me to see you with your beautiful bride. You have always been a great brother, and I know you'll be a dedicated and loyal husband. Amelia, welcome to the family. I'm so glad he found you."

The two brothers hug, and Lola stands to speak.

"Amelia, you've been like a sister to me. I've watched you grow into the strong, independent businesswoman you are today. But more than that, you stayed loving and kind. Take care of each other. Stand by each other and don't ever go to sleep mad. I love you, sis."

Next, Ethan speaks.

"Freddy and Amelia, you two are perfect for one another. You are truly a match made in heaven, or by me." The crowd laughs. "But seriously, always find time for each other. Don't forget to continue to nurture your relationship and date. Listen and communicate. And above all, Freddy, remember—happy wife, happy life," he singsongs, lifting his glass.

Freddy stands and takes the microphone.

"Amelia and I would like to thank you all for sharing this day with us. My bride says I have some instructions to give out, so listen up." The guests chuckle. "The day I brought Amelia out here to show her our land, we burned marshmallows over a campfire. There's a s'mores bar set up in the back corner." He points so everyone can see where it is. "It signifies a very special moment in time for us." I squeeze his hand.

"There's a mountain of cupcakes over there, so everyone please help yourself and take some home in the little boxes provided. We would love for everyone to add their thumbprint to the large picture of the tree by the entrance, if you haven't already done so." Guests crane their necks to try to see it. "Now, if you wouldn't mind joining us outside, I'd like to dance with my new bride." The crowd gives a collective "aw."

Freddy pulls me to stand.

"Why are we going outside? I thought we were dancing in here?" I ask.

"Come with me. I have a surprise for you."

Freddy walks us toward the two big sliding barn doors. As we approach, the doors slide open like magic, and I gasp when I see what he's done. He's had a large wooden dance floor installed. Twinkling lights swoop across the top to form a starry sky. There are Mason jars with candles inside hanging all around the structure, adding soft light to the space. He guides me into the center of the dance floor and pulls me into his arms for a kiss.

"This is gorgeous, Freddy."

"Anything for you, wife." *I love the way he says that word.*

"This day has been everything I ever dreamed it would be and so much more. Thank you."

"It's just the start of our new life together. There are so many more adventures to come, and I can't wait to share them all with you."

As if on cue, "Yours" by Russell Dickerson begins to play. "This is my song to you, Amelia. I will always be yours."

Later in the evening, we dance over to Sasha and Gary, and I ask, "So are you ever going to tell us who that man was you were arguing with?"

"What man?" Gary says, pulling Sasha back to look at her.

"The young guy in the black suit," I say. Sasha glares at me. "It looked like you were having a pretty heated conversation."

"In my line of work, I come across all kinds of people,

Amelia. It's not just women who need my *special* kind of assistance."

"Do you need any help?" Gary asks.

"I might. Let me do my research first."

"Sounds fair." He seems satisfied with her answer. Why aren't I?

"When do you leave for Greece?" she asks.

"After the reception. Vito is taking us on the jet."

"We had a lot of fun on the jet, didn't we, baby?" she coos, shimmying up to Gary.

"We sure did." He plants a heated kiss on her lips.

I look up at Freddy, and he motions his head for us to leave them alone.

We dance away from them, and I tell Freddy I'm worried about her. What if she's in danger?

"Do you know who you're talking about, Amelia? She's a fucking killer. She knows how to take care of herself. She's not stupid. She'll ask for help if she needs it."

"I guess."

"Do you want a drink?"

"No. I'm good. I have a surprise for you too, husband," I purr.

"What is it, pretty lady?" he asks in that sexy cowboy accent of his.

"I like it when you talk all cowboy to me."

"I'll remember that tonight when I have you splayed out on the bed to eat you for dessert."

"We have cupcakes for dessert, remember?"

"Your pussy is much better than those cupcakes." He nuzzles his nose into my neck and makes me giggle. "Ooh, or maybe I can combine the two," he says behind a devilish grin. Chills run down my body, but I have to keep it together. I tug him down to my level and whisper in his ear. A different kind of smile spreads across his face, and it makes me happy to see it.

"Really?" he croons.

"Yes."

He picks me up and spins me around and kisses me fiercely.

Epilogue
Freddy

Three Months Later

Lola and Ethan have been busy with the new baby, Dario Valentino Martinelli. He was born last month. Amelia and I took care of Dom and Alessia for a few days while Lola and the baby were in the hospital. It was fun having them around. We rode the horse, set up a tent in the living room, and slept there all night. We fed them way too much ice cream and candy, but they never cried once.

"Freddy, are you almost done?" Amelia asks, coming into the office. "We're going to be late."

"We won't be late." I stand and take my beautiful wife in my arms. "How's my little man doing in there today?" I ask, rubbing my hand across Amelia's belly.

"He's been kicking the shit out of me. Tell him to stop."

"Sebastian. I'll buy Momma ice cream on the way home from the doctor's office if you stop kicking her," I croon into her belly.

"Daddy's gonna buy Momma ice cream anyway, right?"

"I'll buy Momma whatever she wants. I love you."

The End

Is this the end? The voices in my head are telling me The Martinelli Organization has more stories to tell. It seems that a few dead characters still have a few things left to say too. Not to mention there is a whole new group of characters fighting to be set free. Watch my social media for more to come. This girl isn't done yet.

ACKNOWLEDGMENTS

Thank you to my husband for all of your love and support. For always helping me work through scenes to make sure they would work in real life, if you know what I mean. For being my Creative Content Coordinator.

Thank you to Editing4Indies, Bravia Books, Barren Acres Editing and Author E.M.S. for working with me on all four books in this series. You make my work so much better. Thank you for putting up with all of my questions and changes.

Thank you to Frank for all of the cover work, logo work and 3D printing you have done over the past year. The sherpa is almost to the top of the mountain. Where will we go from here? I think the next mountain should be yours.

Thank you, Austin for being a wonderful son and standing by your mother in all her crazy endeavors.

Thank you, Katie for taking on the role of Personal Assistant. I'm glad we can ride this wave together.

Thank you, Deanna for being the first one to read my work. Your enthusiasm and encouragement helped keep me moving forward.

Thank you, Taylor for coming up with the title to this one. Sorry to make you wait for the last book to use it. I hope Amelia and Freddy check all the boxes. I hope I made you proud.

Thank you, Christy, Ellen Christy Intimate Portraits, for all of your amazing model covers for this series. For all of the lunches we took where we talked so long we were the only ones left in the restaurant. For everything you have helped me with from banners to bookmarks. Thank you for seeing my vision and bringing it to life. Thank you for your encouragement and believing in me.

Thank you, Shae, Beth, Heather, Pam and Christy M. for being my beta readers. Your comments and suggestions helped me so much. Your enthusiasm for the characters made me feel like I was on the right track.

Thank you, Christy M. for becoming my Quality Control Supervisor. You saved my ass so many times on this series, I don't know what I would do without you. I'll always bring the shovel.

Thank you to the Friday Night Dinner Group for encouraging me not to give up on this dream. Even though we don't see each other every day anymore, know there isn't a day that goes by I don't remember something funny we shared or someone we played a joke on. *Oh, I forgot, I'm the innocent one.* For the sweet teas, donuts, cupcakes, no bake cookies and long talks. Having people in your life who you can tell anything to without judgement; who tell it to you straight; and who have your back no matter what, are true friends. I am so glad I found that in all of you.

Thank you to all the readers out there. We've made it to the end of my first series together. I hope you loved The Organization as much as I have enjoyed writing their stories. I wanted these books to be Dark Mafia Romance, but I also wanted the characters to become a family in their own way, and I think I achieved my goal.

About the Author

M.K. Manson began a journey of self-discovery on her 58th birthday. It started her on a path to become a dark romance author. She has been a lover of smut for years. Whether listening to audiobooks or poring over paperbacks, she reads all genres and loves a dark and twisty story. Give her a spicy why-choose romance any day of the week, and she's a happy girl.

With four dark mafia romance books self-publishing in 2025-2026, she is on her way to her life's goal of being a best-selling author. For more information on M.K. and her books, follow her online on Tik Tok and Facebook at authormkmanson. And on Instagram @authormkmanson1.

ELLEN CHRISTY

INTIMATE PORTRAITS
ELLENCHRISTY.COM

Before he stole her heart…
She reclaimed her power.

Ellen Christy Intimate Portraits
Elizabethtown's exclusive boudoir only studio

Every dark romance has one undeniable truth:
POWER IS SEXIER WHEN IT'S YOURS.

At Ellen Christy Intimate Portraits, we specialize in capturing the raw, unapologetic beauty of every woman —through luxury boudoir experiences that feel like stepping into your own seductive novel. Whether you're the queenpin or the quiet force behind the empire, you deserve to see yourself the way the world should: confident, irresistible, unforgettable.

With over 20 custom-designed sets, all-female staff, and handcrafted albums and keepsakes, our studio is a sanctuary where you take back the narrative, frame by stunning frame.

Because every femme fatale has a soft side worth celebrating.

And every woman is the heroine of her own story.

BOOK YOUR SESSION. REWRITE YOUR CHAPTER.

ellenchristy.com | @ellenchristyintimateportraits
Dare to see the woman he would burn the world for.

Visit Us: ellenchristy.com
Contact Us: christy@ellenchristy.com
2791 Shepherdsville Rd, Elizabethtown, KY
270-317-6960

www.ingramcontent.com/pod-product-compliance
Lightning Source LLC
Chambersburg PA
CBHW060517160726
47991CB00001B/70